JAYNE FAITH

War of the Fae Gods

First published by Andara Publishers 2020

This novel is entirely a work of fiction. The names, characters and incidents portrayed in it are the work of the author's imagination. Any resemblance to actual persons, living or dead, events or localities is entirely coincidental.

First edition

ISBN: 978-1-952156-08-3

Cover art by Deranged Doctor Design

This book was professionally typeset on Reedsy. Find out more at reedsy.com

Contents

Chapter 1

LAST TIME I'D been in this very spot, my own people attempted to kill me.

I tried not to dwell on the memory as I sat on my throne, waiting for my cue to address the stone fortress's packed auditorium. It occurred to me that my plan to hand off head of state duties to Maxen Lothlorien wasn't exactly working out. If it had, I wouldn't have to give this damned speech. In fact, at the moment nothing seemed to be going as I'd hoped. While Maxen stood at the podium in front of me and delivered his introduction, I began silently ticking off my lengthy list of stumbles and challenges.

There was the matter of the new subjects I'd recently gained. The hidden ones, as they were called, had returned to Faerie and the fortress to find the former Stone Order of the New Gargoyles had become the Carraig Sidhe kingdom. Good news, except none of them expected me on the throne.

About a hundred and fifty of the hidden ones had trickled in, and the reactions had all been essentially the same. There were varying levels of sorrow and outrage when the newcomers discovered that not only had their beloved New Garg leader Marisol Lothlorien passed away, but I'd been the one to bring about her death.

It was a difficult, sad, and awkward situation, and if there was an easy way to unite the Carraig, I would have done just about anything.

But so far, there was no simple way that I could see.

Add to that the general state of things in Faerie. To say the situation had become perilous would be taking a wildly optimistic and sunny view. The Unseelie were doing their damnedest to crash the Summerlands, the seat of High King Oberon and Queen Titania. The general belief was that the Unseelie were trying to do as much damage as possible, weakening Seelie power to pave the way for the Tuatha De Danann to descend on Faerie in a wave of wrath.

The Tuatha, gods who'd left Faerie in the hands of Old Ones like Oberon, apparently weren't happy with the direction the realm had gone. The gods wanted to come and raze the place and start over, presumably putting the Unseelie at the helm.

And the best part about the Seelie-Unseelie clash? My blood father, King Periclase of the Unseelie-aligned Duergar kingdom, was leading the opposition.

I had to stop running through my list of problems because Maxen was wrapping up his intro.

Maxen half turned toward me. "Champion of the Summer Court, wielder of Aurora, Champion and monarch of the Carraig Sidhe, your Queen Petra Maguire."

I rose. Maxen bowed, and the sound of rustling clothes and shuffling feet filled the auditorium as the entire audience stood. The tone was solemn, and there was no applause. But at least no one was rushing the stage aiming to relieve me of my head. I considered it progress.

I looked out over the crowd, spotlights glaring in my eyes, and waited for everyone to take their seats again. I glanced briefly at the tablet attached to the podium and then began speaking.

"On the chance any of you happened to be in a coma the past couple of weeks, I should inform you that the Carraig Sidhe have dramatically increased in number. It's not a stone blood baby boom, though I'm certain many of you are doing your part to combat our low fertility." I leaned in with a conspiratorial little smile and stage whispered, "Please keep up your efforts. That's a command from the throne."

I paused, my heart nearly stopping. To my enormous relief, there was a smattering of genuine laughter at my joke. It was a tame one for me personally, but pretty damn racy for a queen. Maxen and I had gone back and forth about whether I should cut it from the speech, but I'd insisted that I needed to be *me* in some way. I couldn't just be a wooden figurehead devoid of personality.

I continued in a more solemn tone. "Many of you have been involved in welcoming our brethren and helping them get re-acclimated to Faerie. Your efforts are deeply appreciated. And to those of you who sacrificed nearly everything on the promise of the survival and rise of the New Gargoyles, know that we can never repay you. And know also that we want nothing more than to see you living happy, full lives." My voice broke a bit at the end, and I had to pause to collect myself.

My emotions weren't entirely due to the sacrifice the hidden ones had made. Moving across the hedge to the Earthly realm and cutting themselves off from Faerie completely for decades were certainly worthy of respect, of course. Our newcomers had my most heartfelt acknowledgment for the pain they'd suffered. But I was angry that they'd done it at all. Years ago, before I was born, our former leader Marisol Lothlorien had a vision that led her to command a proportion of our people to hide themselves outside of Faerie. She'd believed that our survival as a brand-new race of Fae depended on it. Perhaps it had, back at the time of the prophecy, but fate had taken some hard turns since then, and I believed the sacrifice had been senseless.

But my opinion on Marisol's long-ago decision didn't matter, now. It was done and in the past. The stone bloods who'd hidden themselves in the Earthly realm had begun to return home, and all I could do was look ahead.

I tried to keep my speech upbeat but respectful, and toward the end I shifted the topic to the larger problems we and the other Seelie kingdoms were facing. And they were significant challenges, indeed.

"Another issue we must urgently address also affects all of us Carraig. We all experienced something seemingly impossible when Finvarra attempted to use the Stone of Fal against us," I said, speaking of the strange hallucination-type episode that swept over us when the former Unseelie leader had tried to force us under his command. "From the accounts we've been able to gather, we all somehow inhabited the bodies of ancient warriors in the Old World for a brief flash of time. It felt real. We believe it *was* real in some sense. I can't reveal more details just yet, but we're working toward uncovering the secrets hidden in this phenomenon. Just know that you didn't imagine it, and we will tell you more as soon as we're able. Until then, no details of the experience will be shared with non-Carraig. That is a command from the throne. The future of Faerie may depend on it."

There was some shifting in the crowd as my subjects took in these revelations. I knew that gossip about it had spread through the fortress, and Maxen and his staff had been staying on top of it as best as they could, trying to ensure rumors didn't go beyond our realm.

I spoke briefly about the ongoing battle in the Summerlands, where Oberon and Titania were struggling to maintain Seelie control in Faerie. Then I wrapped up my speech. Everyone stood and there was brief applause, which I took as a good sign for the overall attitude of the kingdom toward their queen. A few weeks ago, I would have doubted I could leave the auditorium without my sword drawn, let alone get a bit of polite clapping. As difficult as it was to try to win over the hidden ones who were coming back to the fortress to find their beloved leader Marisol Lothlorien gone, dead by my sword, their return seemed to have softened everyone else to some extent. I imagined that having been forced to execute one of my dissenters and exile three others also had something to do with cooling the opposition's fight. The pain of those decisions was still very fresh. But they seemed to have had the desired effect. I couldn't say my opposers openly respected me yet, but at least they weren't trying to oust me anymore.

Maxen and I exited stage left together, and once out of public view, I let out a whooshing breath.

"How'd I do?" I asked.

He inclined his head in a little blow. "You were great. Really. I didn't know you had it in you."

I grinned, drained but relieved. "And the joke? Eh? Admit it. I was right to keep it in."

"You were right," he conceded with a small laugh.

The sparkle began to fade from his sapphire-blue eyes.

I grimaced. "What is it?"

"We have to go to the Summerlands," he said.

We began walking toward the backstage exit, my security detail of two hulking men bearing broadswords on their backs following closely.

"What's happened?" I asked.

"I don't know. Oberon's got something to say. And . . . I get the feeling he's very unhappy."

I drew a deep breath as my pulse bumped up a notch. "Immediate departure, I assume?"

Maxen nodded and glanced down at my gray silk dress and the ornate robe I wore over it. "Change and then come to the Amethyst Room."

He went right, and I continued straight, picking up my pace. Emmaline, a final-year battle school student who'd served as my squire when I'd fought in the Battle of Champions, fell into step beside me.

"Where you off to, Your Majesty?" she asked, giving me a sly look.

I peered at her through narrowed eyes. "How do you know I'm going somewhere?"

"I saw Lord Lothlorien hurry off. And you've got a very purposeful stride going on."

"Oberon's summons," I said. "Why?"

"I just want to make sure you don't go off on some adventure without me, Your Highness," she said. "I want to be part of . . . whatever's going on. I'm very eager to serve, Queen Petra."

She'd been miffed that I hadn't invited her along when I'd led a small group to kill Finvarra not long ago. It wouldn't have been appropriate for her to accompany me on such a mission, but she was one of my most loyal subjects. She and her classmates had stood up for me when I first returned to the fortress as queen, at a time when others were calling for my head. They were literally my only vocal supporters, besides my father Oliver, early on. I did want to include her where I could, but it seemed like everything in Faerie had become critically dangerous, vital to the realm, top secret, or a combination of all three. She was very capable, but I couldn't help my instinct to try to shield her from danger. I hated the thought of putting her in harm's way.

"I know you're ready to serve, Emmaline, and you have my gratitude," I said. "There will be plenty of action in the coming weeks, I'm sure."

She nodded, gave me a quick curtsy, and peeled off. I arrived at the door to my quarters and hurried inside to change. Ten minutes later, I was waiting for Maxen in the Amethyst Room, the only meeting space in the fortress that had its own doorway, a magical portal through which we could instantly travel long distances.

I paced, wondering if Maxen's statement about Oberon being "very unhappy" meant the Seelie High King was upset with us specifically. Last time I'd seen him, he'd been quite delighted with me. His oracle had revealed that my people were key to the Seelie keeping power in Faerie, and Oberon was thrilled to learn there were more Carraig who would be coming over from the Earthly side to join the realm. We'd also discussed the odd phenomenon I'd referenced in my speech, where the other stone bloods and I had experienced the bizarre break of reality.

Eldon, the Fae sorcerer recently turned to the Seelie side, had told us the mass hallucinations meant those of my race had the blood of ancient gods running through our veins. That had made Oberon positively giddy, as he believed having the power of gods on our side might give us a chance against the Tuatha.

The door swung inward, and Maxen walked swiftly in.

"Do we at least get the pleasure of arriving through a doorway within the shield protecting the Summerlands?" I asked.

In the past, visiting the Summerlands meant coming into the area well outside Oberon and Titania's castle. It was a matter of security, but it was also a huge risk because the realm was under attack.

"Yes, in fact," Maxen said, pulling out a small notecard. I glimpsed a row of sigils drawn on it. "But it's not because we're being given any special favor. Apparently, the grounds surrounding the castle have been breached. We'll be arriving in the atrium."

Maxen's face was grim, his mouth pressed into a tight line as he studied the sigils one last time, memorizing them so he'd be able to trace them in the air with his finger. He moved to the archway painted into the mural at the back of the room, and I followed him. Placing my hand on his shoulder, I braced myself for the chill of the netherwhere, the void between doorways. My stomach tightened in anticipation of what news awaited us in the Summerlands.

Chapter 2

WE STEPPED OUT of the netherwhere into a shallow alcove at the back of the Summerlands castle's atrium. I stiffened, my eyes widening, as three guards barred our way. My right hand automatically lifted, going for the hilt of Aurora, the broadsword of legend I wore on my back.

"Just security precautions," Maxen mumbled to me, throwing out an arm in a not-so-subtle move to keep me from reflexively running a guard through with my sword.

As soon as Oberon's soldiers recognized us, they backed off and allowed us to exit the alcove. Stepping into the atrium proper, I scanned the grand room, taking in the activity and the faces of people scurrying back and forth. Brows were drawn and shoulders were hunched. There wasn't a single smile to be seen.

"Everyone looks on edge," I whispered to Maxen.

A deafening boom drowned out his reply and shook the floor under my boots. The entire place continued to tremor for several seconds after the noise of the explosion faded. Dust filtered down from the ceiling, and I cast a glance upward, wary of something coming lose and crashing down on our heads.

The servants barely missed a step through the whole thing. A young female page with the leggy build of a Kelpie jogged up to us.

She curtseyed. "Your Majesty, my lord." She straightened. "If you will please follow me, I'll take you to the High King Oberon. He's waiting for you in his study."

Something about the way she said it made my stomach knot a little tighter. Maybe I was imagining it, but her manner seemed to imply that we weren't going to love what we found when she delivered us to the Seelie High King. Maxen and I exchanged a glance, and his face reflected the concern I was feeling.

Partway to our destination, a familiar black-haired, orange-eyed figure blocked our path.

I stopped. "Hello, Melusine."

The Fae witch, in one of her usual dramatic black dresses, flipped her fingers at our page, shooing at her. The poor girl scuttled several feet away but didn't leave.

"I need to speak to them for a moment," Melusine said irritably to the page.

"But, my lady," the page protested. "The High King Oberon asked—"

"A minute," the Fae witch snapped, and the page went silent and stood against the wall at a respectful distance, averting her eyes.

Melusine herded me and Maxen off to the side of the hall.

"He's very cranky," she whispered.

"Oberon?" I asked.

"Yes. It's going to be ugly in there, Petra," she said.

I shook my head, my stomach sinking even more. "What should I do?"

"You must have faith," she said crisply, looking at me as if her answer was the most obvious thing in the world.

I frowned. "I'm sorry, I don't understand."

"You've got to have faith in yourself, in the future," she said. "You need to believe that you are enough."

I suppressed a sigh. I didn't have the energy to unravel Melusine's riddles. "Can you speak more plainly? Treat me as if I'm an idiot." She shouldn't have any trouble with that request.

But instead of snapping at me again, her face softened. "You need to believe that you are enough, that you *will* be enough, in the coming war. It is absolutely imperative that you have faith because you're going to have to do the impossible. And the only way to do the impossible is through faith. That is what will bring us victory. The only thing that will bring us victory."

I snorted. I couldn't help it. "Melusine, you're talking to the wrong person. Faith isn't going to win us anything. I'm a fighter, and I'll fight as I always have—with my sword and my blood. Faith isn't going to help me win any battles."

Instead of getting angry, her eyes grew worried. But before she could respond, the page called softly from her spot on the wall.

"Please, my lady," the page begged. "I must get Queen Petra and Lord Lothlorien to the High King's office. It's terribly, terribly urgent."

Melusine blinked and backed away. "She's right. You need to go."

I cast her a strange look as we passed her, and her worried expression remained. My insides twisted tighter.

Just before we turned a corner, I thought I heard the voice of the Fae witch repeat the word "faith" behind us. But I didn't have time to think about it any further, as we'd nearly reached the study.

A guard saw us coming and opened Oberon's office door. Inside the now familiar office decorated with large, masculine furniture and murals of hunting scenes, I stopped short. I'd expected that Maxen and I would be meeting with Oberon alone. Instead, we found a room packed with what appeared to be nearly every major Seelie ruler in Faerie. My gaze snagged on a handsome face with golden eyes under reddish-blond hair that was just long enough to begin to curl. Jasper Glasgow. My tension eased the tiniest bit as we locked eyes.

Jasper's presence might have seemed odd at first glance because he wasn't a king, but he was involved in an assignment of utmost importance that would affect all of us.

"Join us," commanded the voice of the High King, jarring my attention away from Jasper.

I licked my suddenly dry lips, realizing that Oberon's invitation carried no warmth. Maxen and I strode toward the dark hearth, where Oberon and the other rulers were gathered. When I caught sight of the High King's face, I nearly gulped.

Maxen bowed and I curtseyed.

"Your Majesty," Maxen said. "We came as soon as Queen Petra finished her address to her subjects."

I quickly peered around at the group, feeling the weight of many sets of eyes on me. The Dobhar King Moreau caught my eye and gave me a slight nod. He and the Queen of the Sylphs, Vida were two of the few who seemed interested in allying themselves with my tiny, newborn kingdom. The King of Gnomes, Lawrence, and Kelpie King Delun stood near each other. Vida and Queen Corrain of the Baen Sidhe sat on a divan next to where Moreau was shifting his weight from foot to foot. The new king of the Spriggan, Trey, gave me his usual cold stare. His father Sebastian and I had gotten mixed up in dealings that ended with Sebastian's death. I wasn't directly responsible, but Trey clearly held a grudge. The Fae sorcerer Eldon was also there. He, Jasper, and Maxen were the only non-royalty present. I took it all in in the matter of a split second.

The energy in the room was tense and solemn. Moreau was the only one who looked even slightly relaxed, but he tended to appear deceptively casual in just about any circumstances.

My attention shifted back to Oberon.

"Speech?" the High King asked incredulously.

"Yes, Your Highness," Maxen said.

"What are you doing making speeches?" Oberon roared at me.

I drew back in a sharp, involuntary movement as if he'd struck me. I wanted to look at Maxen but sensed it would just enrage Oberon more.

11

I swallowed hard and pulled myself up a bit taller in an attempt to project confidence. "We've had a large influx of new stone bloods into the kingdom, Your Highness," I said, trying not to stammer. "My address was part of unifying—"

"Stop," Oberon barked, cutting me off. "I realize you're a new ruler with no qualifying experience, but you of all people should see that the little issues in your realm should not be sucking up your attention at this critical point in time, Queen Petra."

He pronounced my name with something edging on a sneer. I blinked rapidly, trying to ignore the unwavering stares of Seelie rulers while attempting to get a handle on what the hell had turned Oberon's mood so severely. Maxen shifted his weight beside me, his unease practically radiating off him.

"You're absolutely right, Your Highness," Maxen said. An irritated frown tried to crease my face, but I forced my expression smooth as I listened to him. "Queen Petra and I should be turning all of our time and energy to Faerie and the fight against Periclase and the Unseelie."

Part of me wanted to protest, to at least grumble about Oberon berating us in front of an audience. Instead, I forced composure. Of the two of us, Maxen was the lifelong trained diplomat. If he judged that we needed to eat shit in this moment, it was probably the right thing to do.

"My most humble apologies for dividing my attention, King Oberon," I said, inclining my head.

The High King appeared slightly placated, but his handsome face still looked like a storm cloud ready to erupt. He folded his arms and drew a long, noisy breath, looking off to the side at the tall stained-glass window that framed his huge desk. Again, irritation prickled through me. He was treating us like we were naughty children standing before Daddy waiting for our punishment. It was humiliating. But there was absolutely nothing I could do about it.

A few of the other rulers seemed vaguely embarrassed by Oberon's outburst, shifting around uncomfortably or looking anywhere but at me and Maxen. Vida actually shot me a little sympathetic look, for which I was grateful. But most of the kings and queens gathered maintained stony expressions.

Oberon seemed to be waiting for me to declare something, but I wasn't sure what he wanted. I quietly cleared my throat, hoping Maxen would take the lead.

"Your Highness," Maxen began, to my enormous relief. "Starting now, we pledge to devote all of our personal and kingdom resources to the pursuit of uncovering the secrets of the Carraig god blood."

I held my breath as I watched the High King's face.

"Yes, you will," Oberon snapped. "You shouldn't have delayed this mission. The time lost could cost us everything."

Maxen blinked, his forehead briefly creasing. "Your Highness? Has there been an update on the movements of the Tuatha?"

"The gods are in Faerie," Oberon said.

All around the room, rulers reacted. Mouths fell open. There were gasps and a few low murmurs. My own pulse seemed to stall for a second or two, and my blood chilled.

I was still upset about the way Oberon was treating us, but his urgency and anger made a little more sense now.

"Where, King Oberon?" Moreau asked.

Oberon leveled his gaze at the Dobhar king. "One of the remote, uninhabited regions."

My eyes sought Jasper's. In recent months, he'd taken me to such a place, an unclaimed realm. I wondered if his raven shifter friend, Drifte, had seen evidence of the gods' return.

"We need the Chalice of Dagda," Oberon said. He turned back to me and Maxen. "And we need you and your people to unlock the power of the Fomoire blood that flows through you. You must turn all of your resources to it immediately after you leave here. That is an order from your High King. Do you understand?"

"Yes, Your Highness," Maxen and I answered in unison.

"Good," Oberon said. "The two of you can stay to hear our plans to seek the Chalice. Then you will depart."

I wasn't sure if I was glad or disappointed that he wanted us to stay. Part of me wanted to rush out of the Summerlands and dive into our assignment, just to feel like I was doing something to ease Oberon's wrath. The way he looked at me and Maxen sent a cold shiver up my spine. I didn't always respect Oberon's decisions or behavior, but he was an Old One, and I couldn't afford to underestimate him or what his anger might drive him to do. I slid a glance to the side, trying to gauge Maxen's reaction to all of it. He was clenching and unclenching his jaw, his brow drawn low.

A memory of a recent conversation we'd had suddenly surfaced in my mind. I'd made a comment about how the High King must have the good of Faerie as his foremost concern. Maxen had said something to the effect that Oberon had his own personal motives, and he'd warned me not to make assumptions about the High King. It'd been a brief exchange, but it had caused a subtle shift in the way I'd thought about the Old Ones ruling in the Summerlands, one that had faded to the background until now. More and more, I'd gotten the sense that Oberon and Titania ultimately saw the people of Faerie as expendable. I had a vague suspicion they wanted to maintain Seelie rule more to benefit themselves than for the good of the larger realm. Their lack of hands-on involvement over the generations was accepted as the way of things in Faerie, but I was starting to wonder whether such distance was really best.

One thing was certain. Whatever favor I'd had with Oberon seemed to have dissipated. It shouldn't have made me so nervous—angry and embarrassed, yes, for the way he scolded me in the presence of my peers—but the High King and I were on the same side, and he'd admitted that his oracle deemed the Carraig critical to the future of Faerie. Yet I felt tiny tendrils of fear beginning to creep through my gut.

I remained quiet and listened to Oberon and the others discussing the formation of a party to hunt for the Chalice of Dagda.

Information I'd gathered had actually set off this quest. Not long ago, I'd gone to Morven, the Ghille Dubh Fae who operated the Aberdeen Inn in the Duergar kingdom. Morven wasn't a Duergar subject. His race was one of the rare solitary Fae who remained unaffiliated. He'd been alive as long as anyone could remember, and no one ever saw him leave his pub. He was a purveyor of information and was happy to offer it up, if you were able to pay the price he asked. I'd used his services a handful of times, and he'd taken a bit of my magic each time in return. My last visit to him, he'd told me where he'd last heard the Chalice of Dagda was located. I'd passed on to Oberon that Morven believed the Chalice was in the Undine realm, an Unseelie kingdom of water Fae who had fishlike, cold round eyes and a queen with an insatiable sexual appetite. Queen Doinneann had actually propositioned Jasper when he and I had visited her realm. We'd narrowly escaped the Undine kingdom with our lives.

As one of the few in Oberon's trusted inner circle who didn't have a kingdom to rule, Jasper was chosen to lead the effort to find the Chalice. He asked Eldon to join the party. Jasper said he planned to ask Drifte and possibly my half-sister Bryna along as well.

I reflexively curled my fingers against my palms, wishing like hell I could volunteer to go along. I hated the thought of Jasper setting out on a quest without me. But I already knew Oberon would explode if I suggested joining the hunt for the Chalice. And he was right. I had a different mission.

A series of crashes overhead interrupted the discussion. Something exploded outside Oberon's window, and Queen Corrain shrieked.

Oberon pushed away from where he'd been leaning against the wall next to the fireplace and strode to his desk. He lifted the house phone there and spoke into it and then returned to us.

"We'll stop here," he said, his tone short. "Get back to your kingdoms and do what needs to be done."

The office door swung open and three pages came rushing in. Titania was on their heels. Her face was anxious, on the edge of panic, her strawberry-blond hair streaming behind her as she hurried. She barely seemed to see any of us in her haste to get to Oberon.

There were more booms and explosions. My eyes sought Jasper's, and I moved so I could walk next to him.

"How are you holding up, Your Highness?" he asked, his golden eyes intent on me as we made our way out of the royal study.

"Still alive," I said. "I'm just glad Oberon didn't full on paddle my ass in front of everyone. How about you?"

He arched a brow at me. "I wouldn't have minded seeing your ass, but I'd have to object to another man spanking it. Even if that man is the High King himself."

I snorted a laugh. I wasn't sure how he could joke at a time like this, but I appreciated that he'd brought a few seconds of levity into my life.

Someone touched my arm, and I turned. It was Maxen.

"Eldon wants to speak to us before we go," he whispered in my ear.

I nodded, and Maxen moved away to give me a bit of privacy to say goodbye to Jasper. The two of us went to stand next to a giant decorative urn on an oak stand in the hallway outside of Oberon's office.

"I wish I didn't have to rush off," I said to Jasper. I kept my voice low but didn't try to hide my feelings for him. I figured most of Faerie knew we were romantically involved by that point.

He opened his mouth to respond, and a particularly powerful explosion cracked like thunder, and Jasper grabbed my arm to steady me as we both staggered a little. We each looked up as if expecting the ceiling to have cracked open.

"I wish I could steal you away for a week," he said, his golden eyes fixing on my face, roving my features as if memorizing every minute detail. "I hope that after all's said and done, we'll have that kind of time for each other, Petra."

My breath caught at the intensity of his words and his gaze. "Me too," I whispered.

"But for now, we must go."

I sighed. "I know."

I stepped into him as his face lowered. Our lips met in a lingering kiss, and then he rested his forehead against mine.

"Good hunting," I said. "I know you'll find the Chalice."

He crooked a smile at me. "I appreciate your confidence."

I turned toward where Maxen stood waiting.

"Your Highness?" Jasper said.

I looked over my shoulder. He still stood next to the urn.

"I love you," he mouthed.

My lips parted in surprise. Before I could respond, he swiftly turned on his heel and strode away. I had half a mind to chase after him and demand where he got off, saying that to me for the first time in the middle of a busy corridor and then rushing away. But Maxen was already talking to me, and Jasper had disappeared around a corner.

"We need to get out of here," Maxen was saying. "I have a bad feeling things are going to get ugly very soon in the battle for this castle. You and I shouldn't be here when that happens."

I blinked rapidly, trying to focus. "Really? You think the Unseelie are going to breach Melusine's shield?"

"I think it's possible they already have."

That was bad. Very bad.

"Okay," I said, my thoughts scrambling. "Eldon. We need to find him."

"He's waiting over there." Maxen pointed to an alcoved window, and I realized the Fae sorcerer was standing next to one of the heavy, dark drapes.

If Maxen hadn't pointed out Eldon, my eyes might have slipped right past him. I squinted, realizing he was using some of his gloaming magic to make himself inconspicuous.

Maxen and I went to the window and stepped into the shadowy mist.

"No one can overhear us, so have no fear of speaking openly," Eldon said. His usually stoic face was tense. "I wanted to warn you. Oberon is very serious in his anger."

The tendrils of fear I'd felt in Oberon's office became more pronounced. "What does that mean?"

Eldon's eyes flitted back and forth along the hall, his paranoia obvious. "He's becoming a bit . . . unhinged. I overheard him say that if you couldn't figure out how to use your Fomoire power soon, he'd drain the blood of a Carraig and drink it and try to divine the secrets himself."

I stared at him, my eyes widening in horror. "Was he serious?"

"Maybe not. It's sometimes hard to tell with him." Eldon shook his head and muttered to himself for a second. "He may have just said it for dramatic effect, or to blow off some steam. But I learned long ago the hard way not to ignore Oberon's threats. Even if he wasn't being literal . . ."

Eldon trailed off, but the threat was clear.

"So the legendary crazy of the Old Ones is cropping up," I said.

"We *can* be a temperamental bunch."

I blinked. "Oh, uh, I didn't mean—" I'd obviously forgotten for a moment that I was speaking to an Old One. Sometimes it slipped my mind that Melusine was an Old One as well.

It was surprising, in a way, that Melusine and Eldon had become so invested in helping us and such active participants in our struggles. For a couple of reclusive Old Ones who'd kept to themselves for many generations, and could have easily continued doing so, they'd become key to our efforts. Not just key—vital.

"We appreciate the warning," Maxen said tightly. "We're going to do everything we can to unlock the power of the god blood."

"We do appreciate it," I echoed. "And, Eldon, know that I'm truly glad I didn't run you through with my sword when I threatened to."

Eldon let out an odd little bark of a laugh. I'd never even seen him crack a smile before.

"You and me both," he said.

"I honestly don't know where we'd be without you and Melusine," I said. "Especially in light of . . ." I trailed off and tipped my head toward the direction of Oberon's study.

Eldon's already serious face grew even more grave.

"Melusine and I will see this through," he said. "I just hope it will be enough."

"Can you let us know if you hear anything further?" Maxen asked.

Eldon's expression sobered again. "I can't guarantee I'll be able to get word to you."

Maxen nodded. "I understand." He looked up as sounds like distant thunder sent reports around the castle. "We should go."

We stepped beyond the dark mist of Eldon's gloaming and hurried to the atrium, where we used the doorway to return to the stone fortress. I tried to relax into the netherwhere, knowing it might be the only brief moment of ease I'd get for a while. But Oberon's anger and Eldon's words hung heavily on me, even in the void.

Chapter 3

MAXEN AND I rematerialized in the fortress together.

"I need to know about the caves that are part of our holdings," I said to him, the chill of the void still clinging to me. "Morven told me the secret to the god blood was in the caves."

He nodded grimly. "I've had people looking into this since you learned of it. I think we should convene a team right away to figure out what to do next."

I suppressed a groan at the thought of more meetings.

Pinching the bridge of my nose, I mentally searched for a diplomatic way to reject Maxen's suggestion. I lowered my hand. I was too tired to wordsmith my response.

"What if we just take the people you have in mind and go straight there?" I asked.

A frown briefly creased Maxen's features. I tried not to react. I knew what he was thinking: action with no prelude of bureaucracy? Was it even possible? I bit down on my bottom lip to halt a chuckle that wanted to slip out.

His forehead smoothed. "Well . . . why not? I'll send out an urgent summons, and we'll meet back here in thirty minutes."

"Great," I said brightly and strode out before he could decide we needed a meeting to determine whether we could really forgo the meeting.

I had just enough time to return to my quarters, cram some food in my mouth, and get back to the Amethyst Room.

When I arrived, my mood dampened considerably at the sight of Angus, a muscular Carraig of Oliver's generation and one of our newly returned stone bloods. From the time he'd arrived back in the fortress, he'd been vocal about his devastation that Marisol was gone, and he wasn't shy about his feelings toward me. He'd been outraged when he discovered I'd killed his former leader and couldn't understand why I was allowed to take the crown. We'd reached an uneasy truce in the short weeks since he'd led the first large wave of hidden ones back into Faerie.

I flicked a questioning glance at Maxen, but he gave me an absent bow and then turned and began studiously looking down at his tablet—deliberately avoiding me, it seemed. I frowned at his back. I couldn't *wait* to hear why he thought Angus needed to be part of this group.

Angus bowed as well. "Your Majesty," he said. Barely polite, and undeniably cold.

Others began to arrive, saving me from awkward conversation with Maxen while Angus stood by radiating hostility.

Amalie, a distant relative of Maxen's and an administrator who'd trained closely under him and Marisol, was the next to come. Then Oliver, arriving with Murdock and Sanja, two more of the hidden ones recently returned to Faerie. And like Angus, not my biggest fans. Emmaline soon followed. At least I had one ally besides Oliver in the group.

"Okay," Maxen said, finally putting down his tablet. He moved to the arch painted on the wall. "That's everyone. Crowd around the doorway here, and we'll be off."

I thought about demanding an explanation for who Maxen had picked for this little group but decided against a public confrontation. And anyway, I'd always trusted him. He surely had his reasons.

I placed my hand on his shoulder, and the others all made contact with him as well. When he lifted his hand to draw the sigils that would take us to the caves, a curious blurring occurred, preventing me from seeing the gestures his finger traced. I had just enough time to register my surprise—the masking of the sigils indicated we were going to a top-secret location—before we plunged into the netherwhere.

The spot where we emerged was freezing, pitch black, and cavernous by the way our shuffling movements echoed.

"Stay where you are so you don't trip," came Maxen's voice in the darkness.

A second later, a small point of white light appeared, a little piece of simple illumination magic balanced above his palm. It swelled until it was the size of a basketball. He tossed it up, and it hovered in the air above us.

I turned a half-circle, looking around. As I'd expected, we stood in a very large cavern. A stalactite hung above us, bifurcated to form a sort of arch, with the two branched pillars coming all the way to the floor—the doorway through which we'd arrived. The walls of the cavern were pure rock, dark and smooth but with no sheen. There were three openings to tunnels leading away from the cavern.

The arch was situated to one side of the roughly circular room, and I realized the very dark spot in the floor a dozen feet away was a hole. I had the sudden sense that the chasm went very deep into the ground, and something about it made me uneasy.

"Everything you're going to see and everything I'm going to tell you are highly confidential," Maxen said. "It's so vital to our people, I'm going to require an oath from each of you before we proceed."

My brows shot up, and I glanced around again, trying to get a sense of what made this place so special. I began to regret not allowing Maxen to do a preliminary meeting. It might've demystified the people he'd chosen to come with us, and it also probably would have been good to perform the oaths before we left the fortress. I grimaced, suddenly suspicious that he was punishing me for wanting to jump straight to action.

Maxen started with Emmaline, and I sidled over to Oliver.

"Have you been here before?" I asked.

He shook his head. "I knew of the mines, of course, but I don't think this is a mine." He peered around the space. "No, this feels like something different."

It took a few minutes for Maxen to get quick oaths from everyone, but at least there wasn't any pushback, even from Angus. For once, everyone actually seemed united in something.

Maxen pointed at the hole. "Be careful. If you go down, it'll be a very long fall. We haven't yet discovered how deep it goes."

I shivered and resisted the urge to move even farther away from the dark gaping void in the ground.

"Let's go this way first." Maxen tipped his head at the tunnel to my left.

As he moved, the glowing orb stayed above him, lighting the way. The others waited for me to go first, and I caught up with Maxen and walked next to him.

"Are you trying to punish me?" I whispered.

He looked at me, his eyes all wide innocence. "What? You wanted to skip the briefing, so that's what we're doing."

I grumbled under my breath. The corners of his mouth twitched in a tiny grin.

The orb drifted lower as the tunnel narrowed to a tight corridor with a ceiling only a couple of feet overhead. My thoughts flashed back to when Jasper and I had squeezed into the jagged basalt passages in the Giants' Causeway on a mission to rescue Oberon from the Tuatha De Danann. At times I still couldn't believe we'd made it out alive.

The tunnel finally opened up into a small room. In the middle of it was a still pool.

"What's this?" I asked as everyone else crowded around. I went and knelt at the edge of the pool.

Maxen shrugged. "We don't know. It appears to be water, but it's . . . not. It seems to have electrical properties. It causes horrible pain if you—"

I stuck my finger into the liquid. Maxen was right. My body went rigid as a strong electrical force shot through me. Lucky for me, he was there to pull me back.

"Maybe you shouldn't have done that, *Your Highness*," he said through clenched teeth.

I gave my head a hard shake. "You might be right." I stood unsteadily and brushed off my hands. "We should get samples."

"Good idea," he said. He turned to exit the room.

"Wait, that's it?" I asked.

He looked over his shoulder at me. "We've known about this for decades, and we still have no idea what it is."

"Known about it since when exactly?" I asked.

"Before we were born," Maxen said. "It was discovered right after the Cataclysm and the emergence of the first stone blood Fae."

That was interesting, and surely no coincidence.

I caught up with Maxen, squeezing next to him, and lowered my voice. "How was the discovery made?"

His mouth tightened, his posture stiffening. "A dream my mother had." He trained his gaze straight ahead.

He led us back to the cavern and down a different arm. A few feet into the tunnel, a low thrumming from up ahead brought dread creeping through my bones.

"Is that iron in there?" I asked.

"Yes," Maxen said. "Sky iron. You'll see."

We ended up in a similar room, also with a pool in the floor. But this one bubbled silver. I wanted to turn and run away screaming as the drumming terror of sky iron so close gripped me in a tight fist.

"It's molten?" I asked, my breath coming too fast. I was fighting to keep from hyperventilating, and the others weren't faring much better.

"Sort of," Maxen said.

Angus had squatted several feet from the edge of the molten puddle of sky iron. He held out a hand as if testing the heat of a flame. "It's not hot," he observed.

"No," Maxen said. "And yet it bubbles like it's boiling."

"Do we have to stay?" Emmaline's fearful voice floated to us from the back of the group.

"No," I said quickly. "Let's get the hell out. Someone can come back later for samples here, too."

The third tunnel was almost a letdown compared to the other two. It led to a small cavern with walls that glittered various gem-toned colors.

"This is the source of the Brigitstone we use in our mineral sauna at the fortress," Maxen explained.

I would have known even without him telling us. Standing there, I felt the same sense of deep recovery and regeneration I did when I used the mineral sauna in the fortress. I'd never known where the Brigitstone came from, only that it was a powerful healing tonic for Fae with stone blood. It was especially welcome after the exposure to sky iron.

"How'd sky iron get so far underground?" I asked as we all trooped back to the main cavern.

"Great question," Maxen said. "No one knows. It is odd that it's so deep in the ground, though, as sky iron comes from meteorites. And usually not in such large quantities."

"We need to work out the riddle of these caves." Angus asked. "Shouldn't we stay here and try something?"

We all gathered near the arch, and Maxen faced us. "We could. But where would we start? We can't just flail randomly and hope for an answer."

I reluctantly had to agree.

"Let's go back to the fortress, and we can discuss what to do next." Maxen turned to the doorway, and we shifted to stand behind him.

He flipped me a pointed glance, probably to see if I were going to challenge his suggestion. I didn't. He was right, we needed to mull it over and figure out our approach.

A few seconds later, we were back in the meeting room we'd departed from.

Jaci, one of the three assistants who rotated duties in my office, was there waiting. Her eyes were wide, her face pale.

"What's wrong?" I asked her.

"Someone is here for you," she said. "Lord Darion of the Duergar is waiting outside the foyer."

My heart jolted in my chest. "He's *here*?"

Darion was Periclase's brother. There was no love lost between me and my blood uncle, as I'd defeated him in the Battle of Champions while all of Faerie looked on.

"He's outside. He's not threatening and swears he means no harm. He just wants to speak to you."

Oliver appeared at my side. "I won't allow you go to out there," he said to me. He turned to Maxen. "Get Darion something to write with. He can pass a message, but Queen Petra isn't leaving the fortress, and he's sure as hell not stepping foot in here."

My father moved to the house phone, picked it up, and began barking orders about security.

"He's right," Maxen said. He turned to address the group. "We'll discuss the caves later. I'll be in touch soon."

Then he took my arm and strode purposefully to the door. We walked swiftly through the fortress toward the front foyer.

26

"What in the name of the gods is he doing here?" I muttered to Maxen.

"I don't know, but it's nothing good."

"Well, Darion did help us in Palace City when we went to kill Finvarra. Maybe he's changed."

Maxen shook his head. "Men like Darion don't change, at least not like that."

He let go of my arm and went to the front door of the fortress. I trailed after him, suddenly realizing what he intended.

"You're not going out there," I said incredulously.

"He's not going to kill me," Maxen said. "I want to speak to him face-to-face. I'll be right back."

"At least take a couple of guards with you," I insisted. I looked back and beckoned to a pair of soldiers on patrol.

Maxen raised his hand and began tracing sigils in the air. Realizing he was going to ignore me, I hopped forward and grabbed his elbow. I intended to pull him back, but I was a split second too late and instead we plunged through the door together. A second later, we both stood in the Earthly realm on the concrete slab outside the front façade of the fortress, which used to be an Earthly prison.

The familiar smell of the San Francisco Bay Area's marine layer hit my nose. I couldn't even remember the last time I'd crossed the hedge into the Earthly realm.

Darion stood there with his arms crossed. He wore his short sword on his belt but made no move toward his weapon.

Maxen whirled on me but couldn't exactly reprimand me in front of Darion.

"What do you want?" I demanded, looking past Maxen at my blood uncle.

Darion dropped his arms to his sides. My sword hand tensed, itching to reach for Aurora.

27

"At ease," he said witheringly. "I'm not here to hurt you."

I narrowed my eyes at him. "Then why did you come?"

"I have a message from Periclase. He stands on the verge of taking the Summerlands. He's inviting you to join him. Ally the Carraig Sidhe with the Unseelie, and he promises you and your people no harm. When the Tuatha come, you'll be at your father's right hand. You and the Carraig will emerge as leaders in the new era of Faerie."

I scoffed, hot anger shooting through me. "Tell Periclase to screw himself," I growled.

I turned to go back into the fortress.

"You should at least take a moment to think about it, Petra."

Against my better judgment, I paused and looked over my shoulder at my blood uncle.

"Refuse, and Periclase will rain down terror on all the Seelie realms. He'll send servitors on a scale that will make the prior attacks look like a child's birthday party. He won't hold back. He will do everything in his power to cripple every Seelie kingdom. Even yours. You have until he takes the Summerlands to decide. The way things look now, that'll be sometime tomorrow. All you have to do is declare your kingdom Unseelie and pledge to your blood father."

My entire being tightened with the urge to run Aurora through Darion's throat and then keep going until I found Periclase and did the same to him. But killing my uncle would accomplish nothing.

"Let's go," Maxen muttered at me, practically dragging me back through the doorway into the fortress.

I was shaking with rage as I stalked away from the foyer. Maxen jogged a few steps to keep up with me.

"Contact all the Seelie rulers," I said. "Tell them what's happened. Invite those who can come to convene here an hour from now."

An hour and a half later, only King Moreau, Queen Vida, and King Lawrence were able to personally appear at the fortress. The rest declined, citing the critical situation in the Summerlands, to which they'd committed a large proportion of their forces. My kingdom had been spared sending soldiers to that fight only because we were too small to make much of a difference there, and we had to protect against an Unseelie takeover of our small realm. Periclase had breached our walls in the past, and we couldn't let that happen again. The larger kingdoms were carrying the burden of military aid to Oberon.

We met in the Opal Room, along with Maxen.

"Bottom line is, despite what Periclase is threatening, you can't go," Moreau said to me.

I paced. "If I don't do as Periclase asks, every kingdom will be overrun with servitors."

"Any chance he's bluffing on that front?" Vida asked. "We thought the servitors were sent by Finvarra, and he's dead."

I shook my head slowly. "I suppose it's possible Periclase is bluffing. I really don't want to take that chance."

"Here's the thing," the stocky, barefoot Gnome king said in his gravelly voice. "Periclase is going to send servitors either way, if he has them."

My gaze slid to Maxen, and he reluctantly nodded. "I think King Lawrence is right," he said quietly.

I stopped pacing and passed a hand over my eyes. "He's going to try to turn all the Seelie kingdoms against me."

"Everyone knows what he's doing, though," Vida said. "It won't work."

"But if I go, it might delay him," I said. "It might at least give us time to figure out something."

Moreau spread his hands, his gray eyes solemn. "Figure out what?"

"I don't know," I said helplessly. "But there must be options."

"Your Highness," Maxen said to me, his blue eyes earnest. "You've seen the servitors. There hasn't been a damn thing we could come up with to stop their invasions. They came to a halt only because Finvarra decided to stop them."

I chewed my lip for a moment. "I still question whether Periclase has the power to send servitors at all. Finvarra told us he was the source of those attacks."

"Maybe Finvarra got the ability from someone—or something—else, and now Periclase has that power," Maxen said.

My eyes found his. "From the Tuatha?"

He lifted a shoulder and let it drop. "Possibly."

"Why don't they just wipe us all out with the servitors, then?" I asked.

"I don't know." Maxen frowned, a vertical line forming between his eyes. "Perhaps there's some limit on the power."

"Bottom line, you can't give yourself up," Moreau said.

"I strongly concur," Vida quickly chimed in. "Oracles from three different realms all agree that the Carraig Sidhe maintaining independence from the Unseelie is absolutely critical to our future in Faerie."

I folded my arms and dropped my chin to my chest, remembering prior attacks. They'd started on a small scale but had escalated with more violent servitors. Even so, not many had died.

"But we were lucky in the past," I said after a moment, looking up and facing the others. "There were relatively few casualties as a result of the past servitor attacks. Darion all but promised that wouldn't be the case this time, and on that I believe him. The thought of having so much blood on my hands . . ."

"It's not on your hands," Lawrence said. "It's on Periclase's. The Tuatha's, too, if they're granting him the power to conjure servitors. It's not on you, Queen Petra."

His normally gruff face was kindly, and I took a tiny bit of comfort in what he said.

"I won't go," I said finally, my heart aching. "Figure out how to fortify yourselves, please, against whatever Periclase is going to rain down on us."

Moreau, Lawrence, and Vida departed with soldier escorts to take them to the foyer where they could use a doorway to go home.

Maxen and I were alone.

"They're right," he said quietly. "You can't go, even as a stall tactic."

I stood silently for several seconds, staring at the floor, and then turned to him.

"We absolutely have to unlock the power of the Fomoire," I said, my tone an odd, painful mix of pleading and determination. "Not just because Oberon was on our asses about it. We need a secret weapon, and we need it *now*."

He gave a tiny nod. "The god power. We need to resume our meeting with the others who went with us to the caves."

Chapter 4

BACK IN THE Amethyst Room, we all gathered around the table. Angus, Murdock, and Sanja sat in a row to my left. I was at the head of the table, and Maxen, Oliver, and Emmaline sat to my right. It struck me suddenly why Maxen had seen fit to invite Angus and two of the other hidden ones. He wanted to give them representation.

I spread my hands and looked around the table. "Bright ideas? I'm literally open to anything at this point."

"What exactly did Morven say when he told you the key to our god blood lies in the caves, Your Highness?" Oliver asked. It still felt odd for my father to address me that way.

"Nothing more than that, really," I said. "He said Maxen would know what caves I was talking about." I turned to Maxen. "Do you think he really meant some of the other mines?"

"I considered that at first," Maxen said. "But after thinking about it, I realized he must mean that cave."

"Why?" I asked.

"Because the rest of them are just regular ore and mineral mines. There's nothing special about any of them, aside from the value of what they produce. Plus, those ones aren't natural caves. They're mines that we excavated. The only true caves in our holdings are the ones I just showed you, Your Highness."

"Okay." I squinted into the distance, trying to recall the exact exchange of words between me and Morven. "It's just . . . the way Morven said it, he made it sound like the answers would be more . . . obvious."

"Maybe we're overcomplicating it," Oliver suggested.

Maxen lifted a brow and cast me a wry look. "Possible."

"I need to talk to Morven again," I said.

"You shouldn't go back into the Duergar realm," Oliver said.

I spread my hands. "I don't think I really have a choice."

He made a low sound in the back of his throat and then slouched, retreating into grim silence.

"In the meantime, we need to start somewhere with the caves," I said. I turned my attention to Angus. "What do you think?"

His face tightened under my gaze, but he seemed a bit caught off guard by my request for his advice.

"We could take samples of the substances as was suggested," he said slowly. "But I don't think the answer lies in chemistry experiments. Faerie is about magic. Magic that runs through our blood and through everything here. There's something magical, something special about what's in those caves, and I think the answer lies in us interacting with them directly, Your Majesty."

I grimaced, remembering the pool of sky iron and the other water-like substance that caused extreme pain. "An unpleasant thought, considering the materials we're dealing with, but my gut tells me you're probably right. What do you think we should do?"

A bit of the chill melted from Angus's eyes, and he seemed to appreciate being asked for his opinion. "I'd like to spend some time there, if I could have permission to do so."

My brows lifted in surprise that he was volunteering so quickly. I cast a quick glance at Maxen, and seeing no look of protest in his expression, I turned back to Angus. "That can be arranged. I don't want anyone going alone, though. Three people at a time, minimum."

I paused for a second, thinking. I didn't want to assume the worst about Angus or any of the newcomers, but I also needed to ensure the safety of the entire kingdom. If anyone was going back into the caves, I needed to always have at least one person I trusted in the group.

"Oliver and Emmaline, why don't you accompany Angus on his first trip back?" I suggested.

Oliver nodded, and Emmaline straightened in her chair with a barely suppressed grin. Excitement sparked in her lavender eyes.

Maxen shot me a sharp look, maybe trying to tell me I should have handled that with more subtlety, but we didn't have time for tiptoeing around. Angus wasn't stupid. He had to know that his animosity toward me wasn't going to gain him favors or trust. And if he didn't know that, then better for him to learn sooner than later that his choices and behavior toward me had consequences. If it weren't for Maxen, Angus wouldn't even be at this table.

We ended the meeting soon after, as I had to attend to other things.

It was late by the time I was wrapping up official business in my office. Just as I was about to retire to my quarters for the night, my house phone rang.

"Hello?" I answered with undisguised weariness, hoping there wasn't some urgent matter I'd have to stay for.

"It's me," came Maxen's voice. "I just wanted to let you know that a group from today is going back to the caves."

"Tonight?"

"They wanted to get started right away." He sounded almost as tired as I felt.

"Well, that's the kind of dedication we need. Is it the group of three we talked about?"

"Yes. I took them in, as I don't want to give anyone else access to that doorway yet. Well, you and Oliver should have the sigils. But no one else. Not yet."

I closed my eyes and pressed my fingertips over my eyelids. "That's a good idea. I trust Oliver to take other people in with him." I paused. "And about earlier, I know you're trying to make the newcomers feel a part of things, but I still have a lot of dissenters in the fortress."

He let out a long breath. "No, you were right to put two people you trust with Angus."

"Everything okay?" I asked, after the line went silent for a couple of seconds.

"More or less. There's just so much to do."

"Yeah," I said. "But at this point there are really only a couple of things that matter. If you have to, let other stuff fall away for the moment."

"Sure, you're right," he said, but I knew he wouldn't take my advice. Maxen had always worked his ass off, and I didn't expect that to change.

"I'm grateful for everything you're doing, Maxen. You know that, right? I'd be up to my armpits in shit without you."

He let out a soft laugh. "You're hanging in there okay, Queen Petra."

I made a face at the phone. He knew he didn't need to address me that way when it was just us.

"Let me know if they find anything," I said. "Doesn't matter how late it is."

"Will do," he said.

We hung up, and I turned out the lights in my office and headed to my quarters. I cast a longing glance at my giant soaker tub, remembering the few minutes Jasper and I had stolen together, but I didn't have the time for such luxuries. I showered and collapsed into bed.

When I awoke the next morning and realized what time it was, my first reaction was disappointment. Maxen hadn't called, which must have meant that no progress was made in the caves.

I caught up with him after his morning briefing with his staff.

"Angus, your father, and Emmaline stayed there until the early morning hours," Maxen said. The dark smudges under his eyes told me he had likely been up late, too. "They say they got what they thought might be 'flashes' of the god power, but I wasn't completely sure what they meant by that, aside from the experiences being extremely brief. Angus came away with some ugly sky iron burns, and Oliver looked as if he'd been sticking his finger in a light socket, which probably means he was testing the pool."

"I'll give Oliver a couple more hours and then get a more thorough explanation from him," I said. I knew my father wouldn't sleep late, even if he was up all night, but I wanted to allow at least a bit of time for him to rest. "Any update from the Summerlands?"

Maxen blew out a long breath through clenched teeth. "It's bad, Petra," he said very quietly, casting a glance at the others in the hallway and then pulling me off to the side. "Darion wasn't exaggerating. I don't think Oberon and Titania are going to hold the Summerlands through the day."

I blinked a couple of times, not really registering the passersby who aimed little nods and curtseys my way. "Are you serious?"

"Yeah," he said heavily.

I knew Periclase and the Unseelie had done serious damage and the Summerlands was teetering on the brink, but the thought that they might actually drive Oberon and Titania out was difficult to comprehend.

"Is there something we could do?" I asked.

He shook his head. "I don't think so."

"What's going to happen if the Summerlands falls to the Unseelie?"

"Oberon and Titania will seek asylum somewhere else and regroup. And then Periclase will likely declare himself the High King of Faerie."

"Can he do that? Just say it and make it so?" I asked.

"Not exactly. To make it a clear victory, Periclase would have to kill Oberon. That'd be a challenge, considering Oberon's an Old One and

Periclase is just regular Fae like the rest of us. But to win back the Summerlands, Oberon will have to try to oust Periclase. That's a much more difficult challenge than defending it."

"The fighting won't be contained to the Summerlands, I'm guessing."

He shrugged. "That depends on Periclase. It's possible an all-out civil war could erupt between Seelie and Unseelie, with Unseelie attempting to claim Seelie realms by force. But I don't think Periclase will want forces dispersed for smaller fights. I think he'll keep his focus on the Summerlands because it's the seat of authority for the High ruler of Faerie."

"Okay," I said, though everything seemed to be just about as far from okay as it could get. "We need to make sure we're prepared for a servitor attack here. I spoke to Shane last night, and he should be organizing the soldiers into smaller patrols. The servitors will appear suddenly and out of nowhere, so we need armed Carraig everywhere in the fortress."

"Agreed," Maxen said. "And if you haven't already, you should issue a decree that every Carraig stay armed at all times until further notice."

I passed a hand over my brow. "Great. All the easier for someone to try to run me through the ribs."

"I don't think you'll need to worry about that, honestly," Maxen said. "People are scared. Their minds are on bigger things than their disapproval of you."

"Thanks, I think," I said wryly.

He gave me a tight smile that didn't touch his somber blue eyes. "I need to go. We'll reconnect again in a couple of hours."

I went to my office and ordered coffee to be delivered, and then after issuing the fortress-wide decree about staying armed, I reviewed Shane's plan for protecting the fortress again, searching for any ways to strengthen it. I was about an hour in when I got a call from Jaci at the reception desk.

"Critical message for you, Your Highness," she said. "May I send the page back there?"

"Yes, please."

A breathless young woman arrived in my office and passed three sealed scrolls to me. "These just came. The clerk said they were of highest importance, so I ran the whole way here."

I nodded. "Please wait a moment while I read them. I may need you."

My gut strung tight as I broke the wax seal on one of the scrolls. Magic shivered through the air. I glanced at the bottom. It was from the Spriggan King Trey, and it was short.

Frost giant servitors began attacking early this morning. Dozens of casualties so far. Still fighting.

I guessed he'd sent out the same note to every Seelie kingdom. Feeling sick, I quickly broke open the other two seals and scanned the scrolls' contents. Similar messages from King Moreau and the Queen of the Cait Sidhe realm.

I picked up the house phone.

"Yes, Your Majesty?" came Jaci's voice.

"Please summon Lord Lothlorien to my office immediately. You can interrupt whatever meeting he's in."

"Right away, Your Majesty."

I put the phone back in its cradle and looked up at the page, who was watching me with wide, alarmed eyes.

"Is it bad, Your Highness?" she whispered.

"It's not good," I said honestly. "Do you have a weapon?"

She shook her head. I reached down and pulled a sheath containing a karambit from my boot. I held it out.

"Keep this on you," I said.

She took it and curtseyed. "Thank you, Queen Petra."

"You can go," I said. "Be on guard out there. We'll probably see servitors today."

She put on a brave face, curtseyed again, and left.

I picked up my phone again and asked Jaci to get Shane on the line. I quickly told him that the servitor attacks had begun in other realms and to have everyone on high alert.

Maxen arrived, out of breath, right after I hung up. I stood and silently passed the three notes to him.

"I'm going to Morven for anything I can get out of him about the caves," I said.

Maxen squinted. "I'm with Oliver. I don't like the idea of you going into the Duergar realm. Don't you think Morven would have told you if he knew more?"

I shook my head. "I don't know, but I have to try."

My pulse ticked up a notch. He had a strange look on his face, and I wasn't sure what it meant.

"Maxen?"

"Petra, you can't go to Periclase."

I held up my hands in innocence. "I'm not planning to."

He gave me a long, hard look.

"Really," I said. "I just want to talk to Morven. I swear to you, I'm not using this trip into the Duergar realm as an excuse to turn myself in to Periclase. It wouldn't be the right thing to do, and I'm not going to do it."

His expression eased a little. "Okay. But you should take someone with you. Someone to watch your back."

I shook my head. "No. Servitors could attack the fortress at any second. We need all swords here. I can defend myself."

He took a breath, ready to argue, but I cut him off with a sharp shake of my head and strode past him. I went to the Amethyst Room for privacy so no one would see me leave.

I wanted to go in with Aurora drawn, but the sword would give me away at a glance. I left my weapon sheathed but pulled up the hood on the loose poncho-like cloak I'd thrown on. There was an opening in the back that allowed my broadsword's hilt to protrude for easy access.

Tracing the sigils in the air that would take me to the Aberdeen, I whispered the words that opened the netherwhere.

I emerged from the void into the poorly lit haze of Morven's pub, the air heavy with grease, pipe smoke, and the dankness of the very old establishment.

My heart punched my ribs. Something was very wrong. In a split second, I took in the scene. Tables were overturned, chairs smashed, and shattered glass littered the floor. The mirror behind the bar displayed spider-web cracks from hard impacts.

Morven was nowhere in sight. But three men, dressed in Duergar light armor, were picking through the wreckage. For a handful of seconds, they didn't notice I'd arrived. But then one of them happened to turn my way. He straightened, his eyes widening.

"The princess!" he shouted, pointing. "Seize her!"

All three of them began clambering through the broken furniture toward me.

Chapter 5

I WHIPPED OUT Aurora with one hand and turned to the doorway and began furiously drawing sigils with the other hand. I whispered the words and stepped forward, but instead of passing into the netherwhere, the toe of my boot hit the wall.

"Shit!" I ground out.

Someone must have shut off the doorway's exit capacity.

Cursing under my breath, I spun around just in time to swing my sword at the soldier in the lead. He had his broadsword in his hand but pointed down and away. The soldiers didn't want to harm me, but their gleaming eyes said just how much they would enjoy getting credit for my capture.

"Not today, boys," I growled.

I summoned stone armor. Aurora flared with the colors of dawn, and my energy quickened as adrenaline and magic poured through me.

The longer I used Aurora, the faster my reflexes and greater my strength with the legendary broadsword had grown. One swing with the flat of the blade against the first soldier's head, and he was out cold.

I charged forward, disarming the second soldier with a whack to the back the wrist. His short sword clattered to the floor. I kicked it behind me. The third soldier, a massively burly man with beady eyes, tossed his sword away and faced me in a wrestler's crouch.

I flicked a glance over his shoulder. He was the only thing standing between me and the exit.

I beckoned. "C'mon, big guy, let's get this over with."

An eager, sinister grin spread over his face. He growled and charged. All of his momentum was shifted forward, his aim obviously to take me down by using his sizable mass. At the last second, I twisted away, out of his path of attack.

His meaty hand grazed my shoulder blade. He caught the back of my jacket, and there was the sound of ripping fabric as I tried to pull away. Before he could drag me back and off balance, I turned to face him, ducked under his arm, and with my head down, I threw my arms up by my ears and backed up in a swift movement. The loose poncho came neatly off me, turning inside out as I slipped out of it. In the split second of his hesitation as he lifted the garment, seemingly confused that I was no longer inside it, I sprinted to the door.

Sword in hand, I burst outside, my mind whirling. I had to reach another doorway before anyone else got the bright idea to capture me and present me to Periclase. I knew of three other doorways in the Duergar realm that were outside the palace. Two were on the palace grounds. The third was a long way off.

I turned right and began sprinting. The beefy soldier was behind me, grunting in his effort at pursuit. I could outrun him, but there were people on the streets, and I wasn't exactly inconspicuous with my face fully visible and Aurora clutched in my hand.

I veered off into a narrow alley, hoping to at least reduce my exposure.

I mentally calculated the distance and risk associated with each of the doorways I knew. The palace ones were the closest. But I probably wouldn't even make it that far before I had a horde of Duergar soldiers on my ass.

Exiting the alley, I threw hurried looks both ways. Too many people. I sprinted across the street and into the next alley. Shouts in my wake told me people were recognizing me. More would join the pursuit.

If I could find a spot to conceal myself, I could wait for cover of darkness and get to a doorway. I glanced over my shoulder. There were half a dozen people chasing me. I couldn't stay in the streets, or I'd get cornered. And my odds of being able to duck into a hiding place unnoticed were rapidly dwindling.

The commotion behind me was swelling, and when I burst out onto the open street, there were already small knots of soldiers closing in from either side. I pushed through a crowd waiting to get into a café, but I had to slow down.

My options were disappearing. Soldiers were approaching from all sides.

Rising panic mixed with anger at myself for getting into such a predicament. I stopped, widened my stance, and gripped Aurora with both hands. My only advantage was that the soldiers wouldn't want to accidentally kill me. Their king wanted me alive. But from the way they ran with their short swords in their hands, they weren't above injuring me if needed. Maybe I could chop my way through.

I swung Aurora in an arc, pushing magic into the blade. The flaring sword made the soldiers pull up short, hesitant to get within reach of the weapon.

"Stay back!" I thundered. "I am a princess of this realm and the monarch of another. Lay down your weapons, I command you! Ignore me, and your punishment will be death."

I didn't really have the authority to make such a demand, but it seemed to buy me a few seconds.

Something dark and fast overhead snagged my attention. Just as I flicked a glance upward, there was a loud caw from above. I sucked in a breath. A Great Raven was circling over the rooftops of the commerce buildings that surrounded me. Another caw, and the huge bird tilted one eye down at me. I recognized the profile of Mohawk, the Raven I'd ridden many times before.

How had she found me? I had to get higher. I scanned over the heads of the crowd pressing in around me. Half a block away, there was a horse-drawn cart loaded with crates. If I could get to it and climb up the highest stack, I might be able to swing myself up to the second floor. Not a great escape, but it was a start.

I put on my most crazy-eyed, violent expression, screamed at the top of my lungs, and charged ahead, sword swinging.

My act was enough to cut me a brief path. A few brave soldiers tried to grab me from behind, but I spun, snarling and lashing Aurora in blindingly fast, whip-like movements. The soldiers leaned away, wide-eyed.

It was my chance. I howled like a rabid werewolf and ran full speed at the cart. Launching myself from the ground using the full capacity of my stone blood strength, I landed atop a crate. It tipped under the impact. I shoved my boot against the edge, sending it to topple back at my pursuers, and hopped up to the next highest tier.

The shock of my crazed charge had worn off, and soldiers swarmed the cart. One leapt up and grabbed at my ankle, nearly pulling me down. I kicked him in the forehead and backed away from the edge of the crate.

Mohawk was calling to me overhead, swooping lower but not low enough to grab me in her talons. I needed more altitude.

I swung up to the highest pile of cargo and gauged the distance to the building I'd planned to get to. There was a wide window ledge to land on, but I'd misread how far the jump would be. With no room for a running start, I wasn't sure I could make it.

Several soldiers had followed me onto the cart. I went onto one knee to swipe down at them with my blade. I had only seconds before I'd get dragged down.

It was now or never.

I sheathed Aurora and backed up a step to the edge of the crate I stood on. Pumping my elbows hard, I ran forward the scant two or three steps available and flung myself into the air. My fingertips barely hooked onto the ledge, my body slamming against the side of the building.

I quickly swung a leg up and maneuvered onto the ledge. Soldiers were already pouring into the door below. I still needed to get a little higher. Bricks protruding from the building formed precarious footholds. Turning my toes out, I stepped onto the nearest one and reached up for a handhold. The window I'd just been pressed against slammed open, and hands raked out toward me.

I scuttled like a spider out of reach. Looking up, I realized I would run out of handholds before I could reach another window ledge. I made it up the building another few feet and then turned, searching for Mohawk.

"I'm out of room!" I shouted up at the bird.

I wasn't sure if she heard me. She disappeared from sight over the roof of the building across the street.

Soldiers were stepping out onto the window ledges below me. One of them reached for my ankle, and I kicked out and caught him under the jaw.

I was stuck. There wasn't enough clearance for Mohawk to swoop in and catch me on her back if I jumped.

A whoosh of wings and buffet of air made me look up. The Great Raven was hovering just over the rooftops, and something was clutched in her talons and dangling down.

A rope!

She was bobbling in the air, trying to maintain position and get the rope close enough for me to reach. I stretched back as far as I could, but the rope was still beyond my fingertips.

One of the men grabbed for my leg again, higher up this time. Any second, they'd probably be on the roof firing arrows or weaponized magic at Mohawk.

"Screw this," I muttered.

It was time to make my exit.

I looked over my shoulder to make sure I knew where the rope was and then bent my knees, ready to spring back into the air. If I missed, it was going to be a painful drop to the ground, not to mention landing smack in the middle of dozens of soldiers. But I couldn't wait any longer.

I pushed off, twisting in the air and reaching for the rope. My hands closed around it. My momentum sent me swinging out, and the sudden pull of my weight made Mohawk flap wildly. But she gained control and pumped her wings hard, speeding us away. She didn't get altitude quickly enough to clear the rooftops, and the side of my body slammed against the building across the street. But I held on, shaking the stars from my eyes as she dragged me higher.

Mohawk worked hard, putting distance between us and the horde of soldiers, and aiming steeply upward into the clouds. We broke through into clear blue sky. She cawed down at me, seeming to try to tell me something. In the next moment, my stomach tried to meet up with my brain as I started free falling, the rope suddenly slack in my hands. But then Mohawk was under me, and I landed hard on her back, nearly toppling off. Gripping shining black feathers in my fists, I repositioned myself with my knees between her wings. We climbed some more, and I tried to tell my panicked heart that I wasn't plunging to my death.

Then abruptly we passed into the chill of the netherwhere, and all other sensation faded away.

When we emerged, Mohawk arrowed down to a ravine below. Far off to my right stretched the dark expanse of the sea, which reflected the gray of the sky overhead. I wasn't sure where we were until I focused on two figures standing next to the stream that filled the groove of the ravine.

The bird made a steep descent and landed hard in a small clearing. I let out an *oof* as I pitched forward, my face getting buried in the feathers of her neck.

When I recovered, I looked around for the two figures, and my pulse leapt.

"Jasper!" I called, sliding off Mohawk.

He came forward to embrace me, but the other man, who I recognized as Jasper's wild shifter friend Drifte, hung back.

Feeling dazed, I pulled back and looked up into Jasper's eyes.

"Did you have Mohawk following me?" I asked. "She saved me just in time."

"I sent her to look for you," Jasper said. His face and arms were streaked with grime, his clothes rumpled. His cheeks looked hollower than I remembered.

"The Duergar were on the verge of capturing me," I said.

His expression folded into half-frown, half-surprise. "You went into the Duergar realm?"

I nodded. "I wanted to speak to Morven, but he was gone, and the Aberdeen was a wreck."

"Morven is okay," Jasper said. "Or he was very recently, anyway. He contacted me because he wanted to get a message to you."

My breath caught. "What's the message?" I couldn't help wondering why Morven didn't just send a raven to the stone fortress.

"I don't know," Jasper said. He reached into his pocket and then held out something small and silvery. "But this is for you."

I took it and turned it over in my fingers. "A coin?"

"He said you would know what to do with it."

I bit my lip for a second, unsure. Then I remembered the other coin Morven had given to me. I turned, went to the edge of the stream, and tossed the silver disk into the water.

The water at the point where the coin disappeared immediately began to darken, as if a bottle of ink had spilled. The darkness spread, and a face began to take shape—Morven's.

I blinked hard and bent at the waist, squinting into the water as the mirage-like image started speaking.

"Petra Maguire," Morven intoned in his rolling brogue. "I sought ye out because next time we meet, we won't have the luxury of conversation. But I wanted ye to understand."

A chill curled through me.

"For ages, I've collected the magic of all manner of Fae," he continued. "It has been my purpose since my birth, assigned by my people because I was destined to be the last of the Ghille Dubh. The drive to take magic, and the keeping of it, twisted me and filled me until it became all that I am. Don't think I didn't know I was seen as a monster. I always knew that I would be the last of my kind, and that I was to wait for the moment of direst need when I would finally be granted release—and relief. That moment is growing near. I tell ye all of this so that after, if ye survive, ye may pass on my story so I'm not only remembered as a twisted monster. So others know that beneath my thirst for magic lies a love of Faerie, a love of our eternal summer. We will meet again soon. Use the coin at your moment of direst need. In the meantime, I'll see about disrupting the servitor attacks. It's not what my collection of magic was intended for, but it seems a worthy way to use a wee bit of it."

I opened my mouth to respond, to ask him for more information about the caves and the god blood, but the image faded, and it struck me that I'd just witnessed a recording of sorts, not a live communication. With a dry throat, I turned to Jasper.

"Did you hear that?" I asked.

"Hear what?"

I took a deep breath. "It was a message from Morven in the water."

"I saw you staring into the stream for a moment," he said. "That's all. What happened?"

"He seemed to speak to me."

Drifte called Jasper's name, and he turned.

"I have to go," he said.

I blinked hard. "We're in Undine land, aren't we?"

"We are, and we must get back to our hunt for the Chalice of Dagda."

He looked worn, his eyes tired and haunted. I wanted to ask what he'd seen, what he'd endured, but I knew we didn't have time.

"I'm sorry, Petra, but I must go now," he said. "You should go, too."

He stepped forward, pressed his lips to mine, and then turned and jogged to meet Drifte.

"Hey," I called, and Jasper looked over his shoulder. "I love you."

A faint smile touched his lips just as the two of them disappeared into the gloom of the trees.

"Good hunting," I whispered, watching the place where they'd disappeared as my heart gave a little clench.

I went to Mohawk and climbed onto her back.

When Mohawk and I popped back into the world, I recognized the stone fortress down below. I drew a long, shaking breath.

As we neared the ground, I shouted at the gathering Carraig soldiers to stand down. Mohawk landed with a few light hops, and I slid from her back. She took flight immediately, leaving me breathless and windblown, but safe.

"At ease, soldiers," I said. "The Raven is a friend."

I straightened my shirt and went striding into the fortress, studiously ignoring the wide-eyed looks on the faces I passed.

I was glad to be back in one piece but disappointed that I hadn't gained the information I wanted. Morven's message played again in my mind's eye. It was meant only for me, and I wouldn't be repeating it. Not yet, anyway.

I found Maxen in his office and let him know I'd failed in my mission. He went pale when he learned that I'd narrowly escaped.

"You can't take that kind of risk again," he said, his mouth tight and his words clipped.

"I know," I said quietly. "I won't."

"The team went back into the caves," he said. "They're trying to replicate what they felt before."

"Any more reports of servitor attacks?" I asked, not really wanting to hear the answer.

His expression said I was right to dread. "A handful more."

Morven apparently hadn't found a way to stop them yet.

"Casualties?" I asked.

He passed a hand over his eyes and nodded. "These attacks are bloody. And lasting much longer than the previous ones."

Regardless of Morven's promises, we had to be ready. "It's probably only a matter of time, then, before the servitors show up here."

"You're probably right," Maxen said.

My chest tightened at the thought of innocent lives lost, lives that could have been spared if I'd done as Periclase asked and pledged to him.

"I want to try," I said.

He gave me a questioning look.

"I want to go into the caves and see what I can discover."

"Petra, I literally just said you can't take these kinds of risks. And for once, you actually agreed with me."

"People are dying, Maxen. They're dying because we all decided I had to refuse to give in to Periclase's demands. But I can't stand here and do nothing while the Summerlands burns and the Seelie body count rises."

I raised my chin, my jaw stubbornly set. We locked eyes for several long seconds.

Finally, he raised his hands in surrender. "Fine. I'll take you in, and the others can show you what they've discovered."

I nodded, and together we left his office and went to the Amethyst Room. He found a scrap of paper and scrawled a few sigils. "These will

50

take you into the caves, so you can go in later without me if you need to."

I stared at the markings, memorizing them. "Got it."

He took the paper from me and held it on his palm. A little shiver of magic sparked around his hand, and the piece of paper shriveled up until it was nothing more than a dusting of ash that he brushed away.

Maxen moved over to the arch, and I joined him.

"You try it," he said. "To make sure you have them right."

I lifted my hand, but then hesitated. "Maxen, if anything happens to me, now or someday, I know the Carraig Sidhe will thrive under you."

He shook his head. "Don't talk like that."

Whispering the words and drawing the sigils I'd just learned, I tried not to think about worst-case scenarios. We stepped through the arch together and a moment later emerged into the central chamber of the small cave network. Maxen created an orb of illumination magic and sent it over toward me.

I'd been so focused on the three caves and their odd contents I'd actually forgotten about one of the other unexplained features—the large hole several feet away. Maxen had said the depth hadn't been determined. I took a couple of steps in that direction, suddenly curious, but then voices from one of the tunnels caught my attention.

"You might want to call out, so you don't startle them," Maxen said. He was already going back to the arch.

"If there's news, come and let me know," I said.

He nodded and then quickly performed the magic to take him back through the doorway.

I glanced at the tunnel where the voices were coming from, but instead of going to join the others, I went over to the dark, gaping void in the ground. Maxen's ball of light bobbed along above me, lighting my way.

Leaning over the edge, I peered into the abyss. A subtle draft of air rose up from below, a cool current that flowed over my face. Half a minute later, the airflow reversed, pulling down into the hole. I stood there, as still as I could, for a few minutes, feeling the shifting air. It was like a tide, or the slow breath of a slumbering giant.

Vague, barely audible noises seemed to drift up from the depths. When I concentrated, I could almost swear there were whispered words carried on the updrafts. My eyelids drifted closed, and I stood there listening for a long moment. Was it my imagination? Or was there something down there that was trying to speak to me?

The sounds of people approaching pulled me from my focus, and I turned just as Oliver, Emmaline, and Angus emerged from a tunnel.

"Petra? What are you—" Oliver said, cutting off and quickening his pace, his face surprised and then alarmed. "Move away from there."

I blinked and glanced down. Realizing I was literally standing right on the edge of the hole, I backed up and went to meet him. But I did so reluctantly. With an almost visceral longing, part of me wanted to lie down next to the void, close my eyes, and listen to the whispering wind that flowed through it. Perhaps even let a hand dangle over the side to try to feel the darkness.

Oliver was staring into my face. "Are you okay?" he asked, his voice low.

I inhaled a sharp breath, trying to shake off the trance-like sensation that had gripped me at the rim of the abyss.

Oliver looked past me, and then his eyes met mine again. "What were you doing over there?"

I shook my head. "Just looking."

I wanted to ask if any of them had sensed something in the abyss, but my father already seemed alarmed enough about my interest in it.

"I'm fine," I said as Angus and Emmaline joined us. "I came to learn what progress you've made."

The three of them had their own illumination orb floating overhead.

The combined light of theirs and mine helped clear some of the fog from my mind. I resisted the urge to turn and stare at the hole in the ground, my stomach tightening as I realized just how strongly the chasm had seemed to pull at me.

"Lord Lothlorien told me you believe you've induced flashes of the god blood power," I said.

Angus nodded. "Aye, we believe so."

"It felt just like before, when Finvarra tried to use the Stone of Fal on us," Emmaline said, her violet eyes sparking with excitement.

"Like you left the here and now and inhabited a different body?" I asked.

"Yeah," she said. She touched the back of her hand, on which there was an angry red welt. Sky iron burn, I guessed.

I turned to Oliver, who'd been watching me with a studied intensity that made me want to fidget. "How did you do it?"

"Inducing an altered state with sky iron," he said.

I frowned. "You're torturing yourselves until you pass out?"

"Nearly," Angus said. "Then we go into the mineral cave to recover, Your Highness."

"Exposure to the strange liquid pool doesn't have the same effect," Oliver said.

I shook my head. "There's got to be something else." Again, I was tempted to turn and look at the hole in the floor of the cavern.

"We filled some bottles from both pools, and Lord Lothlorien took them, Your Majesty," Emmaline said. "But he told us that when his people went to get them for experiments, the bottles were empty."

My brows rose, and I glanced at the two men.

Angus shrugged. "Apparently the stuff doesn't survive long outside these caves. Only the Brigitstone maintains its integrity away from this place."

"Is there anything else?"

Emmaline shook her head.

"That's about the extent of it," Oliver said.

I took a breath. "Okay. I want the three of you to return to the fortress. We can't have you getting long-term sky iron poisoning."

My father's brows lowered. "And you're going to stay here? Your Highness?" he added belatedly.

"Yes," I said firmly.

I could practically see steam coming out of his ears. "May I speak to you in private, Your Majesty?" Oliver asked, his jaw clenched.

"Of course," I said tightly.

We walked to the far side of the cavern, my illumination orb floating along with us.

"I'm not leaving you here alone," he said.

I looked up into his face. "I'm sorry, but I'm not giving you a choice."

He folded his arms and gave me his hardest stare. "Exactly what are you planning to do?"

"I don't know yet."

We locked eyes, neither of us relenting for several seconds.

"The servitor attacks are spreading," I said finally. "They're bad. Innocent people are dying."

"That's not your responsibility."

"Maybe not, but I still *feel* responsible. I can't hand myself over to Periclase. So I'm going to see what I can do here." I let out a heavy sigh. "I have to do something."

"I won't interfere," he said. "I'll just keep off to the side and let you do what you wish."

I shook my head. "The servitors are going to attack the fortress any minute. I want you there."

His jaw flexed, taking on a stubborn set. "Petra," he said, his tone that of a father warning his daughter not to overstep.

"That's an order," I said quietly.

He cut his gaze off to the side, clearly angry, but he didn't argue any further.

A minute later, my father, Angus, and Emmaline left through the doorway.

Alone in the cavern, I turned to the three dark tunnels leading into the caves. I wasn't going to leave until I'd solved the mystery of the god blood running through my veins.

Chapter 6

I COULD SWEAR the pit was still whispering to me, but instead of going to it, I resisted the pull and picked one of the tunnels. It was the one I least wanted to go down—the one that housed a bubbling pool of sky iron.

I pushed back against the sense of dread that clenched the pit of my stomach tighter, the sensation deepening the closer I got to the iron. My illumination orb lit the small room, glinting off the silvery surface of the liquid. There were a few wide-necked glass bottles, plus a long-handled cup with a pour spout, near the entrance. Residual sky iron clung to the cup, which had obviously been used to sample the pool.

Crouching a few feet from the edge of the liquid, I stared into it, trying to ignore the temptation to turn and run. For Fae, facing this much sky iron was a psychological horror difficult to describe. That much of the substance that was agony and powerlessness incarnate. Fae with stone blood were somewhat more resistant to the pain and physical damage iron could cause, but that didn't make us comfortable with the stuff by any stretch.

As I watched, small pockets of air bubbled to the surface and burst, as if the pool were heated to a simmer from below. But it emitted no warmth.

I went and grabbed the scoop and a bottle. I dipped the cup into the pool and then set down the bottle and carefully filled it halfway. My stomach churned in response to the nearness of the iron, but I tried to ignore it, focusing instead on keeping my trembling hand as steady as possible.

When I touched the bottle to put on the lid, my fingers ached with the throb of the sky iron trapped in the container. I wanted to try inducing the hallucination as the others had, but I couldn't quite bring myself to pour the liquid onto my skin.

I battled my will for a few seconds but then let out a harsh breath and shook my head.

If the only secret the caves held was to give ourselves terrible iron burns and then heal them in the mineral chamber, all for just a brief flash of something we couldn't understand or control, it wasn't going to do us a damn bit of good. There had to be some other secret the caves held for us.

"There's another answer," I whispered to myself.

I capped the bottle and carried it with me back down the tunnel into the main cavern and left the sample of sky iron. Then I continued on into the tunnel to the pool of stinging water. There, I found more bottles and another sampling cup. I half-filled another bottle with the clear liquid and carried it to the central room. Leaving the bottles on the ground, I went empty-handed into the third tunnel.

The room at the end glinted with facets of the Brigitstone that formed the walls. I instantly felt more at ease as I breathed in the soothing mineral scent.

Reaching back for Aurora, I drew the sword, found a slight groove in the wall, and jammed the tip of the blade into the indentation. It took some muscle, but I managed to pry loose a chunk of stone the size of a deck of cards. I carried it back to the large cavern, where I set the piece of stone down next to the bottles.

I lowered myself to the ground, sat cross-legged, and regarded the three items before me. Anxiety tightened my insides, and not just because of the sky iron. I badly needed to discover how to invoke and use the blood of the Fomoire. I tried not to think about servitors ravaging the fortress, of Periclase in the Summerlands, or Faerie turning to ash at the wrath of the Tuatha De Danann. Taking a calming, drawn-out inhale, I ordered myself to focus on what was before me.

"What are you hiding?" I whispered, staring intently at each of the items in turn.

The silence of the caves was peaceful, in its way, but it wasn't giving me any inspired ideas.

A soft draft of air brushed my face and hands, barely stirring my hair. My attention shifted beyond the bottles and stone to the black opening in the ground less than a dozen feet away.

My breath stilled as something familiar trilled through me, a vibration so faint that if I didn't know it like my own face, I might have missed it completely.

Could it really be?

I rose to my feet, and with my heart in my throat, I went to stand at the edge of the pit. Keeping perfectly still, I opened my senses, barely daring to breathe.

There. Another faint shiver.

It felt like a weak echo of my bond with my shadowsteel spellblade, Mortimer, that I'd lost in a crevasse when Jasper and I had gone into the Giants' Causeway to save Oberon from the Tuatha. But that was on the Earthly side of the hedge and halfway around the world. Even when I'd stood directly over the fissure where I'd lost Mort, I could barely feel the sword's presence.

A pang of longing for my old weapon, which was imbued with my own blood, made me pull in my bottom lip and bite down hard. It had to be a trick, perhaps a by-product of stress and proximity to sky iron. It made sense, in a way, to be longing for something that was familiar and comforting in the face of crisis and difficult choices.

I turned away from the abyss. I didn't have time for wishes and regrets.

"*Petra Maguire . . .*"

I froze at the sound of my name, my blood instantly chilling. Slowly, I turned around. It had been quiet, so faint, barely a whisper of words. With careful steps, I went to the edge, my heart thumping uneasily.

"*Healing and agony and the spark that flows between them.*"

"Who's there?" I called. My voice briefly echoed around the cavern. I stayed stock-still as seconds ticked by.

Healing and agony and the spark that flows between them?

What the hell did that mean?

"Hello?"

But no more words came. And the sensation of my bond with Mort, if it'd really been there at all, was gone. Even the current of air seemed to have paused.

The phrase I'd heard echoed around in my mind.

Healing and agony . . . Brigitstone healed. Sky iron was agonizing.

I strode back to the bottles and the rock. I untwisted the caps from both the bottles. Holding one in each hand, I gazed at the liquids.

Here was healing, agony, and water that seemed electrified—the spark? I tipped the bottles and allowed several drops of both liquids to spill out onto the chunk of Brigitstone I'd chipped off.

The liquids mingled on the rough face of the rock, sizzling and spitting. I edged back out of the way of the splatter. The vapor created by the mingling substances wasn't so easily escaped. It looked like only a weak curl of bluish steam or smoke. But when it hit my nostrils, the world reeled as if I'd been punched in the temple. My eyes watering, I sank to my knees and set the two bottles aside before I accidentally dropped them.

I rocked back, cradling my head in my hands and moaning. The pressure in my skull was so intense that the backs of my eyeballs itched and my eardrums felt as if they were bowing outward. My arms were weakening. To my horror, I watched like a bystander as my hands slid from my head and flopped onto the rough floor of the cavern.

Groaning, I sagged over to my side as my muscles went limp. I'd set off a reaction by mixing all the substances together, and I was rapidly losing control of my body. Was it some kind of toxin . . . ?

I lay there with a sideways view of the cavern, wondering if this was it, if I was going to die alone underground in the dark. There was nothing I could do. In the past, I would have struggled. I would have tried to fight it even if the battle was fruitless. But somehow, there was an odd sort of peace in it. As consciousness began to dim, I made the decision to embrace it. I'd die or I wouldn't, and at that moment there wasn't a damn thing I could do about it either way.

My surroundings faded to gray, and my heartbeat and breathing slowed.

Like a flick of a switch, everything went out.

When I came to, it was a sharp, jarring awakening. Every muscle spasmed violently, and I gasped in pain as my spine arched to an impossible angle. The spasms eased after a few seconds, leaving me limp on the hard ground. My heart racing, I stared into the glow of the illumination orb that hovered in the air over me.

I was alive. And I *felt* alive. Energy was zinging through me like I'd chugged a gallon of espresso. I sat up and stretched my arms out, almost expecting to be able to see the vitality that thrummed in my veins.

Or was I hallucinating? Warily, I looked over at the bottles and the stone, which were right where I'd left them. The chunk of Brigitstone had stopped sizzling, but there was a dent where the two liquids had mixed and created the vapor I'd inhaled.

I pulled my feet under me and hopped up lightly. I felt like I could sprint a mile. Wishing I had someone to spar with, I reached back and drew Aurora and summoned magic. Power burst through me, flooding down my arm and into the sword. My eyes widened as the blade flared like a firework, surrounded in a rosy flame of magic and shooting sparks the warm colors of the dawn sky. I stepped through some fencing drills, and my reflexes and strength were so great I nearly tripped as unexpected momentum carried me forward. And it wasn't just my body. Thoughts came fast, as if I could jump ahead in time and visualize the exact muscle flexions I needed to swing the sword with a precision and ease that was startling.

My pulse quickened. Was this the secret of the caves? Would combining the liquids and dripping them on the stone give us the strength, clarity, and skill to defeat the Tuatha?

Abruptly, I stopped. No. Something in my gut told me that enhanced abilities wouldn't be enough to win. There was something more. There had to be something more.

As if in response to my doubts, a wave of dizziness swept through me. I stumbled to one side and hastily caught my balance and sheathed Aurora before I could accidently drop the sword. Vertigo clutched me again, and I reeled, dropping to one knee.

But it wasn't just dizziness. The ground was moving. It was tipping, angling down toward the hole. The floor of the cavern warped, growing steeper and steeper as I tried to shuffle back.

Panic thumped through me. The doorway. I had to get out. I turned my back to the chasm with the aim of scrambling toward the arch. But it was gone. How could it be gone? It was a massive, ancient geological structure. My way out had literally disappeared.

"No," I whispered, confusion and fear mingling in my gut.

Some part of my mind still suspected I was dreaming, but I couldn't trust that assumption. Everything felt too solid, too real. And the cave was still contorting, trying to form a funnel that would spill me into the dark void.

With glassy clanks, the bottles tumbled toward the hole, spilling their contents along the way. They disappeared. The acrid smell of sky iron hit my nose, adding to my panic. The three substances seemed to mingle again, producing the same vapor as before.

I flattened myself on the floor and found handholds as the ground beneath me continued to tilt. The soft current of air from the hole increased to a stiff wind, sucking, pulling at my hair and clothes like a giant vacuum cleaner.

I was strong. I might be able to hold on until everything stopped shifting. I could probably dangle off the wall for a while. But the doorway had disappeared. I had no way back to the fortress.

A deep knowing took root low in my gut.

I was going into the hole. The only way out, if there was a way out, was down.

Seemingly at random, Melusine's plea to have faith flashed through my mind.

Faith.

It meant releasing oneself to the outcome.

Drawing a ragged breath, I let go. Sliding over the rough rock, I bumped and tumbled toward the black void, my frightened cry echoing in the cave as I plunged into the dark.

My stomach rolled and lurched as I flailed in free fall. My illumination orb hovered at the opening of the void, refusing to follow me down. After a few seconds, it was a mere point in the distance.

I realized there was an odd quality to my descent. Under the force of gravity, I should have been falling much faster. I also probably should have been ricocheting off the walls. But my fall was slow, almost gentle. Not quite a float. I tried to twist around in the air to see where I was headed, but only darkness awaited below. Maybe it was better not to know what I was going to land on at the bottom.

Once I'd fallen far enough for the light in the cave to disappear, I began to feel oddly sleepy. I tried to fight it, but it was like I'd been drugged. Just before I unwillingly lost consciousness, I thought I felt another twinge of Mort's presence.

Then I was lost to the world.

When awareness returned, the first thing I noticed was the solid feel of the ground I was sprawled over. I was either dreaming or my fall had finally ended.

Either way, there was a hand shaking me, an unfamiliar voice speaking to me.

"Ethniu," a male voice was saying more and more urgently.

I cracked my eyelids open to blue sky and a face bent over me. The face was unfamiliar except for the eyes. My breath stilled as I focused on the man's eyes. They were the exact shade of gray, with the exact pattern of darker and lighter flecks, as Oliver's.

Chapter 7

THE FACE WITH Oliver's eyes was tight with concern.

"Ethniu? Can you hear me?" he asked.

I blinked and rolled my eyes around, trying to assess what had broken or otherwise been damaged as a result of the fall. But to my surprise, I felt mostly fine. The side of my head throbbed sharply, but it seemed a minor thing compared to how badly I could have been hurt.

I started to push up to sitting. "I can hear you," I said and then froze.

My voice sounded strange. Huskier, and . . . my eyes widened. The words sounded normal in my head, but when I spoke them, they came out in a strange tongue.

I cleared my throat and tried again. "I . . . I can hear you," I said. My mouth still formed the foreign words that I somehow understood.

"Are you hurt?"

"I don't think so."

The man grasped at my arm, his eyes still concerned, and hauled me to my feet. Hair swung across my cheek. Dark-blond hair. My hair was dark brown.

I looked down and reeled dizzily as I realized I didn't recognize the clothes, the arms, the *body*. Oh gods, what was happening to me?

My breath grew ragged as I started to panic. I had no idea where I was. Or who I was. Or why this man was trying to talk to me.

"Who are you?" I asked hoarsely.

The man's concern transformed into fear. "I'm your father. Balor. Do you not recognize me?" He looked past me, shouted a name, and then turned back to me. "You were fine and then a spell of dizziness seemed to overtake you. Another one. I'm getting concerned about these spells, Ethniu."

I twisted and finally started noticing my surroundings. I was outside, but in some sort of wide walled courtyard. Perhaps inside a fortress? There were others around—leading horses, polishing armor, or practicing with swords.

I wanted to insist that it was all unfamiliar, but that wasn't quite true. I knew this place. I knew the man holding my arm. I knew the body I was in. It was all there, somewhere in the remote corners of my mind. I strained, trying to place it all, but I was so lightheaded. I swayed. I was going down.

My knees buckled, and I fell forward into the man, Balor, who claimed to be my father. The world grayed and then darkened.

"Petra!"

I jolted awake, my eyes flying open. When I realized it was Oliver grasping my shoulder and shaking me, I blinked hard and flinched away, not trusting what I was seeing. My gaze swung around. I was back in the cavern. The arched doorway was there. The darkness of the void yawned several feet away.

"What happened?" Oliver demanded.

I forced my focus to his face, the angles of his features highlighted by the illumination orb hovering above us.

"Uh . . . I don't know. Something very strange," I said haltingly. My eyes slipped over to the hole. "I must have hallucinated because I went down that hole."

He sat back on his heels, seeming a little calmer since I started speaking. His gray eyes squinted at me.

"Tell me exactly what happened. What were you doing? What did you see in your hallucination?" he asked, his voice tense.

I hesitated for a second. It wasn't like Oliver to indulge in the retelling of dreams.

Pushing the heel of my hand against the side of my head, I frowned. My attention snagged on the two bottles and piece of Brigitstone nearby.

"I dripped the substances from the two pools onto the stone," I said, pointing. He gave the items a brief glance, but his lack of surprise said he'd noticed them when he'd arrived. "A vapor formed, and I couldn't avoid inhaling it. That's when everything got a little crazy."

I paused. Or had things gotten weird even before that?

"What?" he prompted. I could tell he was trying to be patient, but there was an urgency in his expression that made my stomach tighten.

"Did something happen in the fortress?" I tried to pull my feet under me to rise, but he kept a firm hand on my shoulder.

"Try to remember everything," he said. "It's important, Petra."

I took a breath and then did my best to recount every detail of what I remembered since I arrived in the cavern. The faint sense of Mort coming from the void, the way the air current changed, the hallucination, all of it.

"The man there, the one who was worried about me, he had your eyes," I said. "He said he was my father and called me Ethniu. And he called himself—"

"Balor."

My eyes went wide. "Yes. Who are—were—those people?"

"They're Fomoire. Balor was king and Ethniu was his daughter."

I let my head drop into my hands. "Is this some kind of time-travel shit? Because I don't think I have the intellectual capacity to grasp that."

Oliver didn't laugh. "I don't know. Maybe. But one thing is certain. It's not going to do us a damn bit of good to lose ourselves in hallucinations. We have to force the gods to embody us, not the other way around."

I shook my head. "I'm not sure what that means. But that Balor man? Did you . . . embody him?"

My father nodded. "I saw that place, too. And Ethniu was there. She . . . she had your eyes. I can't believe I forgot that detail until this moment."

"What about Angus and Emmaline? Did they experience the same thing?"

"In very brief flashes, but yes. They seemed to have Fomoire counterparts as well."

My blood chilled as I suddenly remembered that he'd brushed off my question a moment ago. I gathered my legs under me and started to stand. Oliver rose, too, keeping close in case I lost my balance.

"What happened?" I repeated the question. "Servitors?"

He didn't answer.

"Oliver?" I said his name sharply.

"Servitors," he confirmed.

I flew toward the arch, cursing. "Why in the hell are we just sitting here chatting?"

I'd hoped Morven would find a way to intervene and stop the servitors, but maybe something had happened to him.

He hurried after me. "I needed you to remember everything that happened. It fades very fast."

I couldn't respond, as I was already whispering the words that would open the doorway. I hastily drew the sigils and felt Oliver's hand on my back just before I stepped into the void.

We emerged through the doorway in the fortress foyer just as a frost giant let out a deafening roar. Aurora was in my hand almost as a reflex. I pulled magic and the sword flared with the colors of sunrise.

Four Carraig soldiers had backed the frost giant up to the wall opposite the mail room, but they didn't seem to know what to do with it. And the creature was pissed about being cornered. It was swinging its ice-studded club at the soldiers, the swipes telegraphed by the slowness of the giant's reflexes.

In the mouth of the hallway leading deeper into the fortress, I glimpsed the flash of an ogre's battle axe. We were being treated to a variety pack of servitors.

Adrenaline poured through me. I sped across the wide floor of the entry toward the soldiers holding the frost giant at bay.

Oliver followed me, but I twisted to holler at him over the din of shouting and crashes, "Go help somewhere else! I'll take care of this."

He nodded and veered off without question, and I joined the two men and two women facing the frost giant.

One of them noticed me. "How do we dispense with this thing, Your Majesty?"

Frost giants were slow-moving but very difficult to kill due to their size, thickness of fur, and the tough layer of fat under their skin. And if you happened to get in the way of one of their clubs, you'd get crushed to a pulp.

"Great question," I said, jumping back as the giant made a slow, arcing swipe at us with its club. "I'm guessing fire kills ice."

The creature was a servitor, a figment of its creator, but the damage it could do was very real, as evidenced by the nearby circular smash in the tile floor from the giant's club.

Focusing on the center of my chest, I drew magic more deeply and sent it down my arm and into Aurora. Rose-tinged flames engulfed the blade.

"Move that way and distract it," I said, brushing my hand out to the left.

The soldiers shifted away from me. Two of them began shouting, and one banged his sword on the tiles. The giant's attention followed the noise.

Seizing my opportunity, I sprinted forward, getting out of the range of the giant's peripheral vision, and squeezed between it and the wall. The creature's ice-blue fur stuck out in tufts, and its scent of crisp snow and animal musk filled my nose. For a thing conjured completely of magic, it was damn realistic. Its huge, blocky, fur-covered feet shifted as it took a step to swing at the soldiers.

I lunged and, with a two-handed grip, swung Aurora. The sword whipped through the air in a blur. Magic and the sword's innate power combined to make it blindingly quick. I wanted to hit the giant's Achilles tendon, but I was unsure exactly how high up to strike.

Aurora sliced through fur and skin but hit something solid. Damn, too low. I'd struck the top of the bony heel, not high enough to cut the tendon.

The giant let out an enraged roar, the noise shaking the walls and rattling my bones. I jumped back as it kicked and stomped. The creature twisted around, already swinging the ice-studded club. My heart in my throat, I waited until the last possible second to dive out of the way of the club's arc.

Rolling past the foot I'd injured, I smacked into a pillar before I could halt my own momentum. I let out a grunt and scrambled to right myself.

The club had smashed into the wall, sending pieces of ornate stone flying in a puff of dust. The furious frost giant was still putting weight on the foot I'd sliced, which meant I hadn't done much damage in spite of the dark-blue blood pooling on the tiles.

Using the column as a support, I got to my feet and calculated my next move as the giant slowly turned, looking for me.

"Distraction!" I shouted at the soldiers still standing in a half-circle around the frost giant.

They began shouting and clanging their weapons, but the frost giant wasn't falling for it this time. It turned fully, spotted me, and brought the club up over its head in both hands.

I pushed off the column and charged. The frost giant was facing me, so I didn't have a clean shot at the Achilles. I skidded to a stop, jumped on its foot, and gripped a fistful of pale-blue fur with my left hand. Before I could get Aurora around to slice at the back of the ankle, the giant foot rose a few feet and then stomped hard. I hugged the frosty's leg to keep from getting jarred off.

Before the giant could try to kick me away, I whipped my sword around the leg, and throwing as much strength into it as I could, I awkwardly and blindly drew the blade across the ankle.

The giant screeched and pitched. I lost my hold and flew off, smashing into the wall. The back of my head hit, and I saw stars and splotches. Tipping my head back, I looked up at the frost giant as it tried to put weight on the foot. But I must have at least nicked the tendon, because the leg wouldn't hold up. With a high-pitched roar, the giant stumbled. It crashed against the pillar and slid down.

One of the soldiers ran a few steps and then leapt onto the giant's shoulder. The soldier was trying to get his sword around to slice the giant's throat, but the angle was bad.

Still dizzy from the smack to the head, I used Aurora to help me stand.

"The eye!" I shouted. "The hide's too thick. Go for the eye!"

The soldiers heard me, and with all four of them swarming the giant's head and shoulders, one managed to plunge a sword into the eye socket.

The frost giant keened, and then the sound abruptly stopped. The creature stiffened, fell, and then disappeared. Only a dusting of snow was left eddying through the space where the servitor had been.

The soldiers tumbled, limbs askew and swords skittering across the tiled floor. Dazed, they looked around and then began collecting themselves. The foyer was oddly still, but the sounds of battle echoed down the corridors.

"I saw an ogre in the hallway back there," I said. "What else are we facing?"

"Little of everything," one of the women said. "There are small creatures wearing all black attacking with throwing knives, ogres with battle axes, serpents shooting lightning, more frost giants." She ran her hand over her hair. "It's like a zoo was let loose in here."

Snakes shooting lighting. That was a new one for me.

I nodded grimly. "These servitors are going to be more violent than the ones we've seen before. But they're not going to win. Let's take back our home."

I turned and began jogging toward the main corridor leading away from the foyer. The aspect of my personality that relished a fight was eager to engage. But the part of me that felt responsible for my people dreaded what we would find as we made our way deeper into the fortress.

It wasn't long before we stumbled upon our first casualty. A female soldier lay still to one side of the hallway. Blood had pooled under her upper body. I slowed, and with my chest aching, I went to see who it was. Her head was turned toward the wall, but I recognized her even before I knelt to push her hair from her cheek. It was Julie, an older cousin of Shane. I didn't know her well, as she'd been several years ahead of me in school, but my heart clenched at the loss.

Behind me, one of the female soldiers let out a small sound of grief. I heard Julie's name, and a male voice cursing, the words equally angry and sorrowful.

I spared a few precious seconds to fix Julie's face in my mind. She'd been struck on the side of the head, the gash indicative of a battle axe. Carraig stone armor didn't extend over the head, and I spotted a helmet several feet away. It had probably flown off in the battle, leaving her exposed.

Slowly rising, I turned and faced the four soldiers. Their faces were stricken and pinched. Our tiny kingdom had not been engaged in many battles, even before we became the Carraig. We weren't accustomed to losing our own. There weren't many of us, and any loss always hit the entire fortress hard.

"We knew it would be worse this time," I said quietly. "We will take time to mourn later. Now, we must send a message to the bastard who created these servitors. Let's give him a brutal show, shall we?"

Their faces hardened.

"Yes, Your Highness," one of the men said, his voice a vicious growl. I turned and set off at a run.

The fight against the servitors was, in some sense, a relief. I knew how to wield a sword. I could cut down an enemy. Mentally, I shifted into the flow of battle. But even as I fought, there was a part of my mind that snagged on what had happened in the caves. I needed to get back there. If I didn't unlock the connection between me and Ethniu, between the modern stone blood Fae and the ancient Fomoire gods, Faerie would succumb to Periclase and a dark winter of Unseelie rule. If there was any Faerie left after the Tuatha came.

The servitor attack seemed to stretch on for days, though it was probably just a few hours. I lost track of time as I methodically moved from one skirmish to the next. I caught up with Oliver in the training yard, where he and a dozen others were facing off with another frost giant. My momentary relief at seeing him uninjured was replaced by the heartache of three still forms lying in the grass near the entrance to the indoor pool.

Emmaline sprinted past me into one of the gyms.

"I'm going to get training ropes, Your Majesty!" she called as she ran by. "We're going to make a tripwire."

I kept back, assessing the frost giant and catching my breath. After a few seconds' observation, I realized the fighters were right not to try to get close to this giant as I had the other one. This one was smaller than the one we'd killed in the foyer but seemed to be much more agile, the swings of its club swift and dangerous. Perhaps Periclase had learned to make a deadlier variant of this particular servitor.

Wheeling around, I chased after Emmaline. She'd found several ropes used for training games. I helped her drag them out into the yard. The soldiers were doing a good job keeping the frost giant contained, but I kept a wary eye on it while Emmaline and I joined the lengths of rope with knots. We worked quickly, and in a matter of a couple of minutes, we were ready.

Together, we dragged our creation toward the battle.

"I'm going to run the rope around," Emmaline said, her eyes glued to the giant as she studied its movements.

I shook my head. "No, someone from the battle ranks can do it."

She flicked a look at me. "I'm the fastest, Your Highness. Let me."

My jaw tightened. I didn't want to put her in peril, but she was only a few months away from being a fully trained soldier. To deny her would be to insult the lifetime she'd spent training.

"Okay," I said. "Let's move it around first so it'll be easier for you to pull."

Oliver came to help us reposition the length of the rope, and I quickly explained the plan. "Once the giant falls, go for the eye. That's how we killed another one."

He ran off to tell the other soldiers to draw the giant's attention away from Emmaline as best they could.

My heart in my throat, I waited with Emmaline as we watched for the perfect moment for her to take off. Even though I knew she could handle herself, my stomach still knotted with dread. Was this how Oliver felt every time I unsheathed my sword? If this was a taste of how a parent agonized when his child was in danger, I couldn't imagine how he'd kept calm when I'd entered the Battle of Champions. It didn't help my anxiety that Emmaline had shed some of her battle gear so she could move faster.

"Ready?" I prompted her. I clutched Aurora. I was going to back her up, but I didn't want her to get distracted by me. I'd be ready to jump in if she got into trouble. "Go!"

With the rope in her hand, she charged forward. She *was* fast. Especially for a full-blood Carraig.

The giant's back to us gave Emmaline an opportunity to approach. The rope dragged along behind her like a long, thin snake in the grass. As she angled around the creature, the rope pulled against its ankle. It twisted and looked down to see what had touched it just as Emmaline made her turn to cross in front of the giant.

With a surprised grunt, the frost giant swept its club in a downward arc, like a one-handed golf swing. The ice-studded club was headed straight for Emmaline, but she was focused on her run.

My heart jumped into my throat. She was going to get hit.

Charging through the giant's legs, I shoved Emmaline hard. She flew forward, leaving me in the path of the club. I pushed a surge of magic into Aurora and held the sword aloft, side-stepping at the last second and taking a swing at the oncoming club. Bright magic flared, and the blade met the club's head with a bone-jarring impact. For the briefest of moments, heat and light burned my face and eyes.

Spinning away to keep from losing my balance, I blinked spots from my vision. An angry roar drew my gaze up. The giant held the club in front of its face, furious. The weapon was nothing more than hole-riddled husk. Apparently, Aurora had melted the ice within it.

I leapt out of the way as Emmaline and another soldier sped past with the rope. They made it completely around the giant, encircling its ankles with the rope. Others ran forward to grasp it and heave back. I sheathed Aurora and joined them.

We weren't strong enough to pull the creature off balance, but the tightening rope did its job. As the frost giant tried to raise a foot to take a step, it got tripped up. The giant teetered, and then it was going down like a felled tree. The impact shook the ground.

I let go of the rope, drew my sword, and flew at the creature's head. Switching my grip on the blade's handle, I drove Aurora down into the dark pupil of the giant's eye. The giant stiffened and then disappeared in a cloud of swirling snowflakes.

My chest heaving from the exertion, I whirled around to make sure Emmaline and Oliver were okay. My father was grasping her shoulder in a gesture of a job well done. She beamed up at him.

Something caught Oliver's attention across the yard, and I turned to see what it was, expecting an ogre or some other servitor. But it was Shane, the young Commander of the battle ranks.

He slowed and stopped in front of me, giving me a deferential nod. "Your Highness, I'm glad I found you."

"What's the state of the fight?" I asked, my entire body tensed.

He looked exhausted, but he pulled himself up to full height and leveled his chin. "I'm pleased to report that the servitors have been dispensed."

I nodded, slumped, and let out a whoosh of a breath, unable to speak for a second. "Thank the gods." Straightening, I glanced at Oliver and then past him at the dead Carraig. "We need to assess the damage."

"I passed Lord Lothlorien on my way here," Shane said. "He's going to the Ruby Room and asked me to invite you there as soon as you're able to get away."

"You'll join us," I said to Shane. And to Oliver, "You as well."

Shane turned to the soldiers, his face solemn. "You know what to do with our fallen."

With every muscle in my body screaming with fatigue and my heart heavy with the knowledge of loss of life, I walked with Shane and Oliver into the fortress.

Chapter 8

OLIVER, SHANE, AND I arrived in the Ruby Room to find Maxen already there. His rumpled clothing, the dried blood on his cheek, and his tired eyes showed that he'd joined in the fight. Not that I expected anything less. While his mother had always chosen to retreat to safety when danger loomed, Maxen had never backed down from a battle. We'd trained together all through school, and he'd managed to keep up his skills even with all his other responsibilities.

He inclined his head. "Your Highness."

My body weight suddenly felt like too much to hold up. I pulled off my scabbard, propping Aurora's handle against the table, and sank into a chair.

My gaze flicked from Maxen to Shane. "How bad?" I asked quietly.

Shane's mouth worked for a moment. "We lost twenty-three by the most current count. There may be more we haven't yet found."

I propped my elbow on the table and let my forehead fall into my hand. Twenty-three. For the largest kingdoms, that number of deaths would be nothing more than a blip after a serious skirmish. But it was the highest single-event death toll for our people in the history of the fortress. Prior servitor attacks, while terrifying, had been much less deadly. My throat closed as I once again recalled that I could have prevented it. If I'd given in to Periclase's demand of surrender, he wouldn't have sent the servitors. And we weren't the only ones grieving.

In every Seelie kingdom in Faerie, people were mourning their dead.

But I couldn't let the weight of guilt crush me. I forced my thoughts to the alternative, to the prophecies that had come from three different oracles, all saying that if the Carraig Sidhe aligned with the Unseelie, Faerie would fall to Periclase. It wasn't as much comfort as I would have hoped. Prophecies were just words—intangible warnings. Dead bodies and grief-stricken families felt very real.

"It's a terrible spot to be in," came Oliver's voice. I looked up to find his gray eyes on me. "But it was the right decision to refuse the Duergar king's demand."

My father had obviously guessed my thoughts. I appreciated his reassurance, but it didn't change the fact that twenty-three of our people had lost their lives.

"You don't need to stay, Shane," I said to the Battle Master. "I know you have work to do."

He rose, bowed, and let himself out.

"It could have been worse," Maxen said once the door was closed again. "Periclase could have sent an endless stream of servitors. We might still be out there fighting. Our people still dying."

I nodded. "I know. And he may send more yet."

I didn't believe Periclase wanted to wipe us out, though. He wanted to break us down with the hope that I would change my mind and join him.

I paused, gathering my thoughts. "As bad as this was, we can't let ourselves be consumed by it. There's another matter that demands our attention."

It felt callous to change the subject so quickly, but I could almost sense the caves pulling at me. I needed to return there and try to discover more about our Fomoire connection. I hadn't done it in time for this servitor attack. I wanted to be ready for whatever was next.

"Yes," Maxen agreed, his expression turning from sorrowful to grim.

"An update has come from the Summerlands."

My breath stilled. "And?"

"The castle has been breached. Oberon and Titania most likely have already evacuated."

My fatigued body chilled. It had actually happened. Periclase and the Unseelie were taking the High Court of Faerie. Not in full control yet, but it was probably only a matter of days, maybe just hours, before Periclase would declare himself High King. It almost felt as if killing Finvarra had done nothing. That wasn't completely true—Periclase didn't have the universal adoration of the Unseelie that Finvarra had—but I expected the Unseelie would soon unite behind the Duergar king. After generations of Seelie rule, the Unseelie were desperately hungry for a chance to control Faerie.

"Where will Oberon and Titania go?" I asked.

Maxen shook his head. "I don't know. But their military has been decimated, and the support they had from other Seelie kingdoms, well . . . most of their militaries have suffered losses, and now we're all trying to defend ourselves against the servitors."

I made a low, discouraged noise in the back of my throat. Periclase had indeed done a fine job of weakening the Seelie forces all around Faerie. And since Oberon had been ousted, I expected at least a few of the Seelie realms would cut their losses and try to align themselves with Periclase and the Unseelie. Periclase would use his leverage to try to strike deals—no more servitor attacks in return for switching sides.

"Have any of the Seelie kingdoms turned yet?" I asked.

"Not yet." Maxen's thin-lipped expression told me I was right to expect that it was only a matter of time before some of our current allies gave into Periclase.

When survival was at stake, loyalty could get thrown by the wayside.

"There's something else," Maxen said. "Sightings of the Dullahan have been confirmed."

I froze. "Where?"

"Remote regions. Wild lands."

I thought of Drifte and his small outpost in an undeveloped region of Faerie. It was cold there, the mountain peaks snow-capped as the Unseelie winter began to encroach.

"They seem to be growing their army," Maxen continued. "They're targeting the settlements that don't have much in the way of defense. I believe the Dullahan are trying to shore up their numbers in advance of the attack."

He'd stumbled a little, the shock clear on his face even as he said it. I felt just as stunned as he looked.

"It's really happening, then? The Tuatha De Danann are coming soon," I said, feeling a bit stupid about having to ask so literally, but I was struggling to wrap my mind around it.

Maxen took a breath in through his parted lips, as if trying to mentally steady himself. "It looks that way."

I turned to look at Oliver. "I need to go back to the caves. I want you to go, too."

I felt Maxen's attention heighten. There hadn't been an opportunity to explain to him what I'd experienced, how I'd used the materials in the cavern system to bring on a hallucination that took me to the Fomoire's time and land.

I stood, and Maxen rose, too. I picked up my scabbard and pulled it over my head, settling the strap across my chest in a practiced movement I'd done hundreds of times before. The weight of Aurora—heavier than my old sword by a couple of ounces—reminded me of how I'd thought Mort had called to me in the void.

"Wait, what are you going to do?" Maxen asked, his curiosity turning to apprehension.

"Something happened when I was down there alone, and I want to make it happen again. Oliver needs to come with me. I don't know how long we'll be down there. But I know I can trust you to watch over our people and take care of the kingdom. You have my gratitude for doing so."

My father had gotten to his feet as well, but he stayed back, watching and listening to my exchange with Maxen.

"Petra . . . Your Majesty," Maxen protested, following after me as I moved toward the door. "You can't just lose yourself down there. We need you and Oliver here in the fortress. You can't go. You're the queen of this realm, and your people need your leadership. We can send others to continue the investigation."

I turned and faced him so abruptly that we ended up almost nose-to-nose.

"No, we can't send others," I said. "I have to go, and I need Oliver there, too. You need us down there far more than you need us here. And we must do it alone. Don't try to stop us, and don't disrupt us. You have to trust me on this, Maxen."

I looked into his blue eyes for a long moment, silently trying to drive home my conviction about what I had to do. He was still visibly upset, but his shoulders dropped.

"If you're not back in six hours, I'm coming down there," he said.

"Fine," I relented. "But not before then. No one goes down there before then."

As Oliver and I left the Ruby Room, Maxen's alarm reverberated in my head. I was surprised, I suddenly realized, that he was so adamant about not letting me go back to the caves. And then it dawned on me: Maxen wanted me there in the fortress, wearing the crown. Not just as a figurehead for the Carraig—no, *he* wanted me there being Queen. Could it be that he'd come around to a greater level of acceptance about our respective roles in the kingdom? Was it possible that he no longer wished he was on the throne?

Those were questions I'd have to examine later.

When I'd stepped out of the Ruby Room, I'd had a singular purpose driving me: get back to the caves and get to the place where I'd been Ethniu. But as we walked through the corridors of the fortress, I had to slow my pace when my eyes met those of my subjects'. The pain and hope for some reassurance painted on the faces of the Carraig snapped me back to the present moment and time. I couldn't just march to the nearest doorway and disappear. I wanted to go, and it was necessary for me to return to the cavern, but it wouldn't have been right to rush past my people.

I stopped where a pair of soldiers was sweeping up the wreckage of battle. There was smashed pottery on the floor. I recognized the pattern on the shards—the ruined object had been a huge decorative urn that used to be displayed in a tall arched niche in the wall. The marble bench that had always sat under the urn had been knocked over, and one of the corners had chipped.

The soldiers, a man and woman around ten years older than me, paused in their efforts to move the jagged remnants of the urn to the side of the hallway.

"Your Highness," they said, both inclining their heads.

"Evie. Wen." I addressed them both by name, meeting each of their gazes in turn. "I'm relieved to see you made it through the battle relatively unharmed. Which servitors did you fight?"

They gave me a quick recounting of the creatures they'd battled, and as I'd hoped, it seemed to brighten their moods to recall their kills. I expressed my gratitude for their service and skills, and then Oliver and I moved on.

We continued like that through the fortress, pausing to briefly speak to the people helping to clean up or to offer a few words of comfort to those who still looked dazed. In between stops, I glanced up at my father.

"Where would the families of the dead be gathered now?" I asked.

His brow furrowed. "We've never dealt with this many casualties, so I'm not sure. The auditorium?"

I pressed my lips together. The auditorium was too large and open. I went to a house phone, which sat on a small table against the wall next to a nearby staircase and picked up the receiver. An operator answered.

"May I ring someone?"

"Please get Lord Lothlorien on the line," I said.

"Right away, Your Highness."

Half a minute later, there was a faint click.

"I would have thought you'd left an hour ago," Maxen said.

"I realized I couldn't go quite yet," I said, not wanting to articulate how poignant my stops throughout the fortress had been. "Where are the families of the fallen?"

"We've set up a space for them in one of the luxury guest suites."

"I'd like to go there before I leave," I said.

He gave me the location of the suite, and we hung up.

Oliver had been waiting for me a couple of feet away, and I told him where I was headed.

"I understand if you'd rather not come in with me," I said, knowing he wasn't one for emotional scenes.

"Of course I will go," he said, his voice somehow gruff and soft at the same time.

I cast him a grateful look, knowing how much it would mean to the families for him to personally pay his respects.

We reached the door of the suite, where two soldiers solemnly stood watch. I stopped, took a slow, quiet breath, and nodded at each of them. They didn't bow or otherwise acknowledge me, which was the correct protocol for an honor guard. The one on the right stepped out with deliberate, precise movements and opened the door for me. Oliver let me go in first.

I recognized the layout of the suite as being similar to my own quarters. In the front room—a small formal sitting room—the lights were turned low. A long table with a linen cloth over it had been set up with a row of white pillar candles. I didn't have to count to know there was one for each of the fallen Carraig. Soft, solemn orchestral music played on the sound system.

A page stood quietly off to one side, his hands clasped behind his back.

He took a step forward and bowed. "The families are in the casual living room."

Oliver and I continued through the doorway that took us into a short hall. I followed the sound of the people gathered—soft murmurs of quiet words and teary grief. When I reached the room, I paused. I knew many of those gathered by name, and though I hadn't seen a list of the dead, by the people there I could guess who'd fallen.

I moved through the room, clasping people's hands and trying to comfort them. My father did the same, moving through a different area. There was a small part of me that registered the intense discomfort of being in the presence of deeply grieving people, but I tamped it down. This wasn't about how I felt.

When I'd worked my way to the middle of the room, I happened to glance over to the section I hadn't made it to yet. I sucked in a sharp breath when I recognized Emmaline.

My heart clenching, I went over to her. She was sitting on one of the sofas next to a woman who had Emmaline's lavender eyes and auburn hair. They both looked up at me with tear-stained faces that showed the same haunted expression. Emmaline had been leaning against her mother, head on her shoulder, as she stroked the back of Emmaline's hair. She was eighteen, old enough to have rallied her peers around me when I'd first been crowned, when almost no one was willing to publicly show their support for me. But in that moment, she looked like a lost child.

I knelt in front of them. I didn't have to ask. From the way they'd been physically supporting each other, I knew it had to be Emmaline's father they were mourning.

I opened my mouth, intending to tell them how deeply saddened I was that they'd lost someone close, but my throat closed. My lips trembling, I reached for Emmaline and pulled her to me. Her head fell onto my shoulder, her thick hair tickling my face, and a soft sob escaped her.

As I held her, I couldn't help remembering that not long ago I'd been sure I'd lost my own father. A fresh wave of sorrow gripped me when I realized Emmaline was due to graduate from battle school in a few months, and her father wouldn't be there to see the ceremony.

She was the one to pull back first. Her chest hitched once as she struggled to control her emotions.

"We have to kill him," she whispered harshly. One more tear escaped and slid down her cheek, and she impatiently swiped at it with the back of her hand. "We have to make Periclase pay."

Her mother was saying soft words, trying to calm Emmaline's simmering anger, but she shrugged off her mother's hand.

Emmaline's gaze locked on mine.

"We will," I said, my voice nearly a growl. "I will kill him or die trying."

Her face hardened and her chin lifted, and in that moment, I knew that my promise meant more to Emmaline than any words of condolence ever could. She was a fighter, and she wanted revenge. So did I.

I gripped each of their hands, squeezed, and rose. I caught Oliver's eye from across the room, and he gave me a small nod and finished the conversation he'd been engaged in.

Amalie's arrival snagged my attention. She looked solemn and formal, and she had a tablet tucked under her arm. Seeing me, she came and curtseyed.

"I'm going to speak to the families about what will happen next," she said.

"There will be a ceremony honoring their loved ones?" I asked.

She inclined her head. "Of course. We thought it would be nice for the kin to have some say in how we do it. I'm going to suggest a private ceremony as well as a fortress-wide one and see how they feel about it. We will also talk about laying the fallen to rest. I may not get to all of these now. I'm going to see how the discussion goes and what they're ready for."

I reached out and squeezed her upper arm, extremely grateful that someone capable and sensitive was in charge. "You have my gratitude."

Oliver and I drifted toward the door, leaving things in Amalie's capable hands. I supposed I could have made a little impromptu speech before I left but thought it was better that I hadn't. I'd spoken to everyone in the room, and that had seemed the right thing to do. Later, there would be an opportunity for me to speak to them as a group.

With a long, heavy breath, I looked up at my father. "I hope to gods I never have to do that again," I said softly.

"Me too."

We went to the conference room that had its own private doorway. I said the words and drew the sigils to take us to the cavern, and with Oliver's hand on my shoulder, we stepped into the wall. It dissolved into the cold embrace of the netherwhere.

Chapter 9

WE CAME OUT of the void into the cavern, under the stalactite arch. An illumination orb popped into existence over our heads, a useful bit of magic that Maxen had left down there.

"What now?" Oliver asked, peering around.

I pointed at the two bottles that were on the ground where I'd left them.

"We'll use those like I did last time, and unless it was a one-time fluke, they should take us into the world of the Fomoire," I said.

The bottles were empty, I assumed because I had left them uncapped and the substances had evaporated. I picked them up and handed one to my father.

"I'll refill the sky iron, and you can get the spark liquid. I'll get another piece of Brigitstone, too."

He nodded, and we set off down different tunnels to complete the tasks. The illumination orb split into two, one round light following each of us. The sky iron made my skin crawl and my bones throb, and as I stuck the long-handled dipper into the pool, I couldn't help wondering again how sky iron had ended up so deep in the ground and how so much of it had accumulated.

Back in the main cavern, Oliver and I squatted by the Brigitstone with our respective bottles.

"You said something about Mort, before," he said, the glowing orb highlighting the planes of his face. He looked older, the creases in his skin deepened by the angle of the light. "You felt the presence of your old weapon. Doesn't that seem . . . significant?"

I shook my head. "I thought I did. But it was likely just part of the hallucination. Or I simply imagined it completely apart from that."

But even as I brushed off his question, a point of doubt ricocheted through me. I'd felt Mort calling to me *before* I'd mixed the substances and set off the vision. Was it significant? I had no idea. I stilled for a second, listening, reaching out for a sign of my old weapon. The gaping hole in the cavern floor was silent. I felt no signal from Mort.

I reached for the two bottles.

"What can I expect?" Oliver asked before I could pour out the substances.

I lowered my hands, realizing he was on edge, though there were no obvious signs. My father was a master at masking his emotions. The mere fact that he wanted more explanation than I'd already given him was what tipped me off.

"It's uncomfortable, to be honest," I said. "I tried to fight the hallucination but eventually realized I'd have to go through it to get back out. I don't know if it will be the same this time. But my advice is, let it happen."

His jaw muscles bunched, and he gave a curt nod. "Let's get on with it, then." I suspected the gruff edge to his voice was more nerves than impatience.

I took a steadying breath, cast one last glance around, and then tipped both bottles over the stone. The two liquids hit, spreading over the uneven surface, and mingled together. They bubbled, and my heart thumped. My first instinct was to hold my breath, but I forced myself to breathe. Nervous adrenaline flooded through me as the first wisps of vapor began to rise.

My eyes met my father's. "Try to go with it. It's going to happen whether you fight it or not."

His mouth tightened, his nostrils flaring slightly.

Steeling my will, I leaned over the Brigitstone and inhaled sharply. Like I'd just said to Oliver, there was no point trying to resist. After all, this was what we'd come for.

The acrid mist hit my sinuses, and my eyes started watering. The stuff *stung*. I listed, my eyes rolling back as the vapor began to take effect. I'd passed out before. I assumed the same thing would happen again.

The world began to squeeze down into a little point, darkness crowding in. Yep. It was going to be lights out.

Just before I lost consciousness, I managed to lower myself to the ground to keep from smacking my head.

As before, I woke up in the cave. Everything looked normal, but I knew better.

My father was just rousing a few feet away from me. He sat up and pushed the heels of his hands into his eyes, groaning a little.

"Oliver?" I said. My voice seemed to reverberate strangely.

He looked up, blinking rapidly at me. "That was unpleasant."

I gave him a humorless grin. "Oh, just wait."

He brought his feet in, bracing a palm on the ground and pushing the other hand against his knee as if to stand.

Raising my arm, I waved him back down. "Don't bother. It's already starting."

"What's start—"

His question cut off abruptly as the floor bucked and he grunted. The cavern was starting to shift. The walls were distorting. At first, I thought the same funnel would form, forcing me down into the dark abyss in the ground, but something felt different than last time. Instead of the floor sloping down to force us into the hole, the room seemed to be twisting and shrinking. But I could see that the result would be the same. The hallucination—if that's what it was—was forcing us into the void as before.

Despite my warning, Oliver had stood. He braced his feet and held his arms out as he struggled to keep his balance. The ground suddenly bulged under him, popping him up. He landed awkwardly on his side with a loud *oof*.

When his eyes met mine, I let out a sharp laugh. "Told you."

He scowled at me, and I chuckled again.

"Nice to see you find this so amusing," he said.

I stayed on my ass and scooted closer to him. "You should have seen me the first time. I was hanging on for dear life. I thought if I just hung there long enough, it would end. At some point I realized how fruitless it was, and I let go." I closed my eyes and drew a deep breath. "Just let go." I said it as much to myself as to Oliver.

I heard him take a slow inhale beside me. The floor was tipping. I started sliding. My eyelids popped open just as the cavern seemed to narrow and squeeze into a straw. Oliver and I went tumbling, his foot smacking against my shoulder. I curled my arms in and tucked my head under my hands.

I saw the blackness rushing up to meet us, and I tried to welcome it.

"Just Alice your way through the looking glass," I whispered to myself.

As before, I fell through pitch black. Oliver, grunting and swearing, seemed to be above me somewhere.

It wasn't a freefall—more of a drift downward—but I anticipated another loss of consciousness.

Sure enough, a deep relaxation began to take hold, lulling me toward sleep. My eyelids fluttered in the dark. A heavy thrum passed through me, and my heart lurched.

"Mort?" I whispered.

But the Fomoire magic—or whatever was controlling my reality—took over, dropping me into a forced sleep.

I awoke to water dripping onto my forehead. Even before I opened my eyes, I knew I was in the land of the Fomoire, in Ethniu's body. I lay on my back, and though the sky was gray and my clothes and skin were damp from the rain, it wasn't cold. I sat up and looked around.

Spotting a man nearby—apparently unconscious—I inhaled sharply and scrambled on all fours over to him. I recognized him from before. It was the man who'd claimed to be my father. His chest rose and fell, and his eyes darted around under closed lids.

I firmly patted his cheek. "Balor? Oliver?"

I wasn't sure which name was correct. I didn't even know if Oliver had arrived as I had and inhabited the body of the man.

His eyelids fluttered open, dazed and unfocused at first. Just as before, the eyes were exactly like Oliver's, though all other features were unfamiliar.

"Petra," he said, finally fixing his gaze on my face.

I nearly wilted in relief, knowing that Oliver was in there.

"Yes, it's me."

I took his arm and helped him up, and then we stood staring at each other for several seconds.

Oliver looked down at his arms and then the clothes he wore. "This is . . . odd." He looked up and twisted around. "Where are we?"

I turned. We were alone in an area of rolling green hills. The air was humid, and I thought I caught a hint of salty sea on the wind. A couple of horses, outfitted with rudimentary saddles and tack, grazed about a hundred yards off.

"No idea," I said. I pointed at the horses. "But I think our transportation is over there." My voice didn't sound like my own, and it sent a little jolt through me each time I spoke.

We jogged toward the horses, slowing cautiously when we got close and the animals paused their grazing to peer at us. Both horses trotted our way. I'd never been on a horse in my life and knew basically nothing about them. But they seemed to recognize us. The smaller of the two, with a shiny brown coat and black mane, came to me. I tentatively stuck out my hand and the horse nuzzled it.

My eyes on the horse, I called to my father, "Hey, I wonder if they know how to get us back home?"

He didn't answer right away, and when I turned, I found he was already seated on the other horse, a male with black splotches spotting its white coat around the flanks.

He reached forward to pat the horse's neck. "Good boy."

I put my hands on my hips. "Where'd you learn to ride? And when?"

Oliver-Balor shrugged. "I didn't. I just followed my instincts. The other man, Balor, is in here, too, I think." He tapped his temple.

My brows rose. I didn't feel another's presence within me, but maybe I didn't know how to notice it.

I awkwardly grasped the strap holding the saddle of my horse in one hand, and not knowing what else to grasp, I gathered a handful of mane in the other. I stuck my foot in the stirrup.

"Sorry about your hair," I muttered as I hoisted myself up.

The stirrup and saddle slipped a little, and I belatedly realized I should have put more momentum into the movement. I scrambled up and got my leg over and then had to hug the horse's neck to right myself. The animal snorted and bobbed her head, and I could have sworn she was laughing at me.

A glance over at my father showed he looked much more at ease on horseback than I felt. "I don't feel anything. No presence."

"Maybe it'll come," he said. He pointed off in the distance. "He seems to want to go that way."

I nodded. "That's what I was hoping for. I say we let them take the lead."

For the next few minutes, I became absorbed in trying to stay on the horse and get the rhythm of her movement. Once I was fairly certain I wasn't going to tumble off, I relaxed a little and looked up at the scenery. There was mist in the distance off to the right, and my gut told me the ocean was beyond that.

"Cronan," I blurted, the word spilling suddenly out of my mouth. My horse tossed her mane, and I couldn't help a grin. "That's your name, isn't it? Cronan." I flicked a glance at my father. "Maybe someone is in here after all." I tapped my head as he had before.

As we rode, I realized it felt oddly natural to be on a horse, riding across the green land that was broken up with occasional hilly crags. When we saw a flock of sheep in the distance, I suspected we were nearing our destination. The land began to slope upward, and ahead there was a large rocky outcropping. It appeared to be the remnants of a small mountain range, reduced by time and the elements to a crumbling shadow of its former majesty.

We crested a gentle rise and discovered it had been hiding a settlement nestled at the base of the tallest rough, rubbly mountain in the vicinity. A steady, thin mist spilled over the mountain to spread through the settlement, giving it an air of mystery.

By instinct, I gently pulled back on the reins. Cronan stopped, and my father's horse came to stand near us. I peered down at the bustling scene below. A primitive rock wall formed a half-circle around the central area, the two ends of the wall butting up against the mountain. Farmland stretched out far to the left, outside the wall, and to the right livestock roamed.

I didn't recognize anything in particular but had the impression of familiarity. "I think this is where I came before. Or maybe it's Ethniu's knowledge of this place emerging."

My eyes met Oliver's.

"This is where we'll learn to unlock the secrets of the god blood," he said.

"I hope so." Thinking of the coming battle back in Faerie, my heart thumped. "And we need to do it quickly."

Clucking softly at Cronan, I rattled the reins. She responded by springing into motion, and my eyes popped wide as I shifted my weight forward to keep from toppling back. With the horse moving at a quick trot—maybe a canter? I had no idea—and Oliver's horse keeping pace, we were soon at the base of the rise and the start of a dirt path leading to the opening in the center of the wall. People tending to livestock or crops paused to squint at us as we passed. Some nodded when I made eye contact, but most just watched silently. I saw curiosity and respect in their faces. They clearly knew who we were, or they recognized the bodies we inhabited, at least.

There were only a few structures within the walls—not enough to house all the people we saw—and I realized we were not approaching a city but a stronghold that appeared to also serve as a city center.

When we were still about fifty yards from the enclosed area, a boy of about fourteen or fifteen who'd been standing to one side of the gap in the wall looked up at us. He'd been whittling a stick with a short knife, and his hands paused. He tossed the stick aside, sheathed the knife on his belt, turned, and sprinted into the walled area.

Oliver and I reached the end of the dirt road. No one attempted to stop us as we passed inside the wall. But a man strode toward us, and even from a distance I could see his resemblance to Balor, the one whose body Oliver had taken. The man was older by twenty or twenty-five years or so, and I guessed he was Balor's father.

He halted a dozen feet away, and Oliver and I pulled our horses to a stop. The man gave us each long, assessing looks, his face solemn. He had the same gray eyes as Balor and Oliver.

"I see that you are not Ethniu, even though you appear to be her," he said to me. "No, you are the woman of the stone blood who was here before."

He was speaking a thick, rolling language that I somehow understood.

"I'm Petra Maguire of the Carraig Sidhe, the stone blood Fae," I said to him in his tongue. I gestured to Oliver. "This is my father, Oliver Maguire."

The man's eyes tightened as his gaze settled on my father for a long moment.

"I am Burain," he said finally. "We have been expecting you. I will take you to the stables where you can leave your mounts. Then, we shall share a meal and drink."

I peered at Burain for a split second, unable to pinpoint what about him seemed familiar. I exchanged a glance with Oliver, but his expression was unreadable. We both dismounted and, leading our horses, followed Burain.

Chapter 10

AFTER LEAVING OUR horses with the stable attendants, we were taken to a tent. Inside, a carved wood table with six matching chairs were set up. Even though the furniture was rough by my modern standards, I sensed that such furnishings were rare in this time and place. Servants, two women and a man, poured water into metal chalices.

Burain went to the head of the table, clearly intending to sit there, and gestured to the chairs on either side of him.

"Please, sit," he said. "My wife will join us shortly."

I'd barely settled in my seat when a woman with auburn hair, sparkling blue eyes, and dressed in a heavy draping maroon gown that reached the ground hurried into the tent.

"I'm Cethleen, wife of Burain," she said by way of introduction. She placed her hand on her chest and inclined her head.

Oliver stood and gave a little bow. "Oliver Maguire, my Lady. And my daughter, Petra."

She smiled faintly at us, her gaze flicking back and forth between me and my father as she took the seat at the other end of the table.

"I apologize for staring," she said. "It's terribly odd to see my son and granddaughter and yet know that they aren't themselves."

A small laugh escaped my lips. "I can't imagine how disconcerting this must be for you." I gave a little shake of my head. "I have so many questions. For instance, where are Ethniu and Balor if they aren't, well, here?"

"They are still within," Burain said, gesturing at me and Oliver with the back of his hand. "They've simply receded to allow your presence."

I wasn't sure that helped my understanding, but I didn't want to take any more time on the topic.

"Are you the king of the Fomoire?" I asked Burain.

"I am a king of sorts, yes."

As we talked, the servants had been bringing dishes and flatware to make place settings in front of the four of us. I caught a whiff of something fragrant in a steaming copper pot that two of the men were carrying in. They carefully secured the pot's handle on the center hook of a tripod that had hot coals in a ring of stones burning beneath it.

"And you are . . . gods?" I felt awkward saying it, but it seemed important to establish that these people were who we thought they were—the gods who'd claimed Ireland prior to the Tuatha.

"Do we not look god-like?" Cethleen asked, her face serious as she leaned forward on her elbows.

I opened my mouth, but I wasn't sure what to say.

After allowing a few awkward seconds to slip by as I stuttered, she let out a tinkling laugh. "My apologies, I couldn't help myself."

I grinned sheepishly.

"You look like regular mortals," Oliver said, saving me. "You don't take the form of mist like the Tuatha De Danann. You aren't even large in stature like the Old Ones of Faerie."

Burain leaned back, propping an elbow on one arm rest. "We take these forms because they are perfectly suited to be in harmony with the land. These regular mortal forms, as you called us, allow us to experience the full range of the joys and the suffering this land can offer."

He said it with such obvious love for his country, and I couldn't help a faint smile.

"I can't imagine wasting the opportunity of this existence hiding away under a mountain, drifting around as a fog," he said, his mood darkening. Pursing his lips in distaste, Burain picked up his cloth napkin and shook it out more vigorously than necessary before placing it on his lap.

"You're clearly referring to the Tuatha." I squinted. "But forgive me. How do you know of them? From the perspective of your current time, the Tuatha are still many generations away from claiming this land."

My head was starting to hurt with the effort of trying to understand it all.

"Because in your time, our slumbering selves see all from the present to the beginning," he said.

That explanation didn't exactly clear things up. I closed my eyes for a second and then looked at him. "Is this even real, then?" I placed my hands flat on the table and let my gaze dart around the tent. "Any of this? This conversation?"

Cethleen gave another tinkling laugh. "That depends on what you mean by real."

I shot her a wry look, and she winked at me. I'd barely met this woman, but I liked her. Her charm seemed genuine.

"I understand why it's difficult to understand," she said, her smile fading to a more sober expression, but still a twinkle in her blue eyes. "This is not real in the sense that you time-traveled to the past. This is a . . . representation of us, of you. A way for us to interact and communicate. But I would not get too snarled in the mechanics. It's not salient to your current need. Or to ours."

"Let's put the truth on the table, since you brought it up, my Lady," Oliver said. "Your need is to make sure the Tuatha De Danann are defeated so you can once again be the gods who occupy the Old World—Ireland, Scotland, and England, as we call them. You can't oust the Tuatha yourselves. So you want to give us the power to do it for you."

He turned his attention to Burain for confirmation.

"Blunt, aren't you?" The Fomoire man said.

Oliver grunted a noise of consensus.

"Are you going to answer his question?" I asked after a few seconds of silence passed.

"I see bluntness runs in the family," Burain said. He inclined his head just a bit in Oliver's direction. "You are correct in your summary. But are our goals not the same?"

Burain locked eyes with Oliver, and the two men seemed to assess each other for a few seconds.

"In part, our goals *are* the same," Oliver said. "It would be disastrous if the Tuatha were to defeat us. They want to raze Faerie, to terrify us, break us down, destroy our current ways, and set up a new order. They want the Unseelie to rule, and likely at the cost of many lives. So we can't let them win. But what would life be like with the Fomoire as our gods? How do we know it would be any better?"

"We do not plan to burn Faerie to the ground, first off," Cethleen said. "We see no need for that."

"Our primary interest is being able to reemerge to the land we love," Burain said.

"So, you're more interested in returning to Ireland and the rest of the Old World than controlling Faerie?" I asked.

"Yes," Cethleen said. She was leaning forward, her eyes intent. "Ireland, Scotland, and parts of England are our sacred land. Faerie is the offspring of these countries. Faerie is important to us, but it's not our home. We love the Old World lands—your Ireland, Scotland, and England—the way the Fae love Faerie. We only wish to live simply there, similar to how we live here, in harmony with the land and with the current residents. Generations of exile have softened our any tendency toward war or dominance. But we're barred from those lands as long as the Tuatha rule. They defeated us and would never allow us to encroach upon what they view as theirs."

"If you won back the Old World, would you leave us to our own in Faerie?" Oliver asked.

Burain cut a look at his wife before answering. "We would only want to stabilize Faerie to help prevent other gods from using it to rise up against us."

"Does that mean keeping the Seelie in power? Keeping Oberon and Titania on the High throne?" I asked.

"Faerie *is* more stable in the summer reign of the Seelie," Cethleen said firmly. "We have no desire to facilitate the chaos of the Unseelie."

I turned to her. "But what about Oberon?"

Again, wife and husband exchanged a glance.

"That depends," Cethleen said after a brief hesitation.

I leaned forward a bit. "You don't see Oberon on the throne?"

"We want to strengthen Faerie," Burain said, his words carrying a snap of subtle impatience. "If that means new rule, then that's what will have to happen."

I saw the hard look Cethleen gave her husband and knew it meant they hadn't intended to go quite that far in their admissions.

In the second or two of silence that followed, the previous comradery between the four of us seemed to have chilled by a degree or two.

Burain gestured at our place settings. "Why don't we lighten the conversation while we eat?"

The servants had placed crusty bread and chunks of bright-yellow butter on each of our plates and were bringing around bowls of the steaming food in the copper pot.

I wasn't sure whether any of the sensations I felt were truly real, but the smell of the food was making my stomach rumble. Oliver's gaze slid to me, and I gave him a tiny shrug. Why not indulge in this meal, even if it was imaginary?

Cethleen and Burain asked us about the Carraig Sidhe, about our stone armor and the short history of our people. It had to be just polite conversation on their part, asking questions to which they already knew the answers.

To keep my brain from imploding, I had to keep reminding myself that Oliver and I hadn't truly traveled back in time. I decided to see it as a sort of dream, a shared vision, a meeting of mortals and gods, where our hosts had chosen to place us in a historic setting. But unless I had grossly misunderstood, Burain, Cethleen, and the rest of the Fomoire were still alive in the current time. They were in a sort of hibernation under the hills of Ireland, waiting for the time when they could emerge and take back their beloved homeland. It wasn't a battle that would ever make the news on the Earthly side of the hedge. All these conflicts took place in a way that was invisible to human eyes and only left scars on the land and landmarks that those with mystical sensibilities would notice.

I also reminded myself that the Fomoire wouldn't be offering to help us if they could accomplish their goal on their own. They needed us.

Suddenly, the setting made more sense. Burain and Cethleen had chosen human-like forms because it was part of their persuasion. They wanted me and Oliver to trust them, to see what we had in common. To let down our guard and agree to be the Fomoire's pawns.

Could these gods force us to do their bidding if they wanted to? I guessed not. In their current situation of forced slumber, hiding away, they didn't have their full power. They were aware, but mostly powerless to act. That was why they wanted to funnel their power through us, through the Fae with stone blood.

"The Carraig were able to resist the Stone of Fal," I said. "Was that your doing?"

Burain nodded, swallowing his food before answering. "You would be no use to us if you could easily fall under Finvarra's—or now

Periclase's—influence."

"Why not make all of Faerie resistant to the Stone?" Oliver asked.

Burain hesitated. "We don't care to deal with all of Faerie."

Cethleen gave a little huff of exasperation in her husband's direction. "It's also because we could *only* bestow it on the Carraig," she said to me.

"I still don't fully understand," I said. "Can you explain it in terms that mortals would understand?"

She set down her fork.

"Those of you who ended up with stone blood all carried the seed of something in yourselves before the stone bloods were created," she said. "It was the seed of god power, very faint, but there, running through your blood. When there was a magical shift—"

"The Cataclysm on the Earthly side," I supplied.

"Yes, your so-called Cataclysm. That magical shift opened a channel between us and those who had that tiny seed of god blood. We reached out to you, and the stone blood Fae came into being. Like a candle that had been cold was suddenly lit."

"So you created our race," Oliver said.

"In a way, yes," she confirmed.

"And the caves?" I asked. "Did you create them?"

"Yes, we planted the Brigitstone, the sky iron, and the elixir underground and then showed them to your former leader in a dream," Cethleen said. The elixir she referred to was the pool of electric water. "We needed a method for you to reach us, but something that wasn't too easy to access. And we purposely designed it so the sky iron and elixir couldn't be removed and weaponized."

That matched with what Maxen had told me about the caves and Marisol's dream. It also explained why we weren't able to take samples of the two liquids out of the caves. A moment of silence passed while Oliver and I digested what Cethleen had revealed.

"The Cataclysm was decades ago," I said. "Why have you only now tried to contact us?"

"For one, time means something different to us than it does to you," she said. "A few decades are nothing to us. We wanted to time things right."

I nodded slowly. "But the Tuatha are forcing your hand. You can't wait, for fear that the Tuatha may destroy the Carraig, and with us your chances of regaining your foothold in your homeland."

"Yes," she said, her clear blue eyes unblinking. "That is certainly an important factor."

"What else is important?" I asked.

This time it was Burain who responded. "You are."

At first, I assumed that by "you" he meant me and my father, but his gaze held steady on me.

"How so?" I asked.

"You have proven yourself as a fighter, as a woman of principle, and as an individual who is willing to rise above the pettiness that distracts so many Fae in the current era. You, in particular, are the right one. You are most capable of handling the burden, the challenge, of what we may bestow upon you."

"What about the rest of my people? Can they handle it, too?"

"If you can, we believe they can, too."

I knew he was paying me a compliment, and I even believed it was sincere. But I had the distinct impression that there was more he wasn't revealing. The problem was, I could ask questions until I was blue in the face. But the Fomoire weren't Fae, which meant they could lie to me and Oliver. Or they could tire of us and send us away. After all, they were gods.

I rested my forearms on the table. "But there is a cost to your aid, surely."

"There is a danger," Cethleen said. "Channeling the power of the gods is inherently risky. Mortals are not designed for it."

"That's a risk, not a cost," Oliver said. "A cost would be what you expect from us. Or some sort of obligation we will have toward you."

"Yes, there are costs," Burain said, and from the tightness of his eyes, I guessed he was growing impatient again. It only added to my vague suspicion that we were being worked, somehow.

"But before we can bestow the power upon you, before we can worry about costs, there is one final test," Cethleen said gravely.

I tilted my head. "Test? But you just finished telling us that we are the only race who can help you, and that I am, in your minds, the ideal one to receive the so-called gift of your power."

"We believe you are," she said. "But you must understand, we have to be sure."

I wasn't sure I did understand, and I was starting to feel a little pissed off about the whole thing.

"You don't have a choice," I said. "You need us, and you need us now. The Tuatha are coming literally any day. The Dullahan have already been spotted in the remote regions of Faerie."

Burain's eyes clouded. He leaned forward, his cheek twitching as he pinned me with his stare.

"Listen to me," he said, his voice pitched low but somehow thundering. Light flashed in his pupils like little lightning strikes, and I stifled a gasp. "We always have a choice. A century to you is but an hour to us. We've waited for generations. If we have to, we can wait for generations more. We are gods. Know your place, mortal." He snapped the last word with a biting growl, and his voice seemed to echo around in my head.

As he'd spoken, a thin ribbon of fear had started winding through me. The Fomoire could indeed decide to abandon us, because Burain spoke the truth. He and his people had an opportunity, and obviously hoped to take it, but they didn't have to. My people and I, on the other hand, stood a good chance of being utterly decimated when the Tuatha came with their Dullahan army. Even if we didn't die in the battle, the Tuatha aimed to put the Unseelie in power. King Periclase had the Stone of Fal, and he would use it to force loyalty from all survivors. At that point, it would hardly matter that the Carraig Sidhe could resist the magic of the Stone. Every other Fae in Faerie would be loyal to Periclase, and we would be a tiny, pathetic minority.

No matter what, the future was incredibly grim if there was no one to challenge the Tuatha De Dannan.

All of that ran through my mind in the span of a second or two, and Oliver was probably pondering similar thoughts.

"What is the other test we must pass?" I asked.

"You will fight one of our champions," Burain said to me. "If you can best him, we will know you have a chance at beating the Tuatha."

A dozen questions tried to spring up my throat, but some part of me knew the details of the test were almost irrelevant. The terms weren't going to be negotiable.

Oliver had let out a low growl at Burain's proclamation.

"I'll do it," my father said. "I'll fight."

"You will *not*," Burain said, each word dropping like a boulder. He nodded at me. "She will."

My father pressed his lips into a hard line, and I glimpsed a rare flash of defeat in his eyes.

"When will this match take place?" I asked.

"Just after sunrise tomorrow," Cethleen said. Her demeanor, which had been expressive and even warm up to this point, had cooled, her face closed. "We have quarters set up for you. They're not luxurious, but you should be comfortable for the night."

I caught Oliver's eye. He looked irate, and I didn't blame him. I felt the same way. But what choice did we have?

A servant arrived to show us to our beds, and my father and I parted

104

ways with Cethleen and Burain.

Chapter 11

THE SKY WASN'T completely dark yet when Oliver and I were shown to our quarters, and I knew it would be hours before I could sleep, if I could at all.

The servant took us to a small tent toward the back of the encampment near the base of the mountain. Inside the tent, we found two beds set up—essentially mattresses of straw with blankets tucked around them and two more blankets each folded on top. It was rustic but looked comfortable enough. In between the beds was a simple tray made of a rough-cut plank of wood holding a steaming kettle of water a small dish of dried leaves that I assumed was tea, and two earthenware mugs. Also on the floor was a lantern that cast a soothing glow over everything.

I removed my back scabbard, which carried Aurora, and laid it on the ground parallel to one of the mattresses, and my father did the same with his scabbard.

I wanted to speak to Oliver about everything we'd learned and the test I was facing, but the fabric walls of the tent made it too easy for an eavesdropper to overhear. After a few seconds' hesitation, I decided it didn't matter much. We had things we needed to discuss. Most likely none of them would come as a surprise to Cethleen or Burain, if they'd sent spies to listen in.

With a weary exhalation, I lowered myself to one of the mattresses and reached for the tea. Oliver sat across the tray from me on the other mattress, watching as I prepared a mug for each of us.

"So," I said once the tea leaves were steeping and steam was curling gently upward from each mug. "Do you suppose I could actually die if the Fomoire champion defeats me tomorrow?"

I said it casually, but it was a genuine concern. I still wasn't certain of the rules of our presence in this world, or vision, or whatever it was that Burain and Cethleen had created for us to come together.

"That would be very stupid of them to allow it to happen," Oliver said, not bothering with the hushed tone I'd used.

It was still disconcerting to look at an unfamiliar face and body and know that my father was in there. He was probably thinking the same about me. At least the eyes were ones I recognized.

"But don't you get the idea that, ultimately, for the Fomoire, we're disposable?"

My father adjusted his position with an irritated shifting of his weight. "I suppose mortals are always disposable to gods."

I brought my mug up to nose level and inhaled the fragrance of the tea. It smelled like black tea with a hint of something floral. Testing it with a small sip, I found it robust and delicious. I couldn't help thinking how vividly I was experiencing sensations, even knowing that none of it was completely real, not in the way I was accustomed to, anyway.

"Well, there's no way around the fight," I said. "And honestly, I'm okay with that. I welcome it, even. I know how to prove myself with a sword."

He pursed his lips and made an annoyed sound at the back of his throat.

"What's bothering you?" I asked.

"They want to use us. I don't like being used. I refuse to be anyone's puppet. And after, then what? Once they're back in their homeland, will they want to get rid of us?"

I frowned and lowered my mug. "What do you mean?"

"They're not going to want Fae running around with god power coursing through their veins. How do we know they won't use us and then eliminate us?"

I shook my head. "I assumed they would just remove the ability to use the god power."

His face tightened. "We don't even know what this so-called god power is or how it works. Again, I just don't like the idea of being a channel for something I know nothing about."

"But think of what we're facing back home," I said. "Periclase has the Stone of Fal, he's already taken the Summerlands, and the Tuatha are on the verge of descending on Faerie. We need any advantage we can gain. And after . . . well, we'll just have to figure it out when the time comes."

To my surprise, he quirked a small smile at me. "How can you be so calm about all of this?"

I snorted a soft laugh. "I'm not sure it's calm so much as helpless resignation."

"I admire the way you're handling everything," Oliver said.

Our eyes met, and I gave him a small smile.

"I appreciate your admiration, of course, but . . ." I trailed off with a sigh.

"What?"

"I think I'm still a pretty shit queen."

"Nonsense." He waved a hand. "You're finding your footing, and things are getting better in the fortress."

I shrugged and lifted the mug to my lips for another sip.

"No one seems bent on assassinating you anymore. Surely you see that as an improvement?" he deadpanned.

I shot him a withering look through the steam of my tea.

His expression sobered. "Even under perfect circumstances with your subjects, these are challenging times for every kingdom. For gods' sake, the Unseelie have taken the Summerlands. We're going to have to face the Tuatha. There are absolutely no luxuries for any of us these days."

"True," I said. "And that's why I'm here instead of tending to our realm in person. There *are* a lot of things to work out in the fortress still, but those things have to be put on hold for now."

A minute or two of silence slipped by, each of us lost in our own thoughts. The sounds of movement outside our tent were constant reminders that we weren't really alone. I found I didn't mind, though. I didn't have anything to hide.

"How are you feeling about the battle tomorrow?" Oliver asked.

"I think my biggest concern is trying to fight in an unfamiliar body. I'm not finding myself tripping or fumbling, but it still feels . . . foreign." I flexed my arm and looked down at the limb, which was longer and more muscular than mine. I was petite compared to most of the stone bloods back in Faerie, but Ethniu's body was more like the average Carraig—large and powerfully built. "In a battle where I need to rely on split-second decisions and reflexes, I'm not too sure how this is going to work out for me."

"How about some practice?"

My brows arched. "Drills?"

He gave a half-shrug. "Sure, why not? There's a small clear area behind our tent, and there's a bit of light from the torches set up around the encampment. The Fomoire never said you couldn't prepare."

A grin began to bloom across my face. "Yeah. Let's see what this body can do."

Relishing the idea of some physical activity, I stood, brushed off the seat of my pants, and drew Aurora, leaving the scabbard on the ground.

Oliver drew his own sword. Unlike the blade I had, his sword wasn't the one he carried back home. Instead, it looked like a weapon of the current time period we were in. His usual broadsword was large, but his weapon here was even bigger, obviously meant for someone very powerful. I assumed my opponent would be using a similar weapon the next morning.

I held up my sword and watched the light play over the rosy-toned metal of the blade. "Odd that I have Aurora here," I said. "Do you think the real Ethniu might have wielded it?"

Oliver shook his head. "It's possible. That blade has passed through the hands of many fighters over the ages."

Outside our tent, we drew a few curious looks from the people of the settlement who passed by. Fortunately, the foot traffic had thinned out a lot since our arrival. It appeared people had started retreating to their shelters for the night, and those who didn't live within the walls had likely gone home before the sun set.

The temperature had dropped several degrees since our arrival, and a cool draft crept down from the face of the mountain that loomed above us. I hopped on my toes a few times to get my blood flowing and circled my wrist in a quick warmup movement. Then Oliver and I separated and faced off in the clearing. The light of nearby torches played off his blade and danced in his pupils. For a second or two, we were both perfectly still and tensed with anticipation, waiting for the other to make the first move.

Deciding to test the agility of Ethniu's body, I sprang forward into a classic fencing lunge. I didn't move with my usual quickness, fearing that I might misjudge the bulk of the body I wore and fall on my face. Oliver easily deflected my attack and traced a quick C with his blade to counter-attack. A clang rang through the air when our swords clashed.

Not bad. Even though Ethniu was much larger than I was, her body was quite nimble for its size. And I wasn't anywhere near as clumsy as I'd feared.

I shuffled back a couple of steps to regroup, but Oliver wasn't going to let me rest. He jumped into a running charge. I sidestepped and half-turned, cutting Aurora through the air in a downward motion, stopping just short of slamming the flat of the blade into the back of his lower leg as I suddenly realized he wasn't protected by stone armor.

I flicked the tip of my sword down at the dirt and started cursing under my breath.

"What?" Oliver asked, catching my expression.

"No stone armor," I said. "How did I not notice it until now?"

He blinked a couple of times, and his sword dropped, too. "I didn't think of it, either." He let out a loud, irritated grunt. "Well, your opponent won't have it either. And your object is always to avoid a strike, regardless of armor. That was always your training."

I chewed my lip for a second. "I know. But stone armor is part of what allows us to fight as aggressively as we do. That, and our ability to heal quickly."

He brushed a hand through the air. "Bah. You have the skills of a champion. The other things are irrelevant details."

But I could tell the realization had shaken him, too.

"I can't draw magic, either," I said, my heart sinking another couple of inches.

I'd been so caught up in our talk with Burain and Cethleen that I'd failed to notice just how much of my physical nature was different here.

Oliver and I looked at each other for a long moment. He straightened and lifted his sword, taking a ready stance.

"All the more reason to put in a little more practice," he said. He lifted his chin and gave me a stern look.

He didn't want me to wallow, to stress over what I didn't have. He was right, though my mind wanted to worry over how I would pull off a victory with no magic, no armor, and an unfamiliar body.

We started with the most basic drills I'd learned as a young student and worked our way up to advanced. The exertion gave me a place to put my frustration and took my mind off everything but the rhythm of the movements and the flash of the blades. It felt almost indulgent to sink into the physicality of it. It'd been so long since I'd had the luxury of a sole focus. Back when I'd been working as a mercenary on the Earthly side of the hedge, thinking of nothing but my next mark, I hadn't realized just how easy my life was. I hadn't appreciated the simplicity.

I started to tire, and I noticed Oliver slowing down, too. We parted and lowered our blades.

"We probably went too long," I said, panting. "I only meant to practice, not to fatigue."

He pushed the point of his sword into the ground and then leaned his hip against the handle, as if the weapon were a cane.

"I think you needed it," he said. "You've got the night to rest."

We turned toward our tent, and I realized the torches around our makeshift practice arena were the only ones still lit. I had no idea how late it was, but Oliver was right—it had done me good to physically tire myself.

"Are you feeling more comfortable?" he asked, holding back the tent flap so I could go in.

At first, I wasn't sure what he meant.

I gathered my hair—Ethniu's hair, which was thicker and coarser than mine—and held it up off my neck.

"I managed to reach a state of flow for a while." I shrugged. "That's got to be a good sign, right?"

"A very good sign."

Servants had come while we were gone, replacing our tea service with two jugs of water. I sat down on my mattress and took a long drink. Oliver sat across from me and did the same.

He wiped water from his upper lip. "The physical aspect is important, but as you know, the mental part is even more important."

I nodded.

"So," he said. "Is there anything that still weighs on you? Anything that will pull you off your game tomorrow morning?"

I suppressed an amused smile. Was Oliver trying to play therapist?

"My mind is surprisingly clear, considering the threats we face. Maybe it's being in this place, away from other obligations and distractions. In a way, it feels so far from home . . ." I trailed off, looking at the interior of the tent and thinking about the land beyond and how the entire experience wasn't even real, not in the sense of "real" I was used to.

"Good," he said, seemingly satisfied with my answer. "I suggest you try to rest, even if you don't think you can sleep yet."

He rolled one of his blankets into a pillow and then stretched out on his mattress. I imitated him, lying on my back with my ankles crossed and my hands clasped over my stomach. A few minutes later, I heard his breathing begin to even out. I was still wide awake, though.

I hadn't been entirely honest about my state of mind. Though it was nice to be free of my royal duties for the moment, everything felt so foreign, everything I cared about so *distant*. Thank the gods Oliver was there with me, even if he was in a different body. If not for him, I would have felt utterly alone, floating in a strange universe.

A pang arrowed through my chest as I thought of Jasper. The sudden longing for him nearly took my breath away. What was he doing? Was he succeeding in his quest? Was he safe?

I dozed a little, all night in and out of a state that wasn't quite sleep. When I opened my eyes and saw pale light through the crack between the tent flaps and heard people moving around outside, I sat up.

It was time to win the power of the gods for my people.

Chapter 12

A PAIR OF servants arrived at our tent, offering bread, cured meat, and drink. I refused the food and only drank a bit of strong tea from an earthenware pot.

Memories from my fight against Darion in the Battle of Champions—back when I was just Petra Maguire, mercenary vamp hunter on the Earthly side of the hedge—kept creeping into my mind. Those who didn't know me then had underestimated me. Darion had sneered at me because I was a woman. He'd tried to use his brute strength to defeat me. My training, agility, magic, and stone armor had enabled me to win that match. But for the fight I was about to face, I had no armor or magic. I couldn't rely on agility in the large, muscular body I inhabited.

Oliver was right. I had only my training. I hoped it would be enough.

I pulled my focus inward, and my father didn't try to engage me in conversation.

To my surprise, Cethleen came to take us to the site of the battle.

Her expression was carefully neutral, her mood solemn. She walked us through the encampment, explaining what I could expect.

"As we mentioned last night, you will face one of our champions," she said. "Like many of our people, he's a soldier. He possesses the skills and strength you would expect from a fighter with god blood running through him."

"Does that mean he will use magic or power that I don't have?" I asked.

She shook her head. "This is a straight fight. No magic. No god power. Just two fighters and their swords."

That was something in my favor, at least.

"This is a test, not a death battle," she continued. "There will be no fatal blows. The fight will end when either you or he concedes or loses consciousness."

That was all well and good to say, but in the heat of battle, who knew where a blade might fall? This wasn't sparring. Each of us would be fighting all-out. Accidents happened. But then something occurred to me.

"Do you mean that neither of us *can* be killed?" I asked.

"I do. As I said, this isn't about you killing your opponent. It's a test to prove you're worthy."

The front gate of the settlement's enclosure was thrown open, and people were flowing in and out. Many were busy setting up their tents or stands in a space clearly reserved for a market. Beyond the walls, farmers were arriving to tend to their patches of land and herders were taking their flocks out into the hills.

The sky straight ahead was rosy along the horizon, the brightest spot foretelling where the sun would soon peek over. I decided the timing of the fight was favorable for me. Aurora's power was strongest at dawn. Back home, that was true, at least. In this place, there was no magic to empower the blade, and it felt strangely quiet on my back.

Cethleen came to a stop just beyond the gates and pointed to a grassy rise to our left.

"That is where the fight will take place."

The spot was a rounded mound of earth, a bit higher than any of the surrounding hills and covered with young, bright-green grass.

Two men stood on top. One of them I recognized—Burain. The man beside him was larger, both in height and shoulder width. His medium brown hair was smoothed back into a ponytail. We were too far away for me to make out the features of his face.

Cethleen took me and my father around to the side of the rise so we could walk up the gentlest slope. When we met the two men, they both regarded me solemnly.

My opponent was clean-shaven, square-jawed, and might have been handsome if not for a crooked nose most likely caused by a badly healed break and a jagged scar that passed down the side of his forehead, across his temple, and split an earlobe. His bare forearms also bore evidence of many fights.

Burain came forward to hand me a shield. It wasn't large—about as big as an oversized dinner platter. My opponent held an identical one. His thick broadsword was sheathed at his hip, the weight of it pulling at his belt.

Cethleen stepped between the two pairs of us—me and Oliver on one side and Burain and my foe on the other. The sun was just beginning to show itself over the horizon.

"As I explained," she said. "This is not a fight to the death. It's a test. The fight ends when one of you either concedes or loses consciousness."

The big man with the broadsword gave a curt nod and made a noise of assent. His brown eyes regarded me coolly, revealing no emotion. I had no idea whether he'd sized me up to be an easy victory or was still withholding judgment. But I was certain he wasn't just a brute fighter. There seemed to be intelligence behind his reserved demeanor.

"Separate fifteen paces," Burain said, gesturing for me and my opponent to move apart. We each backed up several steps. "Wait for us to move to the neighboring hill. I'll raise my arm. When I lower it, that's your signal to begin. Understand and agree?"

"Yes," the big man said, more of a grunt than a word.

Burain turned to me, and I also expressed my consent to the rules.

Oliver caught my eye and gave me a nod before turning to go with

Cethleen and Burain.

I faced my opponent. "You got a name?"

He squinted at me, not answering for a long moment. "Thander."

"Petra Maguire, Queen of the Carraig Sidhe."

"I prefer Ethniu in her own body," he said in a rumbling brogue.

I gave him a wry look. "I imagine she prefers that, too."

We both turned our attention to our three-person audience, who was just cresting a neighboring hill. They lined up to face us. I reached back and drew Aurora with my right hand and firmed my grip on the shield in my left. Burain lifted his arm. I didn't wait to see him bring it down. Instead, I watched Thander. As soon as he turned back to me, I charged.

Thander's shield flipped up to meet my diagonal slash. Aurora's blade thumped off the leather-covered metal plate. Not used to having a shield, I nearly forgot to use it to defend myself when he lunged forward with his sword aimed straight at my abdomen.

I pivoted, deflecting the strike to slide past me. His momentum carried him forward, and I sidestepped partway around him, but the angle was wrong to try to slash at the back of his legs. It would have worked if I were left-handed, but I couldn't get Aurora around fast enough.

I grimaced. I was wearing a hard leather chest plate, but if he'd landed that blow just right, it could have been very bad for me.

Dancing back, I jumped out of the way of his arcing blade. He was very strong, but so far only average in quickness.

Our swords clashed, clanged, and thumped off shields as we fought at close range for several seconds. After a minute or two, my temples dripped sweat, and my chest heaved.

I crossed Aurora and my shield overhead to intercept Thander's overhand blow. The impact rang through my arms. Ignoring the pain, I whipped my sword down. The edge of the blade caught him below the ear where neck and shoulder meet. He growled through clenched teeth.

Bright crimson seeped through the shirt he wore under his leather armor.

My eyes widening, I tensed, not knowing how he would react. Darion would have gone into a rage. But Thander only seemed to redouble his focus, coming at me with strong, methodical attacks.

Hit by hit, he drove me backward. I was on the defensive and losing ground. I couldn't get too far below him because there was truth to the old saying about winners and high ground. Needing to avoid getting pushed down the hill, I started edging to the right instead.

I was holding my own, and Thander had yet to touch me with his blade, but my arms ached with fatigue. Sweat ran down from my hairline, stinging my eyes. My left hand throbbed from the blows that had landed on my shield. Pain of battle came much sooner without stone armor. My opponent had to be tiring as well, but he wasn't showing it.

After another minute of intense blows and blocks, we parted, both of us panting hard.

"Your teachers taught you well," Thander said. I just peered at him. I didn't have enough breath to respond. "But you won't win this bout. You're missing something."

I squinted, wondering what he meant, but there was no opportunity to ask. He charged, and a second later I realized he'd been holding back. He attacked with precision and force, not trying to run me through with his blade but clearly attempting to exhaust me.

I silently screamed at my body—Ethniu's body—to stay upright, to do anything to gain advantage. But my muscles were shaking, my vision blurring, as Thander continued his attack.

For a split second, I forgot to think of my feet, and I stumbled. I'd gotten too close to the downward slope. Fighting to catch my balance, I flailed. Thander beat at my shield, hitting so hard my hand reflexively flew open. The shield dropped and rolled out of reach.

I went down to one knee and threw Aurora up to deflect Thander's sword, but I knew I was done. He'd pushed me too far down the hill. Either this attack or the next, he would defeat me.

As if sensing his victory, he pulled back.

I looked up at him, anger surging through me but giving me no strength. I attacked anyway. When I got a close glimpse of his eyes, I faltered momentarily. His eyes were tricolored—golden in the centers—just like Jasper's. That split-second cost me, but I probably would have lost anyway.

It was no use. Thander was larger and stronger, and he had the high ground. I managed to intercept his swinging blow but couldn't keep my balance. The impact sent me tumbling backward.

When I managed to stop my descent down the hillside, Thander was there, the tip of his sword hovering an inch from my throat.

I'd lost.

"I concede," I ground out, fury rushing icy-hot through me.

I started to try to stand, but dizziness washed over me.

Thander leaned over me. "Don't return until you've figured out what you're missing. You'll only lose again."

The world began to gray. I blinked hard, but it was no use. Everything began to slip away. I started to fall forward. My muscles were completely unresponsive.

Great. To add insult to injury, I was going to faceplant in the grass.

That was my last thought before I opened my eyes some time later and found myself back in the cave.

I couldn't move. My entire body stung and burned, every nerve on fire. At least it was *my* body. Eventually the sensation receded, and I sat up.

My father was a few feet away, also slowly rousing.

"Oliver?" I said, relieved to hear the familiar sound of my own voice. "You okay?"

He painstakingly scooted around so he could kneel, clearly not quite ready to attempt standing. "I think so."

"I lost," I said dully as the horrible feeling of defeat curled through me.

"I know. I was there."

"I need to go back," I said, looking around for the bottles. "I have to try again."

"You can't," he said. With a groan, he pushed his hands on his raised knee for leverage and got to his feet. "Cethleen and Burain told me we must wait a full day before returning."

A bit of hope sprang in my chest. "But I *can* go back," I said, peering up at him.

"They said you may have a second try. But no more."

I closed my eyes and scrubbed my hands down my face, relieved that I'd get another shot but also ashamed that I needed it. "I'm sorry."

"Why?"

"Because I failed." I looked up at him. "And honestly, I don't know what to do differently next time." My gaze dropped to the rocky floor of the cave as a memory surfaced in my mind. "Thander, the man I fought, said something to me. He told me I was well taught, but that I wouldn't win that fight. He said I was missing something. And right before I came back here, he said not to fight him until I figured out what I was missing. He said I'd only lose again."

"Well, we have a day to think about it," Oliver said.

He extended his hand. I grasped it, and he pulled me up.

I took a deep breath as we turned to the doorway that would take us to the fortress. As my mind shifted to the current world and all its conflicts, my insides began to pull tight.

"Hope the place is still standing when we get there," I said.

"Me too."

I grasped my father's shoulder. He raised his hand, drawing the sigils and whispering the words that would take us through.

Together, we stepped into the void.

Chapter 13

OLIVER BROUGHT US into the fortress into the Amethyst Room with its private doorway.

"Still standing," he said, peering around the empty room. He looked over at me. "I thought it would be better to come in where we could catch our breath for a moment."

I nodded, realizing I still felt slightly dazed. After being in Cethleen and Burain's encampment, the fortress felt overwhelmingly modern—so many objects, textures, and colors. I allowed myself a couple of long, even breaths.

"Okay, let's go," I said.

On the way to the door, I snagged Oliver's elbow. He stopped and turned.

"Thank you for going with me, for being with me," I said. It felt good to say the words to my father, to someone I could trust not to take advantage of them.

He nodded, and a flicker of a smile passed over his face. "I wouldn't have had it any other way."

He pushed the door open, we stepped out into the hall, and the familiar smells and sights of the fortress engulfed me.

It appeared to be business as usual, though faces were tense and solemn as people paused to bow or curtsy.

"I feel like I've been away for a year," I whispered to my father. "We should find Maxen."

I suddenly regretted not calling Maxen's assistant from the conference room to help me track him down. Oliver pointed to a house phone up ahead, and we both angled that way. He picked it up and told Maxen's office that the two of us would be there in five minutes.

I brightened when I saw a familiar face coming toward us. Emmaline's face went white, and I didn't realize until she spoke that it was a sign of her relief.

"Your Majesty," she said, dropping a quick curtsy as she stopped before us. "We were afraid something terrible had happened in the caves."

I searched her weary face, remembering that she'd just lost her father in the servitor attack.

"Emmaline," I said. "I'm sorry we caused worry."

"Did you discover how to channel the god blood?" she asked in a hushed tone.

I traded a glance with Oliver and then shook my head. "It wasn't a completely unproductive trip, but we didn't manage to uncover the secret of the god blood. I will soon try again. What about you? How are you doing?"

Her eyes hardened, and her gaze slipped past me. "Busy, Your Highness."

She wanted to stay distracted. I wasn't going to push her into an emotional conversation when she clearly didn't want one. I'd check in privately with her later.

"What's the news of the past day?" I asked.

She brushed her hair off her forehead in a gesture that conveyed stress, the grief over her father pushed away for the moment. Her lavender eyes were tired. "There was a lot to clean up after the attack. Melusine is here."

The fact that she could speak of the attack—the one that had taken her father—so easily probably meant she was using most of her mental energy to suppress her feelings. Our people were known for being stoic, but I hoped she would let it out at some point.

I frowned. "Why isn't Melusine with Oberon?"

Emmaline shook her head. "I don't know. But the fighting in the Summerlands has stopped. It's completely under the control of King Periclase."

My chest tightened. I glanced at my father, who looked grim.

"I suppose that's no surprise," I said. "Any more servitor attacks here?"

"No, on that front, it's been quiet."

"I'm very relieved to hear that." I touched her shoulder. "I'll let you get on with what you were doing."

She curtseyed again and then scurried away.

We arrived at Maxen's office to find he'd just beat us there.

"What happened?" he asked. "I went to the caves looking for you. I've been sending Angus or Emmaline every twenty minutes since the six-hour deadline passed."

"I'm sorry we caused you worry," I said. "Oliver and I were . . . with the Fomoire."

Maxen sucked in a small breath. "And?"

I shook my head slowly and closed my eyes for a moment. "I failed. But they're giving me one more chance."

He squinted and glanced between Oliver and me. "One more chance?"

I described the entire encounter, from waking up in the grass and riding the horses to Thander defeating me. Oliver helped me fill in details.

Maxen exhaled, his shoulders lowering and his blue eyes focusing on the floor. He looked as dejected as I'd ever seen him.

"I'm sorry," I said quietly.

He looked up. "No, don't say that. I know you didn't hold back."

I spread my hands. "But that's the problem. I *didn't* hold back. I gave it everything I had, and I lost."

His gaze sharpened on me. "You'll win the next one."

I blinked, pulling back slightly at what felt like something very close to a threat in his tone. But then I realized he wasn't threatening me. He was exhausted, but a new ferocity had taken hold. He couldn't accept defeat. I imagined that Nicole and their unborn baby had a lot to do with this deeper level of determination.

"What are you missing, Petra?" Oliver asked, his voice uncharacteristically gentle.

He'd been standing by, watching our exchange. Maxen and I both turned to my father.

Oliver leaned a hip against the wall and crossed his arms. "Thander said you were missing something."

"Uh, my stone armor? My magic?" I shook my head helplessly. "More time getting accustomed to Ethniu's body and not having stone armor or magic?"

"I believe he was trying to tell you something," Oliver said. "I think he wants you to figure it out. I think he wants you to win."

I scrubbed a hand over my frizzing hair. Gods, how long had it been since I'd showered?

The three of us were silent for a short stretch. Finally, I drew a deep breath.

"I'll devote some time to thinking about Thander's comment, and I'll go back tomorrow, of course," I said. "Maxen, is there anything urgent I need to attend to right now?"

"Nothing is more urgent than figuring out how we will defeat the Unseelie and hold off the Tuatha," he said.

"To that end, what's the news coming from the Summerlands?" I asked.

"Periclase has taken the High Court and now occupies Oberon and

Titania's castle," Maxen said, his mouth tight as he spoke. "Word is he intends to declare himself High King first thing in the morning."

"And what about Oberon?"

"In hiding, is the assumption."

There was an urgent and sustained knock on Maxen's office door.

"Come in," he called, his worry lines deepening.

"Apologies for the intrusion, my lord," one of his closest advisors said hurriedly. His eyes flicked to me, and he bowed. "Your Highness."

"What's the emergency?" Maxen asked.

"King Moreau of the Dobhar Sidhe and Queen Vida of the Sylphs are demanding asylum for themselves and their people. Hundreds of people." The man's eyes started to look wild with panic.

My lips parted and a feeling of dismay took root in the pit of my stomach.

"What?" Maxen frowned. "We don't have the capacity for two more kingdoms of people. Queen Petra and I will meet with them now and tell them so."

"We can't," I said.

Oliver, Maxen, and the advisor turned to me.

"I made a deal with the Dobhar and the Sylphs, remember?" I said. "They helped us take back the fortress. In return, I promised them protection if and when the Tuatha came."

Maxen's jaw muscles clenched, and I could hear his teeth grinding.

"The Tuatha aren't here yet," Oliver said irritably.

"No, but the Dullahan have been sighted in Faerie and Oberon's been ousted from the Summerlands," I said. "At this point, arguing with Moreau and Vida on that matter would be splitting hairs. Don't worry, I'll handle it."

Wishing I'd had time to bathe and put on clean clothes, I took off for the fortress foyer. The rulers of our closest ally kingdoms had been given the sigils for the doorway located there. I just hoped Moreau and

Vida hadn't brought too big an entourage.

My ever-present guards—only two of them since no one had tried to kill me in a while—had to trot to keep up with me. When I saw a page, I beckoned to her.

"Please tell Amalie I need her immediately in the foyer," I said.

The girl curtseyed and said she'd do it at once, but I was already rounding the corner before she'd finished speaking.

In the hallway leading to the foyer, I slowed my pace, set my shoulders, and leveled my chin. Pasting on a serene smile, and again wishing I were wearing something a bit more queenly, I stepped into the large entry.

"Queen Vida, King Moreau," I called in a strong voice.

The two rulers had been standing with their heads together, speaking to each other with serious expressions and darting eyes.

Moreau shot me his trademark wolfish smile. "Queen Petra." He made a graceful bow.

I clasped my hands at my waist and stood with the others, reminding myself we were equals. Maybe not in size of kingdom, but in standing.

"I presume you're here to call in what I promised when you gave your aid," I said. No reason to beat around the hedge.

Vida inclined her head. "We are. As you've no doubt heard, we're on the brink of the Tuatha's return." She gave me a narrowed look with her long-lashed eyes. "And we trust you won't try to break your promise."

"Of course not," I said. "However, there is the matter of space."

I flicked a glance to the side when motion caught my eye and spotted Amalie hurrying toward us. As soon as she reached us, I held my arm out in invitation.

"Why don't the four of us go to a nearby private room?"

I led them to the Ruby Room, closed the door, and turned to Moreau and Vida.

"I'm going to be frank with you," I said. "Our space is extremely limited. The Carraig property holding in Faerie is essentially just this structure and the sky above us. We have no grounds to expand on, not even a wooded area to pitch tents."

Vida's full brows lowered. "And what is your current capacity?"

I turned to Amalie.

"We're occupied at seventy percent, your majesties," she said.

I groaned internally. There was absolutely no way the fortress could house two additional—and larger—kingdoms worth of people.

"Hm," Moreau said. "That *is* a problem."

"Yes," Vida agreed. "It's quite a predicament."

I squinted, sensing a proposition coming. My stomach tensed in anticipation.

"I'd like to propose that Queen Vida and I be allowed to bring as many of our people that can comfortably fit," Moreau said. "Our families and topmost officials, primarily."

I sensed an "and."

"And," he continued. "In lieu of not being able to fully make good on our agreement, we'd like to propose an addendum."

"What is it?" I asked, managing to keep the snap from my tone.

"We want a formal allegiance sworn between your kingdom and each of ours," he said to me. "Beginning immediately and lasting in perpetuity, regardless of who wears the Carraig Crown. In addition, we would like a personal allegiance between you, Petra Maguire, and our kingdoms."

The first part of the request made sense, but the second part was odd.

"I can't agree to any formal allegiances," I said. "It goes too far beyond the scope of what's owed between our kingdoms."

"But it works both ways," Vida said. "It's not just about us gaining the protection of the Carraig. You gain the protection of the Dobhar and the Sylphs, as well."

I held up a hand. "I'm sorry. I can't entertain the allegiances at this time. But based on our previous agreement, you may of course bring your people here. Amalie will tell you exactly how many we can accommodate and help you with arrangements. My apologies, but I must excuse myself."

My words came out in a rush, not giving Moreau or Vida time to cut in or protest. I let myself out and walked away from the Ruby Room with an irritable, quick stride.

They'd obviously planned to corner me into the alliances they'd proposed, and it annoyed me. I was also disappointed. I'd considered them allies and friends, and I didn't have many of those. But apparently it was just Faerie politics and manipulations as usual.

A thundering voice coming from the direction of the foyer caught my attention. I stopped, frowning.

"What's going on up there?" I asked a passing page.

He shrugged. "No idea, Your Highness."

The voice came again, this time yelling obscenities. I sucked in a breath.

That was Oberon's voice.

I sprang into a run, going as fast as my legs would carry me.

What was Oberon doing in the fortress?

The closer I got, the more his angry tirade sounded like thundering doom.

Chapter 14

"PETRA!" A VOICE called behind me.

I paused long enough to look over my shoulder only because I recognized the voice as Maxen's. He was out of breath, his cheeks flushed. We hurried side by side toward the foyer and the thunderous, angry shouts.

"What in the name of the gods is going on up there?" I asked, just as Maxen asked me the same thing.

"I have no idea," Maxen said. "I had no warning Oberon was coming. No one has heard from the High King and Queen since they fled just before Periclase took the Summerlands."

In the grand entry of the stone fortress, the ousted High King of Faerie was raving. Clerks had taken cover behind the desk to one side of the foyer, while Carraig soldiers stood by uncertainly.

I strode toward Oberon, a towering figure of fury who glowed with the visible mystique of an Old One.

"Your Majesty," I called in the strongest voice I could muster that was just short of a shout. I curtseyed.

Next to me, Maxen bowed.

Oberon spotted us and stormed over.

"King Oberon," I said, straightening. I had to tip my head back to meet his gaze. "We're honored by your presence and wish we would have had time to prepare for your arrival. Our deepest apologies for not being able to greet you properly."

He was obviously still fuming, but at least he'd stopped hollering. His eyes burned in a way that made my stomach curl into a tight knot. I wanted to skirt a glance at Maxen, but I didn't dare take my attention off the High King for fear it would set him off again.

Oberon's chest was rising and falling quickly, his agitation obviously still coursing through him. He'd come with half a dozen Summerland guards, who stood coldly at his back.

"Would you care to convene in one of our meeting rooms?" Maxen asked, sweeping his arm out in invitation. "The Ruby Room is just down the hallway."

I wasn't sure Oberon had actually heard either me or Maxen.

He leaned over and pointed his finger at me. "I never should have put my trust in you. You were supposed to invoke the god blood. You failed, and now the high seat of Faerie has fallen to the Unseelie. All of Faerie will be decimated when the Tuatha come. The Unseelie will rule, and winter will reign! And it's all because of *your failure*."

His words thundered so loudly, I wanted to slap my hands over my ears. It was all I could do to stand my ground as my heart hammered.

"Your Majesty, we are not done yet," I said, struggling to keep my voice steady. "I *will* earn the power of the Fomoire."

Something was wrong with Oberon. His speech had a raving quality to it, and his eyes gleamed with madness. Remembering how he'd been tortured with sky iron at the hands of the Tuatha under the Giant's Causeway, and what Eldon had said about Oberon's state of mind, I began to wonder if iron poisoning had gripped the High King's blood and we were just beginning to see the effects. The idea chilled me to my bones.

Oberon turned to the rest of the people gathered.

"I should string up all of you like slaughtered cattle," he said, spit flying from his lips. "I should drain you of your blood. I should drink your blood and have the god power for myself! You are too weak for it. But I'm an Old One. I can take the power of the gods. It should have been mine, anyway!"

Carraig soldiers had started creeping closer. I knew they were only aiming to protect their queen, but I was afraid Oberon would take it as aggression toward him. I lifted my hand at my side and flicked it, waving my people off in a subtle gesture.

But Oberon's guard had noticed the movements of the Carraig. They spread out and brandished their hands, palms out with fingers slightly curled. White-hot swirling plasma-like orbs lit in the palms of each Summerlands soldier. It was the magic bestowed by the High King of the Summer Court, Oberon himself. It contained a bit of the sun itself, and it could burn through nearly anything.

Metallic zings filled the air as my soldiers drew their swords.

"Oh, for the love of the gods, stop this nonsense this instant!" came an irritated female voice cutting through the tension.

We all turned toward its source.

Melusine, the Fae witch, came striding in, the skirts of her long black dress swishing around her ankles, bell sleeves flapping at her wrists, and orange eyes blazing.

She came to stand beside me and Maxen, facing off with us against Oberon and his soldiers.

The High King was not happy to see her.

"Show some respect, witch," he groused at her, his raving anger seemed to have cooled to a simmering irritation at the sight of Melusine. "I'm still your king."

"Witch, hm? Is that supposed to be an insult?" Melusine asked. She bent into a deep, flourishing curtsy. "Your *Majesty*," she said belatedly, pronouncing the title with exaggerated care.

He took a step toward us, and magic flashed, zipping from Melusine's fingers to form a huge, glassy gyrating disk. A shield.

"Stop there," she commanded, her words snapping with authority.

Oberon stood with his hands fisted at his sides, his face reddening with frustration.

The High King's attention shifted from Melusine back to me, and I went rigid at the menace in his eyes.

He pointed at me. "The blood of your people would be more use in my veins."

Oberon flicked his wrist, and I just caught the sparkle of a portal jewel before light burst outward, engulfing him and his guards.

When the magic cleared, Oberon and his people were gone.

Melusine turned to me. "Well. The High King is losing his mind. That's a bit of a problem, isn't it?"

I blinked. "You're serious? You think he's really going mad?"

"Most definitely." She pursed her lips and shook her head. "Poor Titania."

"Sky iron?" I asked.

She nodded, her orange eyes sad. "The iron poisoning can take some time to work its way into the brain. A normal Fae would have succumbed immediately. He only lasted this long because he's an Old One."

My chest clenched with sorrow. In spite of the clashes I'd had with Oberon, I didn't want to see him fade away into dementia. And my personal feelings aside, we desperately needed our High King. How could we take back the Summerlands without Oberon?

"What are we going to do?" I asked, my voice small.

"What you were going to do anyway," the Fae witch said crisply. "Channel the Fomoire so we can defeat the Tuatha."

I turned to Maxen, who'd been standing by quietly. "Are the Dullahan riding out yet?" I asked, dreading the answer.

"Not that we've heard. They're still gathering. But it's only a matter of time."

"How much time?"

"Hours? Days? A week? No one knows."

"Melusine, if Oberon isn't fit to rule, will Titania be willing to take the throne alone?" I asked.

Melusine's orange eyes focused on the floor, and the corners of her mouth turned down. "She's capable of ruling, but . . . to be honest, I don't think she could find it in her heart to do so, if Oberon is truly going mad. Despite how their relationship might look to outsiders, theirs is a love that lives in feverish intensity. Titania will never again be herself if Oberon fades away from her. I wouldn't be surprised if she descended into her own madness."

The three of us stood in somber silence for a long moment. I felt a new weight settle over me, adding to the already heavy burden of responsibility I carried.

I left the foyer and went to my quarters. There were a hundred things in the fortress that needed my attention, but I hadn't slept in a day and I'd barely eaten. The sustenance I'd taken in while with the Fomoire didn't stick back in Faerie, it seemed.

In the quiet of my apartment, I ordered a meal and then took the food out into my private, fully enclosed courtyard. Sitting on the grass next to the meandering circular stream that ran around the yard, I took in the late evening. The light coming through the windows behind me cast my shadow in a long slant to my right. The sun had set, and fatigue was beginning to drag at me.

I went inside, shed my dirty clothes, and took a long, hot shower. Afterward, I lay in bed with my hands clasped behind my head, staring up at the dark ceiling.

My body was exhausted, and my mind dragged as I tried to think of how I could ensure winning the power of the Fomoire. I fought sleep for as long as I could, but eventually succumbed.

At some point, I sank into a dream where I was back in the Giants' Causeway where Jasper and I had rescued Oberon from the Tuatha. But in the dream, I was alone. The darkness was complete, but I knew exactly where I was—the cavern with the crevasse where I'd lost Mort. My spellblade had fallen into oblivion, as before, but in the dream I could still sense it far below. The sword seemed to be calling out to me, urging me forward.

My pulse pounded as I took tentative shuffling steps, not knowing exactly how close I was to the edge of the drop-off.

The visceral longing for my blade clenched at my insides. I could feel Mort, which meant it was close enough to activate the blood bond between us. If I spilled enough blood, Mort would come to me.

But if it worked, would I still have enough life in me to escape? I didn't have Jasper there to carry me out.

I stood there for a moment, listening to my own breath and weighing my options.

Then I reached for the karambit on my belt, and without hesitation, I pulled the blade across the back of my arm. Wincing at the kiss of the knife's edge, I gasped and held my breath, waiting until the pain dulled a bit.

Blood flowed, wetting my hand and dripping off my fingers to fall softly to the stone floor. I seemed to stand there for an eternity, and still Mort did not come.

Finally beginning to feel faint, I sank to the ground.

I'd thought Mort was near enough that I could survive the blood loss, but nausea gripped me, and my head began to fog as the minutes stretched. Had I miscalculated?

I moaned softly. It wasn't working. I was going to bleed out.

Sagging over to my side, I cushioned my head with my good arm, and my mind began to drift toward unconsciousness.

But then there was a nudge, the sense of Mort coming loose. My pulse punched weakly. I pushed myself up, my arm shaking weakly.

"Mort," I whispered through dry lips.

The ground shook as there was an explosion far below. Mort was speeding toward me, fighting through the narrow spaces of the crevasse.

I held out my right hand and braced myself for Mort to slam home.

I awoke with a start. For a moment, I wasn't sure where I was. Daylight was just starting to creep through the windows of my bedroom, and the familiar pattern of the wallpaper reassured me I was home.

But my mind was still cloaked in the dream I'd been having. Even as it started to fade, there was an urgency that seemed to be calling to me to remember what I'd dreamt.

I stayed very still, trying to recall any details. But the dream was slipping, dissolving away like mist under the sun.

After another minute, I sighed, threw back the covers, and got up. I was still groggy, not having slept enough to make up for the activity of the past few days. It wasn't until I was in the kitchen with my hand on the coffee pot that I realized part of my dream hadn't faded.

I went stiff, sucking in a breath as my eyes unfocused.

Mort. I could swear the sensation of my spellblade was still there, and I wasn't dreaming. It was very, very faint, but . . . yes. There it was, a faint thrum that echoed through my bones.

The house phone mounted on the wall nearby rang. I sprang to it and snatched the receiver.

"Petra?" Maxen's voice came through the line. "The Gnome King Lawrence is here. I'm not sure how it happened, and I don't completely understand what he's saying, but he—"

"He has Mort," I cut in. "He's brought my sword."

There was a second of dumbfounded silence on the other end.

"How did you know?" Maxen asked.

"I can feel it," I said. "Where is he?"

"The Opal Room."

I raced to my closet, threw on clothes, and then burst out of my apartment. It was all I could do not to sprint through the fortress.

Part of my mind wanted to argue that it was impossible. There was no way King Lawrence could have found my spellblade. I'd dropped it into a crevasse under the Giants Causeway, the fortress of the Tuatha De Danann. The sword had fallen until I couldn't even feel it anymore.

But my heart knew Mort was there in the stone fortress because I could feel the sword, the sensation growing stronger the closer I got to the Opal Room.

When I arrived, Maxen was there with King Lawrence. He held a bundle of purple velvet wrapped around something long and thin. I reached for it, took it, and stood very still for several seconds before slowly unwrapping the fabric and letting it fall to the floor.

For nearly a full minute, all I could do was hold the sword and stare at it. When I finally tore my eyes away from Mort, I looked up at Lawrence.

"How?" I whispered.

The barefoot Gnome king blew out his breath, puffing the fringe of his long mustache.

"Gnomes are Fae of the underground, as you know," he said. "We have an affinity for all things earthen and spend much time in subterranean caverns."

The Gnomes believed that an ancient abandoned dragon's lair existed somewhere deep in the ground, and they had an almost religious devotion to searching for it. Young gnomes, upon coming of an age to leave their parents' homes, often spent a year on underground missions searching for the dragon riches as part of their service to their kingdom.

"One of my people happened upon it at the bottom of a deep well," Lawrence continued. "She recognized it and spent the better part of two weeks surfacing so she could bring it to me."

"I don't know how I can ever repay you for returning my spellblade to me," I said, my voice thick with emotion.

The door opened behind me, and my father strode in. I held up my sword, too choked up to say anything.

Oliver stopped, looked at the blade, and then locked eyes with me. I knew exactly what he was thinking.

"The thing you were missing," he whispered.

I nodded and then pressed my lips together, collecting myself.

I turned to the leader of the Gnomes.

"King Lawrence," I said. I gripped Mort tighter. "You just gave us our best chance at defeating the Unseelie and preventing the Tuatha from burning down Faerie."

His large eyes widened. "I thought you were our best chance at that, Queen Petra."

"Not without this," I said, looking down at my sword. "Thank you, King Lawrence."

I pronounced the words deliberately, knowing full well that I was leaving myself open for him to bind me in an oath. The barest hint of magic shimmered in the air, expectant, looking like glittering mist coalescing in a soft cloud between me and the Gnome king. I heard Maxen draw in a breath.

For a moment, no one spoke. Then Lawrence grunted and waved his hand through the faint cloud of magic.

"You are welcome. It was my duty and pleasure to return your sword to you," he said a bit gruffly.

With those words, he dismissed the possibility of an oath and the magic winked out.

Lawrence gave me a ruddy-cheeked smile, showing a row of large yellowed teeth. I smiled back and gave him a little bow.

"You're a very honorable ally," I said.

"Be that as it may, I must get back to my kingdom," he said.

"I'll take you to a private doorway," Maxen offered.

The two of them departed, leaving me and Oliver alone.

"This is it, right?" I asked. "I'm not deluding myself?"

"If you're delusional, then I am too," my father said. "With Mort, you have a symbol of yourself as you were before you returned to serve your people. And with Aurora, you have the symbol of yourself as leader and servant of the Carraig Sidhe. The two of them together make you whole, Petra."

He was right.

I carved a quick figure-eight in the air with the tip of the blade, nearly shivering with the delicious feel of my magic zinging through my sword. I continued with warm-up patterns I'd learned as a child.

"I don't know how to fight with two swords at once," I said, watching the metal flash.

"I don't think that will be an issue," Oliver said.

I stopped and lowered the sword.

"We need to go back," I said.

My father nodded.

"We have to wait twenty-four hours, though. Has it been long enough?"

He glanced at the clock on the wall. "By the time we get to the caves, it will be almost time."

I quirked a tiny grin at him. "Funny how the timing worked out. I can only conclude that things worked out this way because they were meant to." I paused, thinking again about Melusine's plea for me to have faith. "Can you imagine what would have happened if I'd gone back to the Fomoire to fight again without Mort?"

I shivered at the thought.

"Don't get cocky, Petra," Oliver said. "You haven't won yet."

I laughed. "Not yet. But I will."

Thinking of Burain, Cethleen, and Thander, I went suddenly still as something occurred to me.

"What is it?" Oliver asked, noticing my change of expression.

"Periclase and Burain have the same eyes," I said.

We stared at each other for a long moment.

"Does that mean Periclase will get the god power when you win it?" Oliver asked, his voice low and his face tensed.

"Why wouldn't he?" I asked. "The Fomoire said their connection was with stone bloods in general. There are stone bloods outside the Carraig kingdom."

"You must speak to them about this before the fight," he said.

I nodded, alarm still coursing through me as I realized how close I'd come to letting this little detail slip by.

Oliver came back with me to my quarters, where I took Mort's scabbard from the wall in my bedroom where I'd hung it. He helped me situate Mort and Aurora across my back, and we set out for the nearest doorway.

Word of King Lawrence's visit, and its purpose, must have started to spread through the fortress, because I drew long looks in the corridors.

When Oliver and I rounded a corner and came upon Emmaline and a handful of her soldiers marching in formation, I stopped to salute them. Emmaline stopped, too, her people halting neatly behind her.

Her lavender eyes were fierce as she returned my salute, betraying only the barest shadow of grief over losing her father so recently.

"Petra, Queen of the Carraig Sidhe, wielder of Aurora, sword of the Champion of the Summer Court, wielder of Mortimer the shadowsteel spellbade, we are at our service," she called out sharply.

I surveyed them for a moment and then nodded my approval.

"Carry on with your patrol, soldiers," I said. "And keep the fortress safe in my absence. I'll return shortly."

The way Emmaline's face shone with pride nearly broke my heart.

Oliver and I continued on to the conference room with the private doorway so we could depart in peace. We stepped from the netherwhere into the cool darkness of the cavern.

I inhaled deeply, taking in the moist air of the deep underground. This was Gnome territory, I realized. I wondered if the Gnomes had ever managed to breach this cavern system, unbeknownst to us, creeping through in their explorations.

Focusing on the center of my chest, I brought forth my magic, sending it rippling over my skin and gathering into Mort on my back. I couldn't use my stone armor when I took Ethniu's form to fight for the power of the Fomoire, but I wanted to feel my weapon and my magic together. It was like the most energizing shot of espresso coupled with the thrill of looking over the edge of a high cliff. It felt delicious. It felt like home.

I released my magic and turned to my father.

"Ready to go back?" I asked.

He nodded. "It's time."

He went to fill a jar with electric water while I collected some molten sky iron. We met back in the central cavern. Almost ceremoniously, we knelt next to the piece of stone that was still on the ground where we'd left it last time, and we each poured from our respective bottles.

The choking mist began to rise, and I made no attempt to resist it. I inhaled and held my breath as long as I could before a spasmatic cough forced me to exhale.

Within seconds, the walls and floor of the cavern began to melt and smooth into a highly polished surface. The ground tipped beneath us, funneling us toward the dark hole. I straightened out, feet first, and took the ride down into the void.

As I fell through empty space, sleep pushed at my consciousness. Mort's presence on my back was the last thing I registered before I blacked out.

When I awoke, I wasn't sprawled in the grass as before. Light softened by fabric surrounded me. The uncomfortable lumps of two scabbards and swords pressed awkwardly into my back. I sat up, adjusting the scabbards, and looked around.

"Oliver?"

I reached across the gap between my mattress of hay and the one next to mine where my father—or, who I hoped was my father in Balor's body—lay asleep.

He started and jolted upright.

"Petra?"

I nodded and let out a relieved breath. He took in our tent.

"It seems we were allowed to come straight to the Fomoire settlement this time," he said. "The same one they had us stay in before, if I'm not mistaken."

"Seems so," I said.

A shiver shimmied down my spine as I wondered if the real Ethniu and Balor had fallen asleep here, only to have me and my father crowding them out of their own bodies come morning. I decided it was better not to dwell on it.

It was stuffy in the tent. I stood, pushed the flap open, and stepped outside. My father followed me.

A girl of about seventeen with a high forehead and a long auburn braid was waiting just outside. I did a double take as I realized she had Emmaline's lavender eyes.

"The lord and lady asked me to bring you to them," she said.

She turned, and we followed her through the encampment to the large pavilion-style tent where we'd dined with Cethleen and Burain during our last visit. Our escort ducked inside. A moment later, the couple emerged.

"I've returned to challenge your champion," I said.

Burain gave me a long, cool look, his eyes flicking over the two swords showing over my shoulders.

"So I see," he said.

Cethleen's tight smile was anxious but not unwelcoming.

"But first, there is an urgent matter that needs clearing," I said. I told them of the stone bloods who were our enemies, Periclase in particular.

"Can you hold back the power of the gods and confer it only upon the stone bloods of my own kingdom?"

"If you win the right to the power, it will be done," Burain said with a slight inclination of his head.

Relief spread through me, and I returned his nod. I squared my shoulders. "I'm ready to fight. Where is my opponent?"

"He's ready for you as well," Burain said. "I'll take you to him."

Chapter 15

THANDER WAS WAITING for me on the hill where we'd fought before, and I almost got the feeling that he hadn't left since his victory, though that didn't entirely make sense.

As before, I went to where he stood while my father, Burain, and Cethleen scaled an equally tall hill nearby from which to watch. Oliver had said nothing when we parted. He'd only lifted his chin and given me a slight smile. He seemed confident in my chances of winning this battle.

I faced Thander, and he gave me a solemn nod, which I returned. His eyes passed over the two sword handles over my shoulders in the same way Burain's had.

"You brought something different this time," he said.

I felt my lips twitch in an almost-smile. "Yes. Something I was missing before. Something that is a vitally important part of who I am."

We both looked into the distance, waiting for Burain to raise his arm. But his attention was directed downward to the little valley between the two rises we stood on. The Fomoire were gathering below. Men and women who'd left their fields, flocks, and market stands. They were silently filing in and staring up at us.

Were these gods-in-human-form rooting for me or against me? It was hard to tell from the somber mood.

Burain waited another minute or so and then raised his arm. Thander and I both backed up a few paces and drew our swords. I was starting with only Aurora.

It had been dawn when we'd faced each other before. This time, it was early evening. The sun still hovered above the horizon to my left, casting long shadows for me and my opponent. Aurora gleamed in my hand, but only as a normal sword would. Evening wasn't Aurora's time.

When Burain's arm dropped, I gripped Aurora in both hands and drew my focus in, slowing my breath and blocking out everything but the hulking man in front of me. He moved several steps to the side, and I moved, too. We circled each other until the sun was in my eyes, which was of course what he'd intended. He lunged, faking an attack, but I saw it coming and barely flinched.

He attacked in earnest, and I parried, knocking his blade aside. Our blades clanged a few more times in quick succession, and I had to change to a two-handed grip to absorb the force of his swings. We separated, both of us already breathing hard.

"You're saving it," Thander said.

"Saving what?"

He lifted his chin, indicating Mort's handle over my shoulder. "That blade."

I gave him a cool smile. "Does that make you nervous?"

"No, but it does make me curious. Is not Aurora the more powerful of the two?"

"Yes, if anyone other than me were holding the two swords," I said. "But my bond with my spellblade surpasses the legend of Aurora."

He returned my smile and came in with another slash and lunge combination.

I spun out of the way, coming around to swipe at his Achilles. Aurora nicked the leather protecting his ankles but didn't cut through. I cursed under my breath. In Faerie, in my own body with my Fae magic charging my weapon, I'd have been able to pierce the leather easily with such a blow.

Once again, I had to accept there was no way I would beat Thander using force. He was too large and strong. And I didn't have the advantage of my magic.

I drew a deep breath to calm my pulse.

I needed to be swift and methodical.

Thander came at me again, with more force. I focused on anticipating his attacks and defending against them at the smallest energy cost, all the while being careful not to allow him to force me down the hill.

We fought until both of us were dripping with sweat.

After a brief pause, he narrowed his eyes in determination. I tightened my grip.

He came at me hard, trying to use his bulk to force me back. I kept side-stepping, but I couldn't keep it up forever.

When he pulled back to catch his breath, I faked as if to rest, too.

Then, lightning quick, I switched Aurora to my left hand, charged at the big Fomoire, and reached up to draw Mort.

I'd succeeded in startling him, and he was back on his heels as he defended Aurora with his shield and Mort with his blade. I kept up the attack, my arms flying.

Mort in my hand felt like home, even though it was Ethniu's fingers wrapped around the handle.

Slipping into flow state, everything slowed down. I saw Thander's movements a split second before he made them. There was an opening coming. I just had to keep up my attack.

Thander was grunting with the effort of keeping up with my slashes. He was still back on his heels.

My blades worked faster. My arms screamed with exhaustion. I ignored the pain.

He retreated half a step, now barely on the downward slope. I pressed forward, Aurora beating at his shield and Mort slashing at Thander's exposed knees.

I drew blood once. Again. And again.

There was no fury in my attack, only determination.

I simply had to win.

I raised both hands, ready to crash the blades downward.

As I hoped, Thander raised his shield. For a split second, he blocked his own view.

I dropped my shoulder and charged, slamming into his torso.

He didn't fall, but he stumbled.

I dropped Aurora and dove, wrapping my fingers around the back of Thander's ankle and holding on for all I was worth.

He kicked but couldn't get free of my grip. Like a huge oak, he pitched backward.

I let go, allowing his momentum to do the rest of the work.

He fell, his arms flailing up. He managed to keep a hold of his blade, but I was faster.

In a blink, I was straddling him, the end of Mort's blade at Thander's throat.

I was sucking wind so badly that all I could do was stand there, watching the tip of my sword tremble with the fatigue of my spent arm.

There was a rumble in the distance, and at first I thought it was thunder of a far-off storm. But it wasn't distant, and it wasn't a storm.

"I concede," Thander said. He dropped his blade and held up his empty hands.

My entire body shaking, I withdrew Mort and stepped back so Thander could get up.

I looked out toward the growing noise. It was the murmur of the crowd that had gathered to watch. The sound swelled, transforming from quiet surprise to clapping. Then cheering.

I wiped my brow.

"They're happy I beat you?" I asked, turning to Thander.

He'd stood and his gaze roamed over the crowd.

"They're happy you're worthy," he said.

Tears of relief, exhaustion, and all the fear, despair, and frustration I'd felt since I'd been crowned Queen of the Carraig Sidhe filled my eyes.

I looked to the neighboring hill, finding my father. He raised his fist and let out a shout of victory that carried over the crowd's cheers.

Dizziness swept over me, and I braced myself, expecting to black out and leave the world of the Fomoire. But I didn't faint.

Instead of my vision graying, it was the sky that turned dark. Black clouds boiled in from every horizon edge, and forks of pure white lightning began blasting straight down, touching ground and leaving torched smoking circles. Thunder growled and then roared, deafening and ground-shaking.

The clouds rushed inward, shutting out the sky and plunging us into night-like darkness. The harsh illumination of lightning blinded me every second or two.

I twisted around, looking for Thander. He sat where I'd defeated him. The rest of the Fomoire still filled the valley, and Burain and Cethleen stood on the neighboring hiss.

I thought my heart was pounding in my chest, but I couldn't even feel it through the thunder that drowned out every other sensation, absorbing all but the blinding, jagged forks of light streaking down from the black sky.

I sheathed Mort, found Aurora, and sheathed that sword too, and then whirled around, my panic growing. There was nothing but rolling hills as far as I could see by the light of each lightning strike.

My chest heaved. Where was I supposed to go?

I'd won. Why was I still there?

Then lightning shot from every Fomoire in view, the sound like a thousand whips cracking at once. The bolts angled up into the sky, meeting at a point high over my head.

I tipped my head back, my eyes growing wide.

"Oh, shit," was all I had time to mutter.

The single huge bolt zipped downward right at me. The air crackled with electricity. My hair stood on end. Sparks danced across my lips.

And then the lightning hit me.

An explosion of pain beyond anything I'd ever imagined burst through me.

I went stiff, my spine arcing back at an impossible angle. My lips peeled back, my face twisting in agony. I might have been screaming. In my mind, I was definitely screaming.

The lightning streamed into me for an eternity. I begged my body to lose consciousness. I prayed to the gods for death. Neither my body nor the gods complied.

Finally, blessedly, something changed. The first thing I noticed was the quiet. The thunder had receded to the distance.

There was water.

It plinked on my skin, cooling the burn of the lightning.

The lightning was gone.

I let out a sob.

The pain was fading.

I lifted my face and saw fluffy clouds overhead and blue sky in the distance.

The rain fell more heavily, soaking me, washing away the agony that I'd thought would never end. My tears of relief mingled with the shower from the sky.

I lay there on my side, my head resting on my arm, until the rain stopped.

A bird—a lark, maybe?—alighted on the grass a few feet away. It chirped at me, tilted its head in curiosity, and then poked its beak into the rain-softened ground, coming away with a worm. The bird flew off.

I pushed myself up to my hip to find that although the storm had gone, I was still alone.

I stood, unsure of what to do next. A few seconds passed before I realized I could still feel lightning crackling through my veins. It was uncomfortable, but nothing compared to the pain of the bolt's strike.

I reached my arms out, curling my hands into fists and then stretching my fingers out.

My breath stilled. Those were *my* hands, not Ethniu's.

And suddenly, I understood that the lightning in my veins was the power of the gods.

"How do I use it?" I whispered.

"Speak my name," a voice in my head whispered back.

I stiffened in surprise.

"Speak the name Ethniu to invoke the power of the Fomoire," the voice said. "And no enemy can strike you down."

I took a breath, ready to ask how the rest of my people would invoke the power of the gods, but I didn't get the chance to voice my question.

My surroundings dissolved away, and my mind shut down.

I woke up to cold stone pressing against my left arm and temple. Sitting up with a start, I looked around the cave. An illumination orb hovered overhead.

"Oliver?" my voice echoed in the empty cavern.

No one answered. Where was my father?

My heart in my throat, I rose and hurried to the arch, quickly going through the doorway.

I arrived in the foyer of the stone fortress. The silence was so complete and so strange in the normally busy grand entrance that it brought sharp panic squeezing my lungs.

Then I saw the collapsed forms of my people.

Chapter 16

I RUSHED TO the nearest body and gasped when I realized it was Shane, the Battle Master of our small kingdom.

I shook his shoulder and called his name. When I saw his chest rise with breath and a steady pulse at the side of his neck, I sat back on my heels, swallowing hard.

His eyelids fluttered open.

"Dorth," he said, his voice hoarse.

We squinted at each other.

"What?" I asked.

At the same time, he said, "Petra?"

"You just said something," I said urgently. "What was it?"

He sat up and rubbed his eyes. "Dorth," he repeated. "Gods damn, my head hurts."

"What's Dorth?" I pressed. "Focus, Shane."

He focused on me, his brow creasing. "It's a name. The name . . . the name of a Fomoire warrior."

My heart stopped and then restarted with a jolt. "Did you hear the gods speak? Did the gods tell you that name?"

His eyes widened. "Yes. There was light. Bright light. Then a voice told me the name. The voice said to invoke it in battle, and no enemy could strike me down."

A shiver passed through me.

"It worked," I whispered.

He drew in a slow, awed breath. "You did it. You earned the god power."

"Yes," I said, standing. I looked around at the rest of the still forms scattered where they'd fallen around the foyer. "We need to wake them."

Shane got slowly to his feet, and we went to the people nearest us.

I touched big Angus's shoulder, and he woke a few seconds later, uttering another Fomoire name. We had a short conversation similar to the one I'd just had with Shane.

"Queen Petra," came Shane's voice. He sounded tortured, on the edge of tears.

I went to him. He knelt next to a young woman dressed in battle gear. Emmaline.

"She won't wake up," he whispered.

She lay there, pale with her auburn hair spread over the tiles.

I took her hand. She stirred, and her eyelids popped open. Her lavender eyes focused first on me and then on Shane.

"Torela," she said.

Shane pulled her up into his arms.

"Thank gods," he said into her hair. He looked at me. "I think you're going to have to wake everyone yourself. I don't think they'll respond to me, anyway."

Someone appeared in the doorway leading into the foyer.

"Oliver," I said, pushing to my feet and running to my father. I threw my arms around him, holding him tight for a couple of seconds. I pulled back and looked up into his face. "I didn't know where you went."

"Right after you defeated Thander, I came back here," he said. "I just woke up."

"Did the gods tell you how to invoke the power?"

He nodded. "Using Balor's name."

And then he pulled me in for another embrace, this one nearly crushing me.

It turned out Shane was correct. It took hours to go through the entire fortress and rouse each Carraig. Oliver, Shane, Angus, and Emmaline came with me, explaining and comforting in my wake as I quickly moved on as soon as eyes fluttered open.

Each Carraig awoke with a name on their lips, even the children. It seemed that every one of us had a Fomoire counterpart, a name to speak in battle.

When I was finished, I sought out Maxen. It stuck me like a gut punch that he and Cethleen shared the same sapphire-blue eyes. How had I not noticed it before? Perhaps they were actually Marisol's eyes. It was impossible to know.

"The Dullahan have gathered in the Summerlands," he said, knowing the question in my mind. "And Periclase has the Dullahan skull."

I gave him a questioning look.

"The skull of the first Dullahan king," he explained, his blue eyes grave. "It gives the holder the power to command the army of Bone Warriors."

I felt the blood drain from my face.

"We knew this was coming," I said, giving my head a slight shake. "But it's still . . ."

"Shocking. I know."

"Any chance we can get to the skull before Periclase uses it?" I asked. "Do the Seelie have agents in Periclase's court?"

I didn't know much about the spy network in Faerie, but Maxen did. Our small kingdom even had a handful of spies, though espionage wasn't a Carraig specialty. We were fighters, not secret agents.

The corners of Maxen's mouth turned down. "It's too late. He's already invoked it. The Dullahan are just awaiting his command now."

"But if we can steal it and take control of the Dullahan ourselves—"

"No," Maxen cut me off. "We can't count on that. Periclase will have the force of every Unseelie kingdom to protect him from losing the skull."

I set my chin. "So, we *will* have to fight."

"We most likely will," he said. "Though there is one last, very thin hope."

"Jasper," I said.

He nodded. "If he can find the Chalice of Dagda, it's said to be the only artifact that can render the skull inactive. It also cancels the effects of the Stone of Fal, should Periclase decide to use that, too."

"Any word on Jasper's progress?" I asked, my chest tightening.

I hadn't spoken to Jasper in quite some time, with each of us off on our own vital missions. I knew he could take care of himself and hadn't worried much about his safety but wondered if he even knew we'd run out of time.

"All we know is that he hasn't located the Chalice. We don't know whether he's close."

I nodded, my gaze falling to the floor as I contemplated going to battle against Periclase and the Dullahan. After a few seconds, my eyes met Maxen's.

"We need to ready our forces and coordinate our attack with the other Seelie," I said.

His face tensed.

"What is it?" I asked.

"Now that Periclase has the Dullahan, some of the kingdoms have decided not to fight," he said.

My jaw tightened. *Cowards.*

"How can they justify that?"

He shook his head. "They don't want their entire fighting force turned into Bone Warriors," he said. "They're willing to take a gamble, thinking that if they don't oppose Periclase and he remains High King, they'll find favor with him because they didn't fight."

Anger bubbled through me, and I ran an impatient hand over my hair.

"Gather a list of the ones who are still in the fight," I said. "And summon their leaders here."

"They've already started strategizing, and—"

"I don't care," I interrupted. "Now that we have the power of the Fomoire, the game changes. The Carraig Sidhe are now in charge of the Seelie fighting forces."

Even as the words came out of my mouth, I could barely believe I was saying them. Was I actually strong-arming my way to the forefront of the Seelie command?

Yes. I was. Because it was the only way.

Maxen looked at me in surprise for a moment, but I hardened my expression.

"Yes, Your Majesty," he said. "I'll send the summons right away."

I went to my quarters to shower and change into more formal clothes.

While hot water poured over me, I remembered that the Sylphs and the Dobhar Sidhe had demanded residence in the stone fortress. I'd left that mess in Amalie's hands, and everyone knew there was no way we'd find enough room for two entire kingdoms, but I realized there was a silver lining. Queen Vida and King Moreau would fight with us. They'd more or less already pledged to do so.

So that meant three Seelie kingdoms, at least, in the fight against the Dullahan. I wasn't sure how effectively the dog shifters and the feather blades of the Sylph would be in battle with Bone Warriors, but we needed numbers beyond just the Carraig Sidhe. The stone bloods were fierce, and we had the advantage of the power of the gods, but our headcount was meager.

As I dressed, I ran through the list of other Seelie kingdoms, trying to guess which ones might refuse to fight. I suspected King Trey would hold the Spriggan out of the battle. Not because they were cowards, but because he blamed me for his father's death. Once Trey learned I was in charge of the Seelie army, he'd most likely be out. I thought I could probably count on King Lawrence and the Gnomes, but they weren't a race built for battle.

By the time I met up with Maxen in the Opal Room, I was bracing myself for disappointment.

"Trey refused our invitation," he said.

"I expected that."

"The Gnomes, Kelpie, and Baen Sidhe will come."

My brows rose. "And they're okay with a Carraig command?"

"We don't know yet," he said. "That's what we'll be discussing."

"At least they've agreed to show up."

"Most of the others who haven't responded are small kingdoms with insignificant or even nonexistent military forces."

I puffed my cheeks and let out a slow breath. "We could still make use of people who aren't formally trained fighters. Cat shifters, for example, could wreck some havoc."

"Agreed, but the kingdoms that don't have well-organized militaries may feel as though we're asking them to march civilians to their deaths."

"We're asking *all* Seelie to possibly march to their deaths because everything is on the line here," I pointed out. I hardened my expression. "Literally *everything*. I don't understand the mentality of those who think they can hold back, either out of fear or politics. Those who aren't willing to sacrifice don't deserve to reap the rewards of victory."

"Unfortunately, that's not always the way things work."

The door opened, and Shane, Oliver, and Melusine walked in.

"I hear we're making plans to bury Periclase under his own army of bones and horses," Melusine said, the black fabric of her lacy goth dress swishing as she took a seat across from me. "I want in, of course."

"We're glad to have you, Melusine," I said.

I waited while my head of security and my Battle Master found places to sit.

To Shane, I said, "You are the Carraig military commander, so you should know that I'm demanding that the Carraig lead the Seelie charge."

Maxen leaned forward, and I could sense his discomfort with my phrasing before he spoke.

I turned to him. "Don't worry, I'm not going to put it that way to the other rulers. But I am going to be persistent about this. We have the power of the Fomoire. We are proxies for the gods. We need to command our side."

"I absolutely agree," Shane said. "But I'm concerned that the other rulers won't accept me."

His worry was valid. Shane was younger than me and had only been named Battle Master recently.

"You will lead our forces, and you will advise me," I said. "But I'm going to place myself in the position of overall commander."

It might have seemed like an egotistical move, but I was still the Champion of the Summer Court and wielder of Aurora. I'd been named Queen by Oberon. Destiny was choosing me, and I wasn't about to pawn off the responsibility to anyone else.

"That is as it should be," Shane said, clearly satisfied.

"I'm not kidding about needing your advice, though," I said. "I'm not trained in battle strategy."

"You know I'm at your service."

I nodded and shifted my attention to Maxen. "When can we expect the other rulers to arrive?"

"Less than two hours from now," he said.

We spent the time discussing the various strengths of our allies and how to best make use of them. About fifteen minutes before our guests were due, I called for a break and pulled Maxen aside.

I pulled Morven's coin—the original one he'd given me—from a small pouch on my belt. "This was given to me by Morven. He said I could use it to summon him. I believe he meant me to do it in battle."

"The old Ghille Dubh innkeeper?" he asked. "Wasn't the Aberdeen ransacked? I don't think anyone's seen him lately."

I turned the coin in my fingers, thinking of the times I'd visited him needing information. How he'd taken some of my magic in return for what I needed. And what he'd said to me from the stream.

"He's out there somewhere," I said. "He'll come when we need him."

I tucked the coin away. "How's Nicole doing?" I'd barely had time to think of my twin sister, who was pregnant with Maxen's child.

"Well," he said, his mood lifting. "I'm doing my best to shield her from stress, but it's become a bit hard these days."

"Thank you for taking care of her," I said. I gave him a small smile. "You're going to be a father."

"And you're going to be an aunt."

Maxen would be a father, and I'd be an aunt . . . if any of us were left after the Tuatha and Periclase's Dullahan army came. Neither of us said it, but I was sure we were both thinking it.

Our smiles faded as we both turned our attention to the imminent arrival of Faerie's Seelie leaders.

Chapter 17

"YOU HAVE NO large-scale battle experience," the Kelpie King Delun was saying. His seaweed-green eyes bored into mine, challenging. "None of the Carraig do. You've never been to war."

"You're correct," I said. "But neither have you in the course of your reign, if I'm recalling recent Kelpie history."

"No," King Delun said. "But I'm not proposing to lead the Seelie forces. I'm proposing that someone more qualified than you—or me—do it."

My resolve was starting to falter, and I hated the tightening sensation in my gut. Maxen, Oliver, Shane, and I had been in the Amethyst Room with the Seelie leaders for nearly two hours. Lawrence and Delun had expressed their preference for Melusine to not be in attendance, since she wasn't a ruler of a Faerie realm. She'd quietly complied, which had surprised me a bit. Melusine wasn't one to avoid confrontation or argument, but I suspected she was doing her best to not make things more difficult for me.

Maxen and I had presented our proposition, and we'd been met with lukewarm agreement from King Moreau and Queen Vida, which I suspected was driven only by the prophecies of their respective oracles that said they should align their kingdoms with the Carraig.

The rest of the rulers had fallen somewhere on the spectrum between doubt and outright refusal. I'd expected to have to do some persuasion, but I'd naively thought that having gained the god power of the Fomoire would have given me a lot more sway.

Delun stood with one shoulder against the wall, his long arms crossed.

"I think we should vote," Queen Corrain of the Baen Sidhe said.

I ground my teeth.

"Why not?" she asked.

I did a quick mental calculation. I could at least tie, if I had the vote of my own kingdom, Moreau of the Dobhar Sidhe, and the Sylphs. That would leave the Gnomes, Kelpies, and Baen Sidhe against me. I wasn't ready to take that position yet, though.

"I'll not concede to a vote," I said. "I want to know who you think is more qualified, and why."

Delun and Corrain exchanged a glance.

"King Trey of the Spriggan," the Baen Sidhe queen said. "He was one of his father's top commanders in the Spriggan-Undine battles fifteen years ago."

I sucked a slow breath in through my nose, trying to quell my irritation.

"Trey refused our invitation," I said. "He doesn't want to be part of this."

"Maybe he would, if he knew we wanted him to command the Seelie forces," Delun said.

With a glance at Maxen, I sent him the silent signal that I needed him to take over the negotiations. He'd been mostly quiet, but I needed him. Maxen was a diplomat; I wasn't, and the suggestion that King Trey should lead the Seelie had pushed me to my limits of diplomacy.

"What we really need is Oberon," Lawrence said. "Why has he forsaken us?"

Maxen and I exchanged a look. Apparently, word of Oberon's more recent ranting hadn't spread as far as I'd assumed.

"Oberon was here," Maxen said.

The other leaders straightened, and the attention in the room heightened.

"When?" Corrain asked. "Why?"

"A couple of days ago. He appeared unannounced in the foyer using a portal jewel. He threatened us," Maxen said, clearly reluctant to give the ugly details. "It was much worse than what you all witnessed in his study."

"He said he would string up the Carraig like cattle, drain our blood, and drink it," I said, not in the mood to mince words over the topic. "But it didn't come off as just angry words this time. He meant it."

Corrain gasped.

"What in the name of the gods?" Delun exclaimed.

"It's true," Moreau said quietly. "Vida and I were here. We saw part of the exchange, and Oberon . . . isn't in his right mind."

I sent him a silent thank you for backing me up. I hadn't realized that he and Vida had witnessed any of Oberon's visit.

Lawrence shook his head. "What's wrong with him?"

"Sky iron sickness, we think," I said. "It's not widely known that Oberon was severely tortured with it while the Tuatha held him captive. Apparently, the effects can be delayed."

King Lawrence looked truly stricken. Delun and Corrain sat in shocked silence for a moment.

"We can't count on Oberon's help," Moreau finally said.

"What about Titania?" Corrain asked.

I gave a tiny sigh, reluctant to say what I knew because it would hit hard. But the others deserved to know the truth.

"Melusine told me that Titania is unlikely to take up where Oberon left off," I said. "She said that right now, Titania is unlikely to care about anything but Oberon and trying to stop the progression of the sky iron poisoning. In spite of their quarrels, Oberon and Titania are inseparable, and they belong to each other in ways we probably can't understand. She won't want to go on without him."

"Selfish," Lawrence said, pounding his fist on the table. "Damn selfish Old Ones! How dare they desert us in our time of need? How dare they abandon Faerie?"

"It is selfish, perhaps," I said. "But if Oberon has sky iron sickness, he wouldn't be fit to rule anyway."

"I think . . . I think perhaps Oberon and Titania's time in the High Court may be over for good," Delun said haltingly, as if he couldn't quite wrap his mind around his own words.

At that moment, I faced—truly faced—the reality of Delun's proclamation, which voiced what I'd suspected for a while. Oberon's reign was over. It struck me like an arrow to the heart.

"What's going to happen to the Summerlands with no Titania and Oberon?" Lawrence asked, his face reddening and his expression seemingly torn between anger and despair.

"If we don't defeat Periclase and the Tuatha, it won't matter," I said. "We must focus all of our efforts on that right now. We'll worry about who will rule in the Summerlands later."

What I said was true, but I could almost hear the gears turning in the heads of the leaders in the room. Politics were never fully out of the picture in Faerie, and in the event of a Seelie win, one of the people in the room might very well end up sitting on the throne of Faerie's High Court.

"Queen Petra's right," Maxen said. "We need to settle the matter of who will command the Seelie military."

"We need Trey," Delun said with a stubborn set of his jaw.

Corrain straightened and folded her hands on the table. "I agree. In fact, I insist," she said, casting a cool look around the room, as if challenging the rest of us to defy her.

I ground my teeth so hard my jaw ached. I cast Maxen a not-so-subtle glance.

"We've been at this for a while," he said. "Why don't we take a brief break, and I will send a message to King Trey reiterating our invitation?"

"That message needs to include the fact that he's in the running to command us all," Delun said.

"That's fair," Maxen said, inclining his head slightly. "Let's meet back here in thirty minutes."

He rose and went for the door, and I was right on his heels. I caught up to him in the corridor.

"Why are we bending to them?" I asked, my voice a harsh whisper. "We're not in a position of weakness. We have the power of the Fomoire at our fingertips, for gods' sake. They should be showing us a lot more respect."

"I don't disagree," Maxen said. He kept his gaze straight ahead, and his face was pale and tense. "But they do have one thing correct, which is that we need Trey involved in our plans. The Spriggan military is substantial. The fact is, in numbers and battle experience, it's probably the best the Seelie have."

I forced myself to draw a long breath before responding.

"What if he insists on leading us?" I asked.

Maxen finally looked at me. "Honestly, I'm starting to think that might be best."

My boots scuffed to a halt. "What?"

He stopped a few feet ahead of me and waited for me to catch up.

"I thought you agreed with me, Maxen," I said. "Oberon put me on the throne because I'm not a politician like the others. Fate has chosen us, the Carraig Sidhe, to wield the god power. The prophecies say the Seelie are doomed without us. How does all of this not point to us leading the charge?"

A tiny smile played across his lips.

"What the hell are you smiling about?" I demanded, slamming my hands on my hips.

"You," he said. "Do you hear yourself? Speaking of fate and prophecies, insisting that we are the chosen ones? So unlike the Petra Maguire I've always known."

I folded my arms and shot him an irritated look. "But it's all true."

"Yes," he said. "But think about it. We, the Carraig, are going to be preoccupied with the task of wielding a power so strong that it may kill us. We're going to be the embodiment of the Fomoire. That's . . . huge. Literally the stuff of legends."

"Okay. Go on."

"Why not leave the task of commanding mundane forces to someone who knows how to do it? Someone who isn't going to be steeped in the power of legends?" He sighed. "Look, I thought the same as you, at first. But the more I consider it, the more sense it makes to let a military man or woman do the, well, the grunt work. Because we're going to be fighting in a different plane of existence, for lack of better phrasing, from the rest of the Seelie. We need to allow ourselves to do it fully."

I looked at the ground. Maxen was right. In fact, it seemed so obvious that I felt embarrassed I'd been so insistent on commanding the Seelie. Had my power gone to my head? Was I turning into a greedy, control-grabbing ruler like most of the rest of them?

No. That wasn't me. I just wanted to give the Seelie the best possible chance. The fact was, I still lacked the experience and understanding to be making such huge decisions. I was, after all, still a fighter at heart.

"I think you may be right," I finally said softly. I lifted my gaze to meet Maxen's. "We do need Trey. He's the most qualified. The others in that room don't even want the command."

"Invite Trey," I said. "And . . . if you think you need to make the invitation personal—apologetic, even—from me, then do it."

"His father's death wasn't your fault," Maxen said.

"I know. But Trey thinks it was. So . . ." I shook my head. "Do what you need to do. We can't waste any more time."

He nodded and squeezed my shoulder, and then he headed off down the hallway. I let him go. When I turned, I found my father approaching. He stopped when he got to me.

"It's surprising how tiresome such vital negotiations can be, isn't it?" he asked.

I nodded and passed a hand over my eyes. "And we're not done yet. The fun part is still to come."

He pressed his lips into a line and looked off down the hall. "Trey."

"Yeah. We need him. I see that now," I said. "And I need to eat crow until he agrees to join up with us."

"He will, I think."

"What makes you say that?"

"As angry as he is about his father's death, and his belief that you were at fault, deep down what he really wants is to prove himself."

"Like, prove that he's as good as his father, you mean?"

"Prove that he's greater."

My brows rose. "Well, then our offer should be very appealing to him."

"Let's hope so."

Just as I was trying to decide whether I had time to go back to my quarters and sit in my courtyard for a calming moment, a fortress page approached me.

She stopped smartly and curtseyed.

"This came for you, Queen Petra," she said, offering a scroll with a wax seal.

My pulse quickened as I caught sight of the insignia pressed into the sealing wax. I recognized it as Jasper's.

"Your service is appreciated," I said to the page, dismissing her.

She curtseyed again and scurried away.

I moved to a window alcove and turned my back to the hallway so I could have some semblance of privacy while I read the message. Magic shivered through the air as I broke the seal, recognizing me as the intended recipient of the scroll.

We are close, but in case we don't make it back in time, know that you have all you need already. When this is over, you and I are going to get away from the world for a bit. I love you.

The last sentence brought a small smile to my lips, but it quickly dissolved under the weight of what we were facing. I couldn't imagine how he'd managed to get a message to me, but I understood what he was really saying. He believed he was close to the Chalice of Dagda, but we wouldn't be able to count on it. And I knew something else. His promise of taking me away from the world might never come to pass, because I knew he would give his life to get the Chalice, if he had to.

The note I held might be the last communication I ever got from Jasper.

I closed my eyes, imagining how his hand had written the words, how his fingers had rolled the message and sealed it with wax.

Opening my eyes, I smoothed the paper and then folded it into quarters. I reached into my shirt and slipped it into an inner pocket, which placed Jasper's message near my heart.

I made my way slowly back to the meeting room, as I knew I had plenty of time, taking a route that brought me outside to the training yard where I'd learned how to fight as a battle school student. The bright sun overhead seemed at odds with the heaviness I felt inside.

Current students were drilling in the practice yard. I might have thought it was any other day, except for a new level of intensity. And the fact that they wore full battle gear, as did every trained fighter in the fortress these days. After the servitor attacks, we'd been vigilant around the clock.

As I walked, I thought about my twin sister, Nicole. She'd been kidnapped to Faerie by our biological father, having no idea of the

Fae blood running through her veins. Her relationship with Maxen had progressed quickly, and they were clearly devoted to each other and anticipating the birth of their child with as much joy as anyone in Faerie could feel in the current times.

I had to wonder for a moment if that kind of future might exist for me and Jasper, if we managed to win. Could I even see myself setting down into some sort of domesticity?

I honestly wasn't sure. All I knew was that I wanted to keep the Tuatha from razing Faerie, I wanted to defeat Periclase, and I wanted to be with Jasper. The details would work themselves out later. But Jasper's note had somehow deepened my focus, I realized.

A page came running up, this one a young man.

He stopped, breathless, and bowed, hurriedly passing me a folded note.

"This is from Lord Maxen, Your Majesty," the page said. "He told me to hurry."

There was only one sentence scrawled in Maxen's familiar writing, informing me that King Trey would be arriving at the stone fortress in ten minutes.

I was ready to humbly face King Trey and eat whatever variety of shit he wanted me to eat if it meant he would join forces with the rest of the Seelie kingdoms. I'd be doing it for the people I loved, and for our futures, and what better reason was there?

My shoulders squared and my chin leveled, I walked swiftly back to the meeting room.

I took a slow, deep breath, pausing to center myself before pushing the door open.

Chapter 18

KING TREY, RULER of the Spriggan kingdom, was already there when I arrived. I wasn't sure if I'd hoped to beat him or not, but it didn't matter. He must have come almost immediately after getting Maxen's communication, and I could only hope that was a good thing.

I curtseyed, though I wasn't required to.

"King Trey," I said. "We weren't sure you would come. I'm glad you did."

He gave me a small bow, which I took as another positive sign. His eyes, which reminded me so much of his father's, were guarded, though. It would be grossly overstating things to say that he was happy to see me.

"Queen Petra," he said. "Knowing it is the hour of the Seelie alliance's greatest need, I couldn't turn down the invitation."

"I want you to know that I thought highly of your father," I said, hoping I wasn't muddying an exchange that seemed to be headed in the right direction. "I certainly never wanted any harm to come to him."

Trey held up a hand and briefly closed his eyes. "Please. Let me stop you there. I know of how you saved his life in his night club during one of the first servitor attacks."

My eyes flicked to Maxen. He'd been there when servitors wielding poisoned knives had descended on King Sebastian and his guards in Druid Circle. A couple of Sebastian's men had died, and he might have too, if I hadn't intervened. Back then I'd still been a mercenary vampire hunter working and living on the Earthly side of the hedge and doing my best to avoid Faerie affairs. It seemed like eons ago, though it was less than a year.

"Yes," I said. "And I was glad to save his life."

"Later, my father, well . . ." Trey trailed off. "He got in too deep, mixed up in things that brought unexpected complications. And unhappy consequences."

I blinked. Sebastian *had* gotten in over his head, in my opinion, but I never expected Trey to see it that way or to admit, even in a roundabout way, that his father had brought on his own demise.

"I liked Sebastian, and I mourned his death," I said quietly.

"I believe he admired, you, too," Trey said.

I hadn't exactly "admired" Sebastian and didn't think I'd indicated that, but I wasn't going to correct Trey.

After letting a solemn beat pass, I leveled my chin. "I hope we can honor him with our decisions and actions, so you can continue his legacy in the Spriggan realm," I said with a tone of determination.

Maxen flashed me an approving glance, and I knew I'd chosen my words well.

Trey's expression relaxed into the closest thing to a smile I'd ever seen. "Yes. That is a very nice sentiment, and I appreciate you saying so."

I caught Maxen's eye, not sure if it was appropriate to broach the proposal of Trey taking command of the Seelie military, or if we needed to wait for the other rulers to be present.

Maxen moved toward the door. "I believe the rest should be joining us any moment."

As if on cue, Moreau stepped into the room, holding the door open for Corrain, Vida, Delun, and Lawrence. I expected my father to come, but the Gnome king closed the door behind him. Probably just as well, as I didn't want to appear as though I were trying to outnumber the others on my own turf. I was the only ruler who had an advisor in attendance, which I thought the others likely understood, due to my very short time on the throne and general inexperience. Maxen had always been very well regarded.

The kings and queens exchanged greetings with Trey, and I studied how each one went. Moreau and Vida were carefully cordial. The others were warmer and seemed relieved that Trey had come. King Trey didn't appear to exhibit any special favor toward any of the other rulers.

I wished I'd had a moment to speak to Moreau and Vida before all of us convened with Trey. They didn't know my thinking about putting the Spriggan king in charge had changed. My anxiety rose as I realized I'd probably made an error. I didn't want my allies to think I'd turned my back on them.

"Again, you all have my gratitude for being here," I said, raising my voice a little to indicate it was time to start the meeting proper. I waited while everyone found seats around the table. Even Delun sat, which told me he felt more at ease since the Spriggan king had joined us.

"King Trey's presence here is especially important, as I think we'd all agree." I paused, considering how to express my change of heart without looking wishy-washy or weak. "I'm going to be very frank with you because I don't think I have the luxury of being otherwise. If King Trey is willing to take command of the Seelie forces, I think he should."

Moreau's eyes tightened, and his lips pressed into a hard line.

"Do I have this straight?" Vida asked, her face equally concerned and agitated. "You're saying you *don't* want the Carraig Sidhe to take the lead?"

"The Carraig should lead the charge," I said. "With the power of the Fomoire, we are the most potent weapons the Seelie have. But I believe Trey should be our field commander."

The Sylph queen considered that for a moment and then looked at Moreau. Something seemed to pass between them.

"I'm in agreement," King Moreau said. "But only if the Carraig are on the front lines with Petra in the lead, and my Dobhar and Vida's Sylphs fill the ranks directly behind the Carraig."

He and Vida were clearly still concerned about making sure they followed through with what their respective oracles had foretold would be necessary for victory; namely, that their kingdoms were aligned and fighting with the Carraig Sidhe.

I turned to Trey. "First, though, we must find out if Trey is willing to accept our proposal."

The Spriggan king had leaned back in his chair, crossing one ankle over the other knee and tenting his fingertips in front of his chest. His demeanor was a bit arrogant and relaxed for my taste. In that moment he reminded me strongly of his father, who often postured and tried to appear more powerful than he was. A tiny point of trepidation pinged through me like a shard of glass down a drain. But this wasn't about power plays and posturing, I reminded myself. Trey had legitimate experience that we desperately needed. I didn't need to enjoy his personality to respect that he should take command.

His lips pursed, the bottom lip poking out slightly, and he squinted at me for a long moment.

I kept my expression carefully still, though internally I was beginning to feel fidgety with irritation. Trey clearly knew he had the control in the room, and he was making us wait. I really didn't want to have to beg him.

"I will accept the command," he said at last, and I silently thanked the gods for sparing me having to grovel.

I knew—I was sure everyone in the room knew—that Trey had made up his mind before he'd even arrived at the stone fortress. But as with all things political in Faerie, we had to step through the paces of the dance of bureaucracy.

"We are *most* relieved," Delun said, nodding and then leaning back in his chair and taking a deep breath.

Lawrence stood and came around the table to give Trey's hand a hearty shake. Corrain had placed her hand on the Spriggan king's arm and was smiling ear to ear.

Trey accepted the expressions of gratitude and congratulations, but his wooden expression didn't budge.

Maxen and I locked gazes, and I wondered if he felt the same vague disquiet that was still pinging around in my chest.

Once the chatter settled down, it was time to turn our attention to the business of war. We spent the next two hours discussing strategy, during which I was mostly silent. As I listened, it became even more clear to me that taking myself and my people out of the running for military command had been the right thing to do. Delun was right. The Carraig Sidhe were excellent fighters, but we had no large-scale battle experience.

"Our biggest problem is that we don't know exactly where or how the opposition will attack," Moreau said. "They may rip open doorways in all our realms and let the Dullahan pour in. Or maybe they'll try to draw all of us to the Summerlands, where the Dullahan will try to decimate us and Periclase will use the Stone of Fal to brainwash us to force our loyalty."

"Perhaps the Tuatha will rain down fire on us, and as our kingdoms burn, the Dullahan will collect whoever remains standing," Lawrence said.

"This is why we can't wait until they make the first move," Vida said. She jabbed her index finger onto the tabletop for emphasis. "*We* need to make the first move."

"What would that be?" Delun asked.

"The Summerlands," Vida said.

172

Corrain nodded. "I think I agree with you. We have to force Periclase out of the Summerlands. Whoever holds the castle in the Summerlands has the High Court. We need to get it back under Seelie control."

"Even if that means leaving our respective kingdoms open to attack?" Delun asked.

"It's a matter of priorities," Trey said. "Controlling the Summerlands is more important than what happens in any one kingdom. That is, if we're truly all in this together."

My brows lifted slightly in surprise. He'd voiced one of my concerns—that it would be too difficult to get everyone on the same page, especially if it meant leaving people vulnerable back home. As much as everyone in the room wanted Seelie victory, every ruler also had their own interests in mind. And in Faerie, individual interests usually trumped the good of the realm.

I nodded at the Spriggan king. "Well said, Trey. Can we all agree on what our collective priority is?"

There was some initial hedging, but eventually everyone in the room voiced their consent to take the battle to the Summerlands, even if it meant leaving our kingdoms barely armed at home.

"With any luck, the fighting will stay in the Summerlands," Lawrence said.

"We'll have to do everything in our power to force things that way," King Moreau agreed.

Corrain's plump lips pressed together, and she looked down with sadness. "And we'll all have to pray that we have people and lands to go back home to."

We determined we needed to reconvene with each kingdom's top military personnel in attendance. We'd briefly debated about whether we should press on that night or wait until morning. There were no reports to indicate that Periclase, the Dullahan, or the Tuatha would be making a move in the next twenty-four hours, but because we'd decided we would make the first attack in the Summerlands, we didn't have a second to spare.

Maxen ordered food and drink to be delivered, the others got to work summoning their people, and I excused myself to go look for Oliver during the brief break.

When I knocked the door of my father's quarters, I didn't worry about waking him. He'd never slept much, and given the current circumstances, I knew he'd be on alert even if he was hiding away alone.

The door opened and Oliver appeared. "Petra."

"Can I come in?"

"Of course." He stepped back to let me in.

I quickly filled him in on what had happened with Trey. My father sat on his easy chair—the only seating in his spare living room—and I settled cross-legged on the floor as I used to do when I was young.

"I need to get back to the others," I said. "But I wanted you to know what was happening."

He fixed me with his steady gaze. "It appears that things are falling into place."

"Yes, it appears that way."

"Then why are you seeking reassurance?" he asked.

My brows lowered. "I'm not . . ." I trailed off, my frown deepening. "I feel like we're missing something."

"You probably are. There's no way to truly plan for what we're about to do."

"And there's no time, anyway," I said, standing.

Oliver rose, too, and walked with me to the door.

"You just have to be confident that you've done enough and in the moment you'll know what to do."

"Have faith, you mean?" I asked.

His lips twitched, the barest hint of amusement. "Yes. Faith."

174

I stepped toward him and threw my arms around his neck. He grunted in surprise, but then returned my embrace. I didn't prolong it—neither of us were big huggers—but when I released him and looked up into his eyes, his face had softened.

"Don't be afraid to lean on faith," my father said. "It has its place alongside swords, training, and preparation."

I nodded and left his quarters.

When I returned to the meeting, I suddenly understood the term "war room." The walls of the Amethyst Room—all except the one with the arch designed into it—were covered with projections of diagrams and maps. High-ranking people from our allies' militaries were coming in through the doorway in the wall. The space was growing crowded, the air thick with tension and anticipation.

I sidled over to Shane.

"How are things going?" I asked.

He'd told me how he'd been bringing our people into the practice yard in groups to try invoking their Fomoire powers.

"We've decided there's really no way to get used to using the power of the gods," he said. "It's so intense, we can't waste our energy playing around with it. Everyone knows the name of their Fomoire counterpart and what to do when it's time to fight. After that . . . well, we won't know until it happens."

I nodded, my stomach a little queasy. "We just have to trust we'll know what to do when the time comes," I said, thinking of what Oliver had just said to me. "We have to keep faith the Fomoire have given us something we can wield and withstand."

Even as I said it, I realized I didn't know whether it was true. For all I knew, the Fomoire planned on sacrificing us, using us to channel their power and drive out the Tuatha De Danann, clearing the way so the Fomoire could reemerge into their beloved homeland, and burning us out in the process. The Tuatha saw us as disposable. The Fomoire could very well, too.

Once everyone was gathered—all of us standing, as we'd had to remove the table and chairs to make room—the lights were dimmed. Trey took the lead, and he and the other experienced military people mapped out our attack.

As we'd requested, the Carraig Sidhe would be leading the way. My stomach tightened as I thought about how my people would be going in with no wartime experience and knowing almost nothing about wielding our god power.

"One question," Delun said. "We haven't discussed how we're going to get hundreds of people into the Summerlands."

I stepped forward. "Melusine should be able to help us with that. In fact, we'd better discuss that now."

Maxen sent a page for the Fae witch, and she arrived ten minutes later. The others moved out of the way, creating a path for her. Being an Old One, she towered over all of us, even the tall, leggy Kelpies. The black lace train of her dress trailed behind her, and her orange eyes were solemn as they swept over those gathered.

I repeated our concern, and she clasped her hands at her waist.

"I can use my magic to widen a standard doorway," she said. "But I can only do one. So you must organize yourselves into a single location where you will pass through."

"A single funnel will make us sitting ducks," Moreau called out.

Melusine's gaze whipped over to the Dobhar king, and she gave him a piercing look. "I can create a shield on the other side. But you'll have to move beyond it if you want to make use of any magic." Her eyes found mind in the crowd. "I assume that means the Carraig will need to go beyond the shield to use their god powers."

"We'll be first through, anyway," I said. "So the Carraig will indeed be fighting beyond your shield."

"I know how we can get everyone through," Maxen chimed in. "It

176

will take some coordination, but it should be simple enough. We'll use the fortress as our corridor for bringing in the soldiers from all the other kingdoms. Melusine's doorway emerges from here in our territory into the Summerlands. I'll have the logistics written up immediately."

Pride, anticipation, and nerves stirred in my chest.

This was it. The time for planning was done. We were going to storm the Summerlands.

Chapter 19

WE PLANNED TO stage our attack before sunrise to have the element of surprise on our side. Some portion of the Unseelie kingdoms' forces still seemed to be residing in their respective kingdoms, though most had sent large numbers of soldiers to help Periclase in the Summerlands.

Word had spread that he'd already named Oberon and Titania's former stronghold the Winter Palace and was still considering what the realm would be called, as Summerlands obviously wouldn't do.

It was a small thing, but it irked me deeply. Periclase hadn't truly won yet, but he was already trying to put his stamp all over the High Court of Faerie.

There were some delays in coordinating the Seelie forces to stream through doorways from their kingdom and into the stone fortress to queue for our attack. There were also some last-minute changes, which rearranged the order of the attacking forces, putting the Spriggan at the very back. King Trey also decided to hang back instead of coming through with the first charges. I didn't have the knowledge to question the changes, and neither Maxen, Oliver, nor Shane seemed concerned.

The Carraig, Moreau's fighting Dobhar Sidhe, and the swordspeople of the Sylph were all stuffed into the training yard of the stone fortress, representing the first wave. The other kingdoms' fighters would come after, streaming in through the other fortress doorways and funneling into the practice yard.

We were waiting for one last update on the Summerlands. I didn't know the particulars, but some of our allies had spies there.

Melusine was at the wall of the practice yard where there was an existing doorway, mentally preparing herself to break open a magical tunnel between here and the Summerlands.

There was some jostling in the crowd of soldiers and shouts to make a path. A breathless page came running up to Maxen, who was at the head of the pack along with myself, my father, Shane, and our most skilled fighters. Trey also stood with us, though he wouldn't be going through the doorway with the first wave. He would come through after the Sylphs, on horseback so he could take stock of the battlefield and what we faced.

The page, a blond girl of about fifteen, handed a scroll to Maxen. He quickly broke the seal to a shiver of glittering magic. I watched him scan the words on the rolled message.

"The Dullahan have gathered in the Summerlands," he said, his gaze whipping up to mine. His tone was grim, but his eyes were uneasy—almost fearful. "The entire army of Bone Warriors is just standing there, surrounding the castle."

My mouth went dry. "They've just . . . come suddenly?"

If the Dullahan had amassed around Periclase within the span of the past few hours, could it possibly be a coincidence? Or did he know we were coming? Either way, he was ready for us.

"No matter," King Trey said crisply. "The Seelie will attack with the same goal as before: to keep the battle in the Summerlands instead of in the individual realms. Good hunting to you all."

He turned before we could reply, going back to take his position at the rear of the Sylph swords.

"No word from Jasper?" I asked Maxen, though I already knew the answer.

He shook his head.

Without the Chalice of Dagda, everyone but the Carraig would be vulnerable to Periclase's Stone of Fal as well as to the touch of the Dullahan. We didn't expect Periclase to invoke the Stone right away. He'd certainly wait at least until Seelie forces had filled the Summerlands, maximizing the number of people who would be exposed to the Stone's power.

Periclase might also save the stone for later, perhaps as a safeguard if it looked like the Unseelie might lose. Information brought in by spies indicated that Periclase had been commanded by the Tuatha to wait, to allow the Dullahan to deal with us first. The rumor was that the Dullahan would be aiming for the Carraig because we were the only ones known to be able to resist the Stone. The Seelie agents hadn't been able to discover whether Periclase knew we'd acquired the power of the gods. We could only hope it would come as a very big surprise.

"How much longer?" I asked Maxen, my hands twitching at my sides.

The soldiers in the yard in front of us were trying to keep a respectful distance, but with more people crowding in behind, we were getting squeezed up closer to the wall and the arch where Melusine waited to open a gateway.

"Only a couple minutes more, I believe," he said, his eyes cast up at the dark night sky. "A raven will come to Melusine when we've amassed as many soldiers as we can in the queue."

There hadn't been time for rousing speeches or much preparation at all, really. Shane had briefed all our fighters about the Dullahan and made sure all the Carraig who would be fighting knew their Fomoire counterpart's name to speak to invoke their gods-bestowed ability. But we were untested and inexperienced with wielding such enormous power.

I turned to those gathered behind me and drew Aurora from my back with a soft metallic zing. With the sword of the dawn held aloft, the nervous chatter died.

"Raise your swords!" I called over the crowd.

The thrilling whoosh of hundreds of blades being drawn filled the air, and then metal bristled overhead.

"We are stone bloods, we are Carraig Sidhe, and we are Seelie," I said, projecting my words powerfully. "Today, we fight for who we were, who we are, and who we will be. And we do it with the power of the gods running through our veins. We are fighters of legend!"

A roar went up just as a dark shape flapped overhead, coming to circle over Melusine's head and then land on her shoulder.

It was time.

Melusine raised her hands, and the raven squawked and took flight.

My heart pounded as I watched her lips move with silent words. Her hands flew through the air, drawing sigils I didn't recognize. The arch in the wall began to glow as if heated from within.

The doorway shimmered and melted, the solid surface under the arch giving way to Melusine's magic. Sparks burst outward, and I squinted and drew back as a prickling shower of magic hit my skin.

The Fae witch's fingers stilled, but she held her hands palms out and moved them in slow circles. The doorway swirled as if her motions stirred it. The edges of the arched doorway began to bow outward, stretching to either side as Melusine widened it.

I stole a glance at my father, and his gaze turned to meet mine. His eyes shone with the fiery reflection of Melusine's magic. An excited roar began to go up in the crowd, but I heard Oliver's words clear as day.

"Fight as I know you can, daughter," he said.

I nodded at him, my heart swelling in my chest. "See you on the other side."

The doorway grew wider and wider until it was nearly the length of the wall where the arch had been carved. If we squeezed together, we could probably go through thirty at a time.

My stomach twisted at the thought of the Dullahan waiting on the other side.

"The battle is yours now," Melusine's voice boomed above the noise. "Good hunting!"

Raising my sword, I charged forward into the blinding light of the doorway with Oliver to my right and Shane and Maxen to my left.

Instead of the cold void of the netherwhere, I plunged into the plasma-like veil of Melusine's magic. It clung to my skin like hot wax and peeled back as I passed through.

Bursting into the Summerlands, my first thought was that we'd taken longer than intended because the light of daybreak was beginning to pale the eastern sky. My second thought was less a thought and more a horrified impression.

The Dullahan, skeletal riders on horseback, spread out as I could see.

Melusine had let us through just inside the outer wall surrounding the castle's grounds. A pearlescent bubble of magic stretched out before us as we charged. The Dullahan riders edged away from it, the horses tossing their heads and prancing back. The Bone Warriors couldn't touch us as long as we were protected by the magic, but we also couldn't invoke our god powers from inside the bubble.

I was nearing the edge of Melusine's shield. Taking a breath and holding it, I plunged through. It slipped over my skin like a sticky film.

I'd intended to call out Ethniu's name as soon as I was free of the shield, but I faltered when I caught sight of a man mounted on the largest warhorse I'd ever seen, standing still on top of a gentle rise.

"Periclase," I growled.

He saw me. Even from a distance, I could feel the second my blood father's eyes locked on mine.

Behind him, the ranks of his own kingdom's fighting force lined up, ready with their shields and short swords. But they made no move to join the fight. Not yet.

Periclase raised his arm, and for a heart-stopping second, I thought he was going to invoke the Stone of Fal. But the thing he held was larger than the stone. Greenish mist spilled from the object like a fog of dry ice. It was a skull. The skull of the first Dullahan king. The artifact that gave the owner command of the Bone Warriors.

"Dullahan, attack!" Periclase commanded, his voice carrying out over the rolling hills of the castle grounds. He thrust the skull higher.

I had just enough time to plant my feet, grip Aurora in both hands, and scream Ethniu's name at the heavens.

The sky cracked open overhead, and lightning spiked down, hitting me in the forehead, and for a long, agonizing moment, obliterating everything I felt and knew.

Only one thing lingered in my power-singed brain: the fear that while I stood there paralyzed, the Bone Warriors would hurl their skulls at me. The childhood tales of the Dullahan flooded me with dark terror.

Don't let them touch you, or you'll join their ranks forever.

My vision cleared, but the lightning filled my veins. It was pure pain, pure power.

Strikes rained from the sky all around.

A blur of white bone sped at me. I knocked it away, and it shattered into dozens of pieces on Aurora's impact. Two more skulls aimed at me met the same fate. They weren't destroyed for good. They would slowly reassemble themselves and make their way back to their owners.

Feeling rather than seeing the presence of my father, Maxen, Shane, and other Carraig next to me and behind me, I stormed forward.

A volley of skulls arced toward us. I batted them away, my sword a blur.

I started to think the Dullahan were too wary, that they would keep their distance. Then I heard Periclase's call for them to charge.

The front line of horses sprang at us with frightening speed. In one blink they'd seemed to be standing there almost casually. In the next, they were streaking at us, their skeletal riders letting out screams that must have originated from beyond the grave.

Skulls rematerialized under the arms of the Dullahan who'd thrown their detached heads at us.

Ethniu's strength filled me. I switched Aurora to my left hand and drew Mort with my right. My blades blurred, cutting down horses and riders as the Dullahan tried to crash through our ranks.

A rider came at Oliver from his blind spot, and I lunged. My blade severed the skeletal arm that reached for my father, but in my haste to protect him, I didn't see the skull flying at me. It hit me in the cheek, and I turned, stunned, to look at the bony orb that had landed on the ground next to my foot.

My heart stopped. I'd been touched by the bone of a Dullahan. For a moment, terror overwhelmed the god power. I was just Petra, suddenly and deeply fearing that I'd come to my end.

More skulls came at me, and I reflexively cut them out of the air. Seconds passed. Minutes. I fought, even as my mind was screaming that at any moment I would join the ranks of the Bone Warriors.

But it didn't happen.

I saw other Carraig get nicked by skulls, and they didn't change, either.

A cool smile touched my lips even as my swords whirled faster. I was still standing. The god power was keeping the Dullahan from turning me into a Bone Warrior. When I realized the truth of it, the pain of the lightning searing my insides became a welcome agony.

And it truly hit me: we didn't need to play defense. We could go after the Dullahan with full force. We could mow them down on our way to Periclase.

"Periclase!" I shouted at Shane. "We need to get to him. Can we form a smaller attack group?"

I wasn't sure how to reorganize in the middle of a fight, but Shane began shouting orders at the nearby Carraig, calling out for some to stay behind and others to start forging ahead.

Behind us, all the Carraig fighters had made it through Melusine's portal. Dobhar, in their canine forms, were grabbing the Dullahans' horses by the throats and shaking their riders off. Then Carraig and Sylphs would race up to hack the Bone Warriors to pieces.

But we were losing some. The Sylphs and Dobhar were vulnerable to the Dullahan. I watched one dog get surrounded by riders, pelted with skulls, and then fall into a still heap. At some point, that Dobhar would rise and join the Bone Warriors.

The Kelpies were beginning to come through, armed with their back quivers full of slim throwing spears.

"We should take a couple of spears," I called to Shane, sparing him only a quick glance as I kept advancing on the Dullahan.

Shane gave a nearby Carraig the order to go back and bring up three Kelpies.

As triumphant as it felt to know the Dullahan couldn't kill me or my people, my heart ached for the others who didn't have such protection. Loss of life was a cost of war, but it still hurt. I tried to push away the thought of casualties, focusing instead on fighting at my father's side, starting to carve a path through the Dullahan.

It struck me that the Seelie forces far outnumbered the Dullahan. It would be only a matter of time before Periclase sent his own soldiers, along with the other Unseelie armies I spotted lined up behind his Duergar, to fight us. He was probably just waiting until the Bone Warriors had mowed through some of our ranks.

I sucked in a breath as a realization hit me. If we let out all the Seelie forces on to this battlefield, they would be slaughtered. The Bone Warriors would go after all but the Carraig, and Periclase's Unseelie army would finish off the rest. It would be a hard fight, and many Unseelie would fall, but . . .

"Shane!" I screamed over the din.

He glanced my way, but neither of us could stop fighting. I maneuvered a little closer to him.

"We hold back some of the Seelie forces," I said.

"Why?" he panted.

"Because Periclase wants to draw all of them out. He wants all the Seelie soldiers here so he can decimate them all at once. He's going to—"

An explosion behind us cut me off. I stumbled forward as the ground shook and nearly lost hold of Aurora as I tried to keep from pitching into my father, who'd moved in front of me.

My ears ringing and throbbing, I whirled around.

The doorway was closed. Melusine's wide arch was gone, and so was the protective bubble that she'd formed in front of it. My confused gaze swept the Seelie forces. All had made it through . . . except the Spriggan.

My insides clenched.

Something had gone wrong.

Everyone on the battlefield, even the Dullahan, was still reeling from the magical explosion. My people seemed generally okay, but many of the other Seelie had been knocked out cold by the blast.

"Petra!"

I tipped my head back at the sound of my name from above.

An enormous Great Raven was circling overhead. And on its back . . .

I gaped in surprise. "Bryna?"

My blond half-sister rode the Great Raven. Something dropped from her hand—a scroll. I tucked Mort under my arm so I could catch it. I ripped the wax seal.

King Trey has betrayed you. He's on the side of the Unseelie. Periclase is going to use the Stone of Fal to turn all the soldiers to his side. He'll keep some as his minions and slaughter the rest.

Our commander was a traitor. With Trey's desertion, the Seelie army was reduced by half. And we'd been abruptly cut off from Melusine's help and protection.

I looked up, scanning the Dobhar, Sylphs, Kelpies, Gnomes, Baen Sidhe, and the handful of other Seelie race representatives who'd joined our fight.

"They're all going to die," I choked out.

Chapter 20

I SHOVED THE scroll at Shane.

I could tell by the way his face paled that he'd come to the same conclusion I had: the Carraig Sidhe might survive this battle, but most likely no one else would. And we couldn't fight by ourselves forever.

Oliver had come and grabbed the note from Shane's hand. Maxen joined us.

Carraig were milling around looking stunned, trying to rouse and help our non-Carraig allies to their feet.

"What do we do?" I asked helplessly.

With a glazed numbness, I looked around at the battlefield, where the fighting had temporarily died down after the blast.

"We have to fight," Oliver said. "There's no way out."

"But they're all going to die," I repeated.

Shane set his jaw. "They're soldiers. We're all soldiers. We all know the risks."

I looked helplessly at Maxen.

"We need to get the Stone from Periclase," I said. "The skull, too."

"He may not even have the Stone on him," Maxen said. "If that note is correct, he's not planning to use it on us. Not here on this battlefield."

I looked into the distance at my blood father. He'd been knocked off his horse by the blast, and his commanders were helping him up. One of them was Darion, Periclase's brother and my blood uncle.

"He has it," I said. "I would bet my sword on it."

"Even if he doesn't," Oliver said. "He's got the Dullahan skull. If we can get it away from him, we can turn the Bone Warriors against the Unseelie."

I tipped my gaze up to the sky. Where had Bryna gone? I really could have used an air drop to Periclase's hill. The Unseelie had archers who used magic to direct their arrows true, though, so I didn't blame her for not lingering.

The fighting was beginning to resume. And it looked as if Periclase was getting ready to advance his forces.

"We need to go on with our plan. The Carraig need to cut a path to Periclase," I said.

Shane nodded. Oliver's mouth hardened. Maxen's eyes were haunted as he looked back at our allies.

The three of them retreated to spread the word to our people. I gripped my swords and turned my attention to the lightning inside me, the electric, painful power that I'd barely tested yet.

"Ethniu," I said under my breath. "I need everything you have."

The electric power surged in response to my plea. I ground my teeth as my spine arched in pain.

Oliver, Maxen, and Shane had returned, and by their expressions I could tell something about me had changed. When I looked down, I saw double. My body was shifting, pulsing—one second I saw the arms I recognized and the next Ethniu's larger, more muscled ones. Then the two blurred together as another zip of lightning seared my insides. The Fomoire warrior and I had merged.

"We fight," I said in two voices, two languages—mine and Ethniu's.

The Dullahan had recovered from the blast. Six of them charged me. I walked forward, my swords cutting through the air, the horses, the skeletal riders, all with the same ease.

Ahead, Periclase spotted me. He shouted to his commanders. I couldn't hear the words in the noisy fray of the battle that was picking up around the grounds. But a moment later, Darion gave a signal and a hundred Duergar raised their short swords in the air and then charged. Periclase was intensifying the attack.

The line of Duergar soldiers moved with precision, splitting in the middle and skirting around the Dullahan to join the left and right flanks of the battle.

The next line of a hundred Duergar moved up. They charged on Darion's command. They crashed through the Dullahan, some of the Unseelie mortals accidentally brushing against the Bone Warriors and then collapsing. I couldn't help wincing.

Still, I forged ahead, the grunts, clangs, and yells of my people following in my wake.

More Unseelie forces joined the fight. Arrows began to rain down from the sky. Undine with their electric tridents raged forward with savage stabs. Salamanders in their reptile forms breathed fire. Ogres swung battle axes. All manner of Unseelie races battered us with their magic and weapons.

But I only had eyes for Periclase. I'd halved the distance to him when I saw him draw something from his pocket. He placed it to his lips and blew. An eardrum-splitting tone pierced the noise.

With head-spinning abruptness, his forces stopped mid-fight, wheeled around, and began racing back to him. All but the Dullahan retreated as if wrathful gods were hot on their heels. Periclase was calling for retreat, which meant that something else was coming.

My pulse surged. Only a few dozen Dullahan stood between me and my target. I redoubled my efforts, charging and slashing.

I was close to breaking free, to reaching the open ground between the last of the Dullahan and the rise where Periclase stood.

But I never made it.

Fog began to pour down out of the sky, so thick it blocked out all light.

It surrounded us in vertigo-inducing whiteness. When I inhaled it, my lungs spasmed, and I coughed until my eyes watered.

"Oliver!" I shouted. "Father! Maxen!"

I could hear voices, but only barely. The mist was dampening the sounds of the soldiers around me.

I turned and began stumbling through the blinding mist, hoping to collide with one of my people.

The air cooled until crystals formed where moisture had condensed on my skin.

And then it struck me. This wasn't any ordinary fog. I'd felt this mist before when I'd been under the Giants' Causeway—it was the preferred form of the Tuatha De Danann. Periclase had called the gods. He was asking them to finish us off.

Just as the realization struck me, the lightning of the god power in my veins sputtered. It flickered three times, like a failing lightbulb. And then it was gone.

I cried out at the sudden absence of the Fomoire power.

"Petra?" a voice came through the mist.

"Oliver!" I nearly sobbed my father's name.

Then, suddenly, he was there, grasping my wrist. His arm faded away at the elbow. He came closer until we were nearly nose-to-nose. Even then, I barely believed he was real.

"It's the Tuatha," I said, wishing I could keep from inhaling the fog of the gods. "This is the form they take because they don't want mortal eyes to see them."

"But nothing is happening," he said, his voice strangely distant even though he was inches away from me.

"Maybe it is happening, and we just don't know it yet."

Despair was filling my insides, seeping through me and replacing the agonizing zing of the Fomoire power.

"We need to forge ahead," Oliver said. "Get out of this, if we can. I know which way to go."

His hand slipped down to grasp mine.

"But the Dullahan," I said. "We don't have protection anymore. If we touch one, we're done."

"We can't just stand here."

I swallowed hard. "You're right."

He started to tug me forward.

"Wait," I said. "Hold onto me so we don't lose each other. I need to get something."

I'd already sheathed both swords, for fear of accidentally injuring an ally.

Oliver grasped my elbow, and I loosened the string on the pouch at my belt. Reaching in, I found what I sought—Morven's coin. My pulse quickened.

"We have to find water," I said. "I can summon Morven."

"What will that do?"

I shook my head, carefully placing the coin back in my pouch. "I don't know. But he's been siphoning magic from Fae for eons. He gave me the coin and said to summon him. He can help us, I'm sure of it."

"There's a moat around the castle," my father said.

New hope zinged through me. "Yes, we have to get there. You know which way?"

"Yes," he said.

My father always had an uncanny sense of direction. I was so directionless from the fog I was almost nauseous with vertigo. But if he believed he knew where the castle was, I had few other options but to trust him.

"I'm keeping my sword drawn ahead of me," he said. "Be ready with one of your blades to defend the rear."

I almost reached for Aurora, but instead took Mort into my right hand. My magic quickened in my blood and slipped into my spellsword. I'd nearly forgotten that in the absence of the Fomoire power, I could use magic. The familiarity of Mort and my magic brought some measure of calm.

Magic, followed by stone armor, flowed over my skin.

"We have our magic back," I said. "Arm yourself."

I considered shouting to the others to arm themselves, but I didn't want to tip off the enemy. In the muffling fog, I wasn't sure anyone would hear me anyway.

Oliver took my free hand and began to walk. He moved slowly at first, but encountering no obstacles, he sped up.

The silence was eerie. I could hear voices every so often, sounding incredibly far off. I couldn't help suspecting the mist of the gods aimed to open impossible distances between us, leaving the Seelie to wander alone through the fog. I hoped some of my allies had found each other in the blinding white.

We walked up a rise and then down the other side.

Where was everyone? Where had all the Dullahan gone? More important, where the hell was Periclase?

It seemed like my father and I could walk forever, lost in the whiteout. The thought chilled me to my bones. But that wasn't the worst possibility. The mist wasn't just about disorienting us. The Tuatha surely had something else planned.

I moved to my father's side, walking with my shoulder brushing his arm, close so we could hear each other.

"Something else is coming," I said. My words were muffled, as if I spoke into a fluffy pillow.

"I know," Oliver responded. "But we're close. Do you smell the water?"

I inhaled deeply. The mist had a chill to it, but it wasn't damp like a normal fog. Oliver was right. There was a very slight undertone that hadn't been there before—the scent of moist banks and murky water.

"How far?" I asked.

"Not sure. But at least we seem to be headed in the right direction."

Something rippled over my stone armor, and it was so subtle for a second I thought I imagined it. Then it came again.

The sensation filled me with dread.

I was just about to ask Oliver if he felt it too when I realized the mist was thinning. I blinked hard and then squinted, trying to peer through the white veil, but I still couldn't see anything ahead.

My father had slowed. He stopped, his hand still grasping mine.

"Something's changing," he whispered.

My gaze rose, and I sucked in a breath. I could make out points of light overhead. Were those . . . stars?

"I can see the sky. Stars," I said, confused. "But it's not supposed to be nighttime."

Oliver looked up, too.

"I don't think those are stars," he said, his voice edged with dread.

For a long moment, we just stood there, hand-in-hand, with our heads tipped back.

The mist was clearing, revealing a dark sky. It was wrong. All wrong. We'd attacked in the wee hours of the morning. We should be able to see the sun. There was no sun. Only inky blackness punctuated by . . .

They weren't stars. It was a hailstorm of fire streaking down toward us.

A horrible, nightmarish thrum reverberated through me. Low, like a whisper, but strong enough that I knew what it was.

"It's a meteor shower of sky iron," I said. "Flaming sky iron."

"We have to run." Oliver yanked me forward as he sprang into a sprint.

My heart in my throat, I raced after him, stumbling and then catching my balance. The mist was still swirling around us, obscuring our way, though it had cleared overhead.

The smell of the water was growing stronger, but I could barely focus on it through the horror of the sky iron. My eyes were glued to the heavens, watching as the flaming "stars" grew larger. And suddenly, I knew that Periclase was gone. He'd escaped with the Unseelie and the Dullahan to take cover and wait while a hellish meteor shower destroyed the Seelie army.

With dread and terror surging through me, I picked up my pace. Oliver let go of my hand so we could run faster, and I fought to keep him within my sight. The damn mist was still thick around us.

I could hear the sky iron meteors crackling overhead, and I slid a look upward. Oh gods, they were close, and they were *huge*.

When I looked down again, I didn't see my father.

I sped up, thinking he might have pulled ahead of me.

"Oliver!" I screamed into the fog. But my voice seemed to die just beyond my lips.

The whine of an object coursing through the air blasted down from above, and the fog lit with an orange glow. Screaming, I looked up as a molten boulder of sky iron the size of a car pounded down to my left. The impact rocked the ground and blew me sideways. I landed hard on my knee and elbow.

Pure terror raced through me.

The moat, the moat, the moat!

I had to reach water. Morven would come. He would help.

Another sky iron meteorite hit somewhere behind me. Screams pierced the air, even cutting through the fog.

The mist was thinning. Or maybe I was reaching the edge of it. I had no idea. But I could see a turret of the Summerlands castle up ahead.

I pushed as hard as I'd ever run in my life. The air grew hot as more molten sky iron rained down. Breathlessness, panic, and toxic iron seared my lungs. I struggled to draw breath as I raced toward the castle. I didn't dare look up. Only ahead.

I was close. Only another hundred and fifty feet.

A hundred and thirty.

I tried not to think about my father, whether he was still alive.

One hundred.

Fifty.

I switched Mort to my left hand and dug the fingers of my right into the pouch. The solid roundness of Morven's coin squeezed in my palm reassured me.

Forty feet.

Something was screaming overhead. A fireball.

Oh, shit.

It hit, exploding outward with heat and dread. The impact knocked me off my feet, throwing me forward.

I tried to tuck and roll, but I didn't want to let go of either Mort or the coin.

Just as I crashed to the ground, another meteorite hit.

So close. I flew like a rag doll.

I landed, my head flopping hard against stone.

Everything went black.

Chapter 21

WHEN I AWOKE, one arm was deliciously cool. The rest of my body was a mess of singing pain. My body was angled down, blood throbbing painfully in my head. I smelled burning hair.

My eyelids cracked open. My vision blurred so badly I felt my bile rise. I squeezed my eyes closed.

The only part of me that wasn't screaming in pain was my left arm from the elbow down. I tried to move my fingers, wanting to trail them through the coolness, but they didn't respond.

Water!

My eyes flew open again. Overhead, upside down, I recognized the walls of the Summerlands castle.

The meteorite blasts had thrown me to the moat, and I'd flopped head down on the steep bank. My left arm was submerged.

My head hurt with such intensity I wondered if I'd literally cracked my skull.

I had to get to Morven's coin.

I started to move, scooting around so I could reach my belt and the pouch there. Tears sprang to my eyes when the pressure changed in my head. But the pain in my skull had only distracted me from something else: my left arm was hanging, loose and useless. When I tried to shift, the exquisite red-hot nerve pain made me cry out.

I stopped, breathing through clenched teeth.

The dreadful throb of sky iron still buffeted me, and the booms and shaking ground told me the hellish rain wasn't over yet.

Struggling to move with one bum arm, I twisted and then pulled myself up to the edge of the bank.

Mort was there. Nearly sobbing at the sight of my spellsword, I reached for it and dragged it next to me.

Breathing hard, with sweat dripping down my face, I loosened the pouch's drawstring and found the coin.

"Morven!" I shouted and hurled the coin into the water.

I slumped, pain overcoming me again, to wait for whatever the coin would bring.

Seconds ticked by. I wondered if Morven was dead, if I'd pinned my hopes on a ghost. I reached for Mort, clutching the familiar handle in my good hand.

At first, I didn't really pick out the rumble under the pulse of sky iron and the blasts of fireballs.

I blinked several times, trying to clear my still-doubling vision. The ground under me was vibrating. Tiny ripples disturbed the surface of the moat.

The water was glowing, an eerie crimson bubbling up from under the surface.

The quaking grew stronger, and the water began to churn.

Dragging Mort with me, I started to scoot backward.

The churning increased to boiling, more furious by the second, turning the moat into an angry soup as debris, objects, and fish were roiled to the surface.

Steam curled from the water, which had turned blood-red. It mingled with the white mist of the Tuatha, driving back the fog of the gods.

The turbulence and quaking intensified, the ground shaking so hard my teeth rattled together. There was a pause, as if the energy of the water were briefly pulling in on itself.

And then, the blood-red moat exploded in a geyser.

I tried to scramble back away from the banks of the moat, but I was too injured, too disoriented to move quickly. The spew of the geyser arced into the air, curling outward like a giant tidal wave with an impossible volume of water.

And it was going to crash over me.

Something large and black swooped down at me. There was a great flurry of feathers and wind, and then I was being lifted from the ground. A Great Raven had come to my rescue. It arrowed sharply upward.

Sharp claws dug into my shoulders, and I screamed and bucked reflexively as pain lanced down my injured arm.

The movement caused the raven to lose its grip. But not before we'd crested the top of the tidal wave. I'd caught a quick glimpse of the castle grounds beyond the outer wall.

Periclase, the Dullahan, and the Unseelie forces were gathered there.

I was falling. I was going to drown in the raging dark red water below.

My fall stopped abruptly as I landed on a glossy black back.

The Great Raven arrowed upward, rising above the mist. I held on for dear life with my good hand.

"Stay here," I shouted. "Don't go through a doorway. I have to stay!"

Messenger ravens and Great Ravens had their own system of doorways, and I was afraid this one would try to spirit me away. But I couldn't go. I knew where Periclase was, and I had to get to him.

The Raven circled, and below, the mist of the Tuatha shrank away from the bloody water that had exploded around the castle.

There, where I'd thrown the coin, a figure was rising—a huge, hulking figure with a white beard.

Morven.

Rivulets of red water poured from him as he stood. Morven had transformed into a giant.

Once he'd straightened to his full height, he was taller than the highest turrets of the castle.

He looked up, finding me on my Raven, and my blood ran cold.

"Petra Maguire," he breathed. Brown smoke, the magic that always leaked from him when he took some of my power, puffed from his mouth. It misted from his ears and eyes, too. "I come to do your bidding. I cannot kill, and I cannot raise the dead, but I am yours to command."

My eyes widened. Mine to command?

I looked over the wall at the Unseelie forces gathered there. I couldn't ask Morven to level them, if he wasn't allowed to kill.

"Vanquish the Tuatha from Faerie, give me a clear path to Periclase, and heal the injured Seelie," I said, the words rolling out as if they'd been waiting deep in my heart, as if I'd always planned to say them.

He drew a deep breath, an inhale that seemed to go on and on, until his chest was impossibly inflated with air. Then he puffed his red Santa Claus cheeks and began to blow.

The magic that flowed out of his mouth was almost indescribable. It seemed to contain every type of power known to Faerie—all the magic he'd been siphoning for ages—strands of it curling and gyrating as it streamed outward on his breath. I caught the briefest impressions of it as it flowed, so many varieties my brain could barely register them individually.

The horrifyingly awesome rainbow of magics fanned out, darting through the air and disintegrating the mist of the Tuatha De Danann. The sky brightened as the fog cleared. The hailstorm of sky iron ceased.

I'd had my doubts that Morven possessed the power to rid Faerie of the Tuatha De Danann, but my reservations began to dissolve as I watched him.

Morven reached the end of his exhalation, and the entire battlefield was cleared of mist. The sun broke through fluffy clouds overhead, and I squinted up at the calm blue sky.

He wasn't done yet. Twisting around, he balled his hands into giant fists and then smashed them through the closed castle gate. Splinters of wood and buckled metal bracings flew everywhere. With a finger, he flipped the drawbridge down. It landed with a crash across the moat.

Through my awe, I recalled the words he'd said to me from the stream. For centuries, Morven had been collecting power, waiting for the moment when he could fulfill his destiny as martyr and savior.

Through the flying dust and debris, I glimpsed Unseelie scurrying around in the foyer of the castle.

Morven reached over the wall with his index finger extended. He plucked a figure from the crowd.

"You're not going anywhere," the giant Ghille Dubh's voice purred.

He'd grabbed Periclase and held him like a toy figurine in his hand.

A flurry of arrows flew at Morven, but most didn't even pierce his skin. The few that did, he didn't seem to notice.

He bent down and knocked Unseelie soldiers aside, clearing a space in the middle of the grand entrance of the castle. Then he set Periclase in the center. Blowing a stream of magic, Morven surrounded the Duergar king in a shimmering bubble. When a few of his people tried to run to him, they bounced off the shield.

"Only you may pass through, Petra Maguire." Morven's eerie voice was somehow a whisper and a roar at the same time. "But first, I shall heal you."

He held out his palm. My Great Raven descended, landing on Morven's hand. I slid off the bird and it took flight, ruffling my hair with the motion of its wings. Looking up into the giant's face sent awe and fear lacing through me. His irises swirled like kaleidoscopes, and a rainbow of magic leaked from his lips, ears, and the inner corners of his eyes.

He leaned in, sending his breath and magic spilling around me. The itch of healing agitated the superficial scrapes on my face and the areas of my hands that weren't protected by armor. It settled in my head, and for a moment the healing was worse than the concussion. I ground my teeth until the itching burn moved to my shoulder. Nerves screamed as they repaired.

I'd fallen to my knees on Morven's palm, my vision graying. But the pain receded, and I came back to my senses.

When I could see clearly again, Morven bent and reached into the water he stood in. He felt around for a moment and then lifted something.

Mort.

The giant handed my sword to me, carefully pinched between his thumb and forefinger and no bigger than a butter knife next to the scale of his hand.

I looked into his eyes, my fear diminishing and only awe remaining.

"Thank you," I whispered, taking my spellblade.

He only grunted. It struck me that this service could be the end of Morven because the Ghille Dubh I'd known wouldn't have hesitated to use my words to try to bind me in an oath, or at the very least, take more of my magic. But his magic collecting days were over. He was serving his purpose, emptying himself of all the power he'd accumulated. There was no longer any need for him to manipulate, to collect.

He set me down on the paved path that led to the drawbridge, which none of the Unseelie had dared try to raise. Periclase, trapped in the bubble of magic, waited for me just inside the castle atrium.

Morven leaned over the castle walls again, like a child peering into his toy, and breathed magic. He formed shimmering walls to keep the Unseelie back, giving me unobstructed access to my blood father.

I walked toward the drawbridge, looking back only once as Morven stepped out of the moat and went onto the battlefield, where he knelt to breathe magic over a writing soldier. I forced myself to face forward, because if I saw that Oliver had fallen, I was afraid I wouldn't be able to do what needed to be done.

With Periclase in my sights, I stalked into the Summerlands castle.

He was dressed in ornate armor befitting a king. One arm hung at his side, gripping the Dullahan skull. He reached with the other for the short sword on his hip. I clutched Mort in my right hand and drew Aurora with my left.

As I approached, Periclase tossed the Dullahan skull to the side as if it were worth nothing. He was right. It wasn't going to save him. Reaching over his head, he grabbed a small shield that had been strapped to his back.

"How does it feel to know you've failed?" I called.

Periclase gave me a cool smile that touched only the flesh side of his face and even managed a chuckle, but I could see wariness in his hard eyes.

I stopped a dozen feet away from him.

"Look around you, daughter," he said. "This isn't failure. Oberon has gone mad. Winter is descending on Faerie. Even without the Tuatha, the time of Unseelie rule here has already dawned. The old gods have done their work. There's no turning back now."

The mention of Oberon sent a chill through me, because on that point, Periclase was probably correct. But that was a concern for later.

"You're wrong," I said. "You will not see nightfall on the High throne. I might accept your surrender, if you ask politely. It wouldn't be a nice life, but at least you'd have one."

At that, he threw back his head and let out a sharp laugh.

"Petra, you really are my blood," he said almost affectionately. "In spite of our clashes, I do feel pride that you're my daughter."

The terror I'd felt when Oliver had been tortured at the hands of Periclase and Finvarra rushed in. I narrowed my eyes at Periclase, hot anger replacing fear as I imagined Oliver injured—or worse—out on the battlefield.

"You shouldn't have said that," I growled, stalking forward a couple of steps.

I drew magic, sending power into Mort and shielding my skin with armor. Aurora blazed with the colors of dawn.

I sprang into a run, letting out a yell and swinging Mort as hard as I could at the Duergar king's neck.

Periclase saw it coming and lifted his shield to deflect my hit. He stabbed at my middle with his short sword, but the blade slid away.

I backed up a pace and then drove at him again, both blades flying. The fury of my attack seemed to throw him off guard, which only drove me harder.

Every shred of fear, anger, frustration, and heartache I'd felt in the last year seemed to surface. I blinked tears from my eyes and hurled myself at Periclase, beating at him with brutal hammering swings. Periclase had always been a formidable enemy. But with the good power flowing through me, I was invincible. And I had not a speck of sympathy toward this man.

Blood flowed from a deep gash in the forearm of his sword hand. I aimed for the wound and added to it.

He roared in pain, his hand spasming. His short sword dropped to the ground. I hastily kicked it back behind me with a swing of my heel.

My chest was heaving with ragged breaths, my pulse pounding through every blood vessel. I was suddenly aware of his people surrounding the bubble watching the fight.

I backed off a couple of steps. "Last chance," I spat at him.

He squinted at me. "Truly, Petra? You would kill your own father?"

I wasn't sure if he sincerely wanted an answer or just needed to stall. His sword arm was dripping crimson.

I went at him again, but this time it was with all the cool methodical moves of years of training. In a matter of minutes, I'd backed him up to the edge of the magical bubble. Bashing him with overhead blows, I forced him down to a knee.

I tossed Aurora behind me. With a devastating two-handed swing of Mort, I batted Periclase's shield away.

I teed up again. He raised his arms in defense, but instead of another battering hit, I drove my sword forward into the V of his ribcage. I threw all my weight and momentum behind the thrust. Mort pierced his armor and drove through his diaphragm.

"I'm *not* your daughter," I whispered, my face only inches from his.

His mouth opened in a soundless scream. His heels scrabbled against the tiles, and he clawed at the sword, at my face and arms.

I leaned back and pulled Mort free. Periclase sagged slowly to one side, the life fading from his eyes.

The Unseelie were going mad, bashing against the magical shield and screaming at me, their mouths working and their faces reddening. I couldn't hear them, and I was grateful for that.

I felt no remorse for killing my blood father.

I knelt and began searching his clothes, looking for the Stone of Fal. My agitation grew as I went through every pocket and pouch. I tore off his armor and ran my hands over his clothes.

I searched him again. A third time. Then I sat back on my heels, shaking my head.

The Stone wasn't there.

Frowning, I retrieved Aurora and sheathed both swords. An examination of Periclase's shield yielded nothing. I inspected his sword, thinking maybe he'd had it made so the Stone could be hidden in the handle.

I was just about to stick the shortsword through my belt, thinking surely the Stone must be concealed in it, when I realized there was a figure standing very still on the other side of the magical barrier, just behind Periclase's limp form.

It was Darion, the dead king's brother. In the riotous fury of the Unseelie trying in vain to get to me, Darion was the only one unmoving.

He raised his hand. Pinched between his thumb and forefinger was the Stone of Fal.

I felt the blood drain from my face.

With his eyes locked on mine, he raised the Stone.

"No," I yelled, the word strangled.

Whirling, I spotted the Dullahan skull. I raced to it, sliding on the tiles and scooping it up. I had to activate it before Darion invoked the Stone. If I could command the Dullahan riders to attack, I might be able to stop him.

As soon as I touched the skull, greenish magic began leaking from it. I turned, desperately looking for the Dullahan and clutching the skull.

"Attack that man!" I shouted and pointed at Darion.

The Bone Warriors had been assembled in the shadows of a wide corridor leading away from the castle's front atrium. When I held the skull aloft, they began to move toward me.

The rioting Unseelie either got out of the way or were touched by bone and collapsed. The riders cut a path to where I was. They knew I had the skull, but they weren't responding to the commands I screamed.

And it was too late, anyway.

I caught the form of a Great Raven high above just before it winked out of sight through a doorway.

Light exploded from where Darion stood. He'd activated the Stone. The magic blasted upward. I tipped my head back and whirled around, following the path of the magic as it spread up and beyond the castle walls. It probably wouldn't affect the Unseelie, who were already loyal to each other. The Dullahan would be immune. But the Seelie still alive on the battlefield—all except the Carraig Sidhe—would blindly follow Darion as soon as the Stone's magic touched them.

My chest constricted.

Tucking the skull under my arm like a football, I raced out of the protective magical tunnel Morven had formed for me.

The giant Ghille Dubh was on the far side of the battlefield, presumably having worked his way around to heal everyone he could.

"Morven!" I waved frantically. He twisted toward me, still down on one knee as he tended to one of the injured. "Stop the Stone of Fal!"

I think I knew in my heart there was nothing he could do. The light of the Stone had already faded, and everyone on the field who wasn't of stone blood was turning toward the castle. I turned to look, too.

Darion had somehow found a way up onto one of the castle's ramparts.

Everything went silent and still.

"I am the holder of the Stone," Darion called out. I wasn't sure if his voice carried clear to the end of the field, but I was in the middle and heard him clearly. "And by the Stone, I proclaim myself the king of the High Court."

Everyone seemed to draw in a breath.

"I command you, my followers, end the Carraig Sidhe!" he bellowed.

My pulse skipped a beat. I would have to call on the power of the Fomoire to fight the very people who'd been my allies only moments ago. It was that or die.

It was going to be a massacre.

I drew both swords.

Chapter 22

KING MOREAU'S DOBHAR dogs—the ones who'd survived the battle—were shifting into their canine forms and loping ahead of the other Seelie toward the Carraig Sidhe, who'd been at the forefront of the charge into the Summerlands.

My heart jolted with relief when I saw that one of the Carraig taking up arms was my father.

Our allies, now brainwashed to believe they were loyal to Darion and the Unseelie, were beginning to clash with my people. My chest tightened at what we were going to be forced to do.

"Use your god power to defend rather than kill, if you can," I shouted. "Work your way to me!"

It was impossible to tell how many Carraig heard my command, as the sounds of battle were already filling the air. I wasn't sure what I'd do with them once I'd gathered all of us together, but I wanted us to be able to defend ourselves as a group.

I shoved the Dullahan skull into the back of my shirt, hastily securing it in the diamond shape formed by scabbard straps across my back. Tipping my head to the sky, I invoked Ethniu's name. Lightning struck my forehead, and for a moment I lost all sense of the world as I drowned in the excruciating pain of the god power.

I came back to my senses just as a Dobhar dog leapt at me.

In a blink, I sheathed Aurora. Sidestepping, I threw a punch at the dog shifter's neck, throwing the god power and my own natural strength behind it. The Dobhar yelped, flew, and landed. He stumbled, but quickly wheeled around to lunge at me again.

"Don't make me do this," I muttered under my breath.

Two more dogs were approaching. Reluctantly, I drew Aurora again. I started both blades whirling, hoping the threat of the flashing metal would keep the Dobhar at bay.

"Petra!" Maxen's voice came from beside me.

In my periphery, I saw him move around to put his back to mine so we could defend each other's blind spots. I made swipes at the dogs' legs when they came closer to challenge me, trying not to injure them too badly.

Morven was standing at the far edge of the field, close to where the other Seelie and I had come through Melusine's doorway. The doorway was gone, and I had no idea what had become of the Fae witch.

"Morven, can you help us?" I screamed over the din of battle.

He was oddly still, his arms limp at his sides and his eyes unfocused. I could only spare him flicking glances as I fought, but there was something odd about the way he looked.

On another look, I realized what it was. Morven seemed to be dissolving. I could see the line of the distant mountain range cutting across his chest. The giant Ghille Dubh was growing transparent. My heart sank as it hit me that he'd done all he could. He'd come when I'd summoned him, he'd fulfilled my requests, and he'd served his destiny.

"Goodbye, Morven," I whispered.

I didn't have time to fully process the Ghille Dubh's disappearance, though.

"Darion is commanding the rest of the Unseelie into battle," Maxen said, his voice tight.

I was facing away from the castle, but Maxen had a view of what was going on there.

"Where are they coming from?" I asked.

"The drawbridge. Morven's magical walls are gone. The way is clear for them to get out."

"We need a doorway," I said, desperation leaking into my voice. "We have to get out of here. If we stay, we'll have to kill every last one of them. I don't know if I can physically last that long, even with the god power."

More Carraig had joined us, and we stone bloods formed a circle facing outward, fighting off our attackers.

"Here they come," Maxen said, his words high with alarm.

Battle cries and the rumble of many boots rose up. Darion's Unseelie crashed into us like a tidal wave, breaching the Carraig circle and trying to trample us. I nearly lost my breath in the onslaught of bodies. Pounded from every angle, I began to fear that I'd literally drown under a mountain of Unseelie.

They couldn't kill me as long as I was channeling the power of the Fomoire, but what if I got knocked out and lost my connection?

I threw my elbows out, struggling to make space. Through the pain and power that seared through me, tendrils of panic started to creep in.

There wasn't even room enough to properly swing a sword.

Black spots danced in my peripheral vision as bodies jammed tighter against me.

If I got crushed and the air squeezed out of my lungs . . .

Something dark passed overhead, but it was out of range too quickly, and I couldn't move enough to catch it with my glance.

Was someone calling my name from above?

Yes.

My pulse jumped. I knew that voice. It was Jasper.

With renewed strength, I fought harder to free myself, stepping onto people in my effort to get just a little higher.

There.

I broke through and tipped my gaze up.

A huge black bird swooped down. A Great Raven! And Jasper rode its back. The Raven that had disappeared right before Darion activated the Stone of Fal must have gone to Jasper.

The bird circled tightly overhead. Jasper was trying to tell me something. I couldn't understand him, but he held an object aloft.

A large, golden goblet.

Tipping it, he began to empty its contents. A silver liquid poured out, spreading into drops like fine rain droplets in the air and falling onto the people around me.

It had to be the Chalice of Dagda. And if the liquid coming from it was true to legend, it should dissolve the spell the Stone of Fal had cast upon the Seelie.

The smell of moss, oak, and metal hit my nose. Jasper kept circling, pouring down a seemingly endless supply of liquid from the Chalice over the battlefield.

The crush of bodies below me and around me was moving, easing. Seelie were looking around dazedly, as if they'd just snapped out of a deep sleep.

The Unseelie, loyal to their side without any need for magical tricks, fell upon the glassy-eyed Seelie, and the battles began anew.

Even with our allies back on our side, the Seelie were outnumbered. The Spriggan army was against us. It would be a gruesome fight with high death tolls, regardless of the outcome. I didn't want that. We had to find a way to defeat the Unseelie swiftly.

The skirmishes were rearranging themselves as Seelie came back to their senses and began to fight Unseelie instead of going after me and the other Carraig. It opened up a little space. Using my blades to cut a path before me, I fought my way to the rise where Periclase had stood when the battle first began. From there, I could see the drawbridge was still down.

The Dullahan skull had miraculously stayed in place on my back. I crested the hill, sheathed Aurora, and worked the skull out from under my scabbard straps with my free hand while fighting off a Spriggan soldier with Mort. The power of the Fomoire made me practically psychic, able to easily see my opponents' moves coming. I managed to fend off the Spriggan, as well as a couple of fish-eyed Undine, as I got the skull into my hand.

As soon as I'd touched the skull, a cool tingle had spread over my skin, and the artifact was once again oozing green magic.

Turning, I ran toward the castle. Darion was still up on the rampart, overseeing the battle. Archers lined up to either side of him and sent a bristling rain of arrows at me. I dodged them with ease.

My blood uncle furiously screamed an order to take up the drawbridge, but I was already on it.

Channeling the strength of the god power, I fought off a few of his men and reached the foyer. Going to the little room to one side of the entry where the drawbridge mechanism was housed, I found a man and woman still working to pull up the bridge. Both were Spriggan.

"Out, or I'll run you through," I growled at them.

Both froze with wide eyes. They were armed but made no move toward their weapons.

I brandished Mort, and they jumped and then fled past me.

With a few slashes, I destroyed the pulley system, making sure the bridge would stay down.

In the main area of the foyer I found that Periclase's body had been dragged away, leaving a trail of blood on the tiles. But the Dullahan still lurked in an adjoining corridor, the whiteness of their bones glowing eerily in the gloom.

I lifted the skull of the first Dullahan king.

"To me," I commanded.

A chill spiraled up my spine as the horses began to move. Silently, the

Bone Warriors emerged, many of them holding their own skulls under their arms, with grotesque clouded eyeballs peering out at me from the eye orbits. Before, Morven's magic bubble must have insulated me from the Dullahan, preventing them from hearing my command.

I had no idea how much they would understand, or what exactly to say to them. Darion's fighters backed off as the Dullahan surrounded me. The riders' attention was fixed on me so intently I shivered.

"You're now on the side of the Seelie," I called out, hoping all of the Dullahan could hear and understand. "I order you to protect the Seelie on the battlefield. Use lethal means against the Unseelie only when necessary."

The horses pranced, seeming eager to go and carry out my command.

I pointed out to the battlefield with my sword.

"Go!" I commanded.

In one unified motion, all of the horses sprang into action, as if they were coiled springs that had been waiting to be let loose. Galloping around me and past me, their hooves on the tiles were almost deafening for a moment.

Once the last rider was out, I turned and ran after them, Mort in one hand and the skull in the other.

Jasper was still circling overhead, and my heart leapt at the sight of him. Another black bird flew with him—not as large as a Great Raven, but bigger than a messenger raven. It had to be Drifte, the wild shifter with the solid black eyes.

Something flashed at the far end of the battlefield, drawing my attention. My spirits flew again as I recognized the long, white hair of Eldon, the Fae sorcerer. He'd joined the fight, and with our allies back and the addition of the Dullahan on our side, victory was suddenly within reach.

I waved down Jasper, and his Raven swooped toward me. Jasper pointed to a nearby hill, and I ran that way, meeting him there.

He slid off the bird and grabbed me around the waist with one arm, pulling me off my feet, the Chalice of Dagda still in his other hand. His mouth covered mine in a quick, rough kiss that nearly stole my breath.

"I'm so glad you found it," I said, pointing to the Chalice. "And I'm so fucking *happy* you're alive."

He grinned at me. "Me too."

"I need to get back in the fight, but I don't want to carry this." I shoved the Dullahan skull at him.

He blinked, looking down at it.

I stepped around him to slash at an Undine who was running at Jasper and brandishing a magically electrified trident.

"But you'll be passing its power to me," he said.

"I know."

I twisted to swing Mort at a Duergar. She leaned out of the way, and I shoved my foot in the middle of her stomach, sending her tumbling backward down the hill.

"Just tell the Dullahan to keep doing what they're doing and then whatever else you see fit to help the Seelie campaign," I said. "You'll have a better vantage point for command from up there, anyway."

I knew he wanted to join the fight on the ground—and we could have used someone with his skills—but he was the keeper of the Chalice of Dagda, and now the Dullahan skull, and he needed to stay clear of the enemy's grasp.

The corner of his mouth quirked. "You're really going to put the command of the Dullahan in the hands of an Unseelie?"

I pushed Jasper toward his Raven. "I really am."

Jasper was no traitor. He'd never turn on the Seelie the way Trey had.

We traded quick smiles, and then he was off to the sky and I was back in the thick of the fight. The fallen sky iron pushed the skirmishes into a handful of individual battles throughout the field. I ran toward the nearest fray.

With Aurora in my left hand, Mort in my right, and the sharp lightning of the Fomoire power surging through me, I fell into the rhythm of battle. There was incredible relief in knowing that the god power made my people nearly invincible. And there was unimaginable freedom in fighting with the protection and strength of the gods flowing in my veins.

I lost track of time as I mowed through the enemy. Every time I recognized an Unseelie ranking officer, I told them they could still surrender and no more of their ranks would be killed. None of them took me up on my offer, and they fought stubbornly on.

By late afternoon, it became obvious that the day belonged to the Seelie. Duergar battle horns sent out a series of staccato sounds. The Unseelie still in the fight stopped, turned to the castle, and then raced that way.

Victory shot through me on a wave of adrenaline, and I let out a shout that was echoed by my people and my allies.

I already knew Darion was going to escape with the remaining Unseelie through a doorway. I was okay with it. I had no desire to take any more lives, and once they were gone, we could have Eldon secure the Summerlands doorways so enemies couldn't sneak back in.

The last of the living Unseelie soldiers disappeared into the castle. Darion was already gone from the rampart.

I sheathed my blades and released the Fomoire power.

Back to my mortal self, I stumbled and fell to my knees, suddenly overcome with fatigue. My vision grayed for a second, and I took deep breaths until the dizziness passed and I could see clearly again.

All around the battlefield, Carraig Sidhe were releasing their Fomoire power as well, stumbling and falling as it left them.

I stood and turned slowly, surveying the grounds. The triumph I'd felt only a moment ago drained away. There were so many still bodies—Seelie and Unseelie.

I took a long, solemn breath and went to meet Maxen, who was trudging toward me. His broadsword was crimson-stained, his clothes covered with dirt and blood spatters.

"We did it," he said, turning to survey the field. "We've taken back the Summerlands."

I nodded. "We did."

Shane joined us, looking as exhausted as I felt.

We stood there, looking around and catching our breath.

"I'll set up patrols to sweep the castle," Shayne said. "We'll also have to figure out how to dispose of all the sky iron."

The meteorites the Tuatha had sent raining down on us had cooled into lumpy, dull silver boulders. I'd been in their presence so long in the course of the battle that the ugly pulse of the toxic metal was barely more than background noise. It still made my stomach turn and tighten every time I focused on it.

An idea struck—if we could break up the sky iron and get it down into the caves, we could toss it in the liquid pool. Once melted there, it could never be removed and weaponized.

"Yes," I said. "Let's first work with the other rulers to take care of the dead. And find a way to get the Unseelie fallen back to their respective kingdoms."

As if they'd known I was speaking of them, King Delun and King Moreau began making their way toward me. Overhead, I saw Jasper disappear on his Raven and realized he couldn't land until he'd found a place to stash his cargo.

No, our work definitely wasn't done yet. We were going to have to figure out what would become of the Summerlands and who would rule the High Court. Maybe not that night or even in the next few days. But the political maneuvering was sure to begin immediately.

We'd defeated the Unseelie. But would the Seelie be able to work out peace with each other?

Chapter 23

THE OTHER SEELIE rulers who'd participated in what had quickly been named the Battle of the Gods agreed that we would postpone any decisions about the High Court until the dead had been attended to. But the reality was that would only buy maybe two or three days. It was already clear that the politicking had begun in the background. Back at the stone fortress, I'd asked Maxen to meet with me so we could determine what position we should take.

It was early morning after the battle. We'd spent the night tending to the fallen and securing the Summerlands castle. I'd caught maybe three hours of sleep just before dawn, but almost wished I hadn't bothered.

I gulped my third cup of coffee, hoping the caffeine would lift the weary heaviness in my head.

"Any report on what became of King Trey?" I asked before diving into the topic of the High Court.

"He escaped and he's alive," Maxen said.

I clenched my jaw. "Darion still has the Stone of Fal, and Trey slipped away. These are things that will have to be dealt with."

"Yes, but for now we must focus on the High Court." Maxen paused. "You know, there's a decent argument for nominating you."

I nearly spit a mouthful of coffee across the conference table.

"Oh, no," I said through a cough. "No *way*. Don't ever say that again. Even if I could get enough backing, I'm not a good choice for the High

Court."

Maxen gave me an amused but tired smile.

I reached for a napkin on the coffee service tray and wiped my mouth.

"What about one of the Old Ones?" I asked.

"We already sent out a call to the ones who live in seclusion or prefer not to mix with common Fae," Maxen said. "So far, there isn't a single bite. Melusine and Eldon are the only Old Ones who appear to have any interest in being involved with us, and neither of them would be, ah . . ."

I gave a short laugh. "It's okay, just say it. They'd be absurd choices to rule."

"Not to mention that they don't want the High Court."

"Who's vying hard at this point then?" I asked.

"King Moreau is in the lead. He's got the endorsement of the Sylphs, which makes him a very strong contender."

I scrunched my mouth to one side.

"You don't like him for the High Court?" Maxen asked.

"Not really. I can't even say why, exactly. He's a strong ruler. We have a good relationship with the Dobhar. I like him as a man. I just . . . I don't know, I guess I'd rather see someone who's unaffiliated take rulership, you know? That's why it'd be fitting if an Old One could step in."

"We can try to persuade Titania," Maxen said, but his doubt about the chances of success was clear in his tone.

"I suppose we could," I said.

Slumping, I stared at the wall with my brows drawn down.

"What about Jasper?" I asked, lifting my gaze.

Maxen's face registered surprise. He tilted his head. "Character-wise, I wouldn't have a single argument against him. But he'd never win in a vote."

"Why?"

"He's Unseelie by heritage. He's Finvarra's son."

I waved a hand. "Technicalities."

Maxen snorted. "Maybe so, but they're enough to prevent him from being a viable candidate."

I sighed, knowing he was right. I wasn't completely disappointed. As deeply as I believed Jasper would make an excellent High King, for my own selfish reasons, I didn't want him consumed by the duties of the High Court.

"Are we going to have to support Moreau then?" I asked.

Maxen drew a slow breath. "If we want to support the strongest candidate. If there's someone we like better, though, we do have clout. It's known throughout the kingdoms that we have the power of the Fomoire. That gives us some considerable standing among the Seelie."

I'd invoked Ethniu's name when I'd woken up that morning, just to test whether the Fomoire had retracted their gift of power. They hadn't. Maxen and Oliver had reported the same result. We'd had no direct contact with the Fomoire, but rumors were already spreading that the Giants' Causeway, the longtime hiding place of the Tuatha De Danann on the Earthly side of the hedge, had been vacated. I expected the Fomoire were allowing us to keep our power only long enough to be sure the Seelie had secured the High Court. Time would tell.

Even though we were no longer actively at war with the Unseelie, I knew Maxen was right. The Carraig Sidhe had a connection with the gods. We were virtually immortal while we channeled the gift from the Fomoire. There was also the fact that we had, by all appearances, fulfilled the prophecies of three different oracles, which said that we were vital to Seelie victory. There was a certain awe factor in that.

I leaned forward, and my armrests hitting the edge of the conference table made Maxen startle.

I stared him in his sapphire-blue eyes.

"You, Maxen."

He squinted at me.

"*You* should put yourself in the running." My breath came faster as the implications fully formed in my mind. "Yes. It's perfect. You're not a king. But you understand ruling and politics. Everyone respects you. More so than probably any other ruler, if they were really being honest."

I stood abruptly, and my chair went flying back on its wheels, bumping into the wall.

"Maxen Lothlorien, you should be High King."

For a long moment, he just stared at me, his lips parted in surprise. I slumped. "What, you don't want it?"

"No, I . . ." He blinked rapidly, shook his head, looked down at the table and then back up at me.

I pressed my lips together, suddenly hit by a punch of emotion as I realized what he was thinking of: his mother.

"I think Marisol would agree with me," I said softly. "I'm not just saying that to try to persuade you. I hope you know I'd never use the memory of her that way. I truly think she would believe you perfect for this role. I think she would see, as I do, that perhaps you were born for this."

He broke eye contact, bowing his head. Even though his expression was hidden from me, I could see his jaw muscles working.

Marisol Lothlorien had groomed her son—her only child, the apple of her eye—to take the throne of our kingdom after she stepped down. That had been her dream. Things had turned out so terribly different from what she'd hoped, and her prophecies had been partly derailed, but . . . I thought this was better. Prophecies weren't everything. They could be defied.

Maxen was one of the best people I knew. He worked tirelessly for the good of others. His moral compass was inarguable and his reputation in Faerie above reproach. He *should* be ruling. Faerie deserved him. We needed him.

"Maxen?"

After a moment, he met my gaze. We stared at each other for half a minute.

"Okay," he said. "I'll make a run for High King."

I ran around the table, and he stood just as I crashed into him, wrapping my arms around his neck and planting a loud kiss on his cheek.

When I stepped back, he let out a laugh that was part delight and part confusion. "A hug? That's not the Petra I've always known."

"I know," I said. "But I'm no longer the person you grew up with. You're not just going to make a run for High King, Maxen. You're going to take the crown."

Once the decision was made, there was a whirlwind of activities to prepare for positioning Maxen as a candidate for High King.

Over the next few days, I represented my people by attending services in all the other Seelie kingdoms who'd lost soldiers in the Battle of the Gods. Each event was a reminder of just how lucky we were because we'd only lost three Carraig who'd been crushed by sky iron. Each memorial service in the other kingdoms were also opportunities to feel out the opposition.

The Dobhar Sidhe King Moreau was not happy when I informed him of Maxen's candidacy.

"You're going to split the vote, Petra," he said to me in a private meeting. "In the end, it will weaken Seelie strength in Faerie, no matter who ends up leading the High Court."

"We may split the vote," I conceded. "But I don't agree with your other assessment. I believe putting Maxen on the throne in the Summerlands will be the best thing for Faerie long-term. I'm not saying that because he's Carraig. I believe he was born for this. We're no longer going to be ruled by a demi-god. Faerie will be ruled by mortals from now on. We don't know exactly what that will ring, but things will change. Maxen is the right man to usher in this new era."

Moreau argued with me, but I could see in his eyes that he knew Maxen was a formidable candidate. And even though the Dobhar king wouldn't say it out loud, I knew Moreau was smart enough to see just how ideal Maxen was for the job.

The Sylph service for their dead involved a lot of beautiful music played by an orchestra of wind instruments—Fae versions of flutes, bugles, and other horns and woodwinds I didn't recognize. Two rows of a hundred Sylph sword bearers with their slim, feather-shaped swords lined up facing each other. On Vida's command, they drew their blades, lifted them in the air, and then the two rows angled toward each other, tenting the blades over a path of honor down which came a procession of coffins.

Afterward, I asked Queen Vida for a moment so I could tell her about Maxen.

"I heard," she said, her long lashes lowering partway as she cast me a shrewd look.

"Please don't take it as a desire to see the relationship between our realms erode," I said. "We consider the Sylphs some of our most valued friends in Faerie, and that won't change regardless of who goes to the Summerlands."

"The Sylph kingdom will be officially supporting Maxen Lothlorien," she said, her words clipped and formal.

My mouth fell open, and I blinked.

"You . . . but what about Moreau?" I asked.

"Maxen is the better candidate," she said. She looked down, adjusting the folds of the exquisite emerald-colored velvet gown that hugged her curves. "And our oracles have advised me to support him. Even before Moreau contacted me to tell me about Maxen, the oracles were banging down my door."

"Oh?" was all I could manage.

I didn't think much of prophecies by that point, but at times they had worked in my favor. This was one of those instances when I wasn't going to argue with the declarations of oracles.

I couldn't help wondering how it would look for Vida to make this switch. But that was her issue to deal with.

"Yes. Now, let's get Lord Lothlorien on that throne," she said with determination.

I nodded a couple of times, still trying to process my surprise. "Yes. We're going to put everything we have behind this. And know that the Carraig Sidhe—that I personally—deeply appreciate the Sylph support."

She touched my arm and then strode away.

I waited until I was back in the stone fortress to let out a little shout of victory. With Sylph support, Maxen would be much harder to beat. Queen Corrain of the Baen Sidhe hadn't endorsed any candidate yet, but Maxen believed the banshees might get behind him because Corrain and Marisol had always maintained close ties. I believed King Lawrence would support Maxen as well. The Gnome had taken it especially hard when Trey had betrayed us and had been effusive in his praise and gratitude for how the Carraig had carried the Seelie to victory.

After telling Maxen of the Sylph support, I dispatched a couple of fortress pages to track down my father, who hadn't answered the phone in his quarters when I called.

Oliver came to my apartment as I was pausing for a midday meal. Knowing he probably hadn't taken the time to eat, I forced half my sandwich into his hand.

I caught him up on my meetings with Moreau and Vida.

"How will it be for you to lose your most trusted advisor?" he asked.

I paused my chewing for a second, and then swallowed. I'd been avoiding the thought of ruling the Carraig without Maxen in the fortress.

I took a deep breath and then let it out slowly, wiping crumbs from my fingers with a linen napkin.

"It will be hard," I said. "Even painful. I expect there will be times I question whether it was in the best interest of the Carraig Sidhe to let him go."

Oliver watched me intently.

"But it's best for Faerie," I continued. "And I think Maxen deserves it. For a long time, he was the rightful heir to the throne here. He probably still is, really. But now I see there was a reason he didn't get it. He was meant for something bigger."

My father gave me a tiny smile. "Wise. And selfless."

"I wouldn't call myself either of those things," I said wryly. Then I brightened a bit. "But I have Amalie. She was groomed by Marisol and Maxen. Amalie is incredibly capable and couldn't be more devoted to her work. I've been wasting her talents in her current position. She'll make a superb top advisor."

"That's good to know."

I shifted in my seat, suddenly feeling uncertain. "Are you worried about our kingdom if we lose Maxen?"

"No, I think the Carraig kingdom will survive just fine," Oliver said. "And it's not as if Maxen would never speak to you again. I'm sure he'd offer advice if you asked for it. He's a stone blood, even in the High Court. He'll always want us to succeed. No, I'm not worried about the kingdom. I'm concerned about what you're taking on, though."

I tilted my head. "What do you mean?"

He spread one arm. "All of this. Being queen."

"But that's what I am."

"Because Oberon forced you to be. It wasn't what you wanted."

For a moment, I was still, turning inward and searching my feelings.

"You know," I said quietly. "It honestly hasn't occurred to me to try to pass the crown to someone else. I guess . . . I guess that means I've accepted this role. I've internalized the responsibility. I . . . *want* it."

We stared at each other for a few seconds.

"Can you believe I just said that?" I whispered.

Oliver threw back his head and laughed. It was short-lived, but it was a level of emotion I'd rarely seen from my father. It startled me at first, but then I grinned.

"And what about your Duergar man?" Oliver asked. His tone was carefully even, but his eyes guarded.

"Jasper? What about him?"

"What does the future hold for the two of you?"

I reached up and scratched the back of my neck, a faint sense of agitation prickling through me.

"Petra, it's a father's right to ask such a question."

"It is," I relented. "Jasper and I haven't had a chance to talk about the future. All I know is that I want to be with him."

"That presents a bit of a difficulty, doesn't it?"

I nodded reluctantly. "He's technically still a Duergar subject. Those oaths aren't easily retracted."

"If I were you, I'd call upon your Fae witch friend. I bet her magic could solve your problem."

For a moment, I peered at my father. "Does that mean I have your true endorsement for my relationship with Jasper? For something . . . permanent?"

A small part of me was tempted to add that I didn't need my father's approval, but I held my tongue. The old Petra would have said something defiant like that. I was no longer the girl who needed to rebel against her father at every turn.

The corners of his eyes crinkled in the faintest movement. It could have been either a grimace or the barest hint of a smile.

"Jasper Glasgow is the man you've chosen, and I think he's worthy.

You have my blessing."

I couldn't answer right away, as my eyes misted and a lump suddenly rose in my throat.

I inclined my head in a tiny bow. "Thank you."

"Do you think you can persuade him to become one of your subjects?" Oliver asked.

My brows lifted, and I let out a tiny laugh. "I suppose it could be odd for him to be with a queen, but I'll do my best. There is a problem, though."

"What's that?"

"He can't form stone armor. Traditionally, that was the one requirement to demonstrate sufficient stone blood to join the Stone Order."

Oliver leaned back and waved a hand. "You're queen. You can change those rules."

"But that was one of Marisol's dearest tenants about our people. She wanted to make sure we kept a certain level of purity."

"Yet now we have a queen who has a bit of human blood in her. And blood daughter of a Duergar on top of that."

My breath stilled, and I stared at him. "My mother was part human?"

"She was," he said. He pressed his lips into a thin line and looked off to the side, and it took me a second or two to realize that he was fighting back emotion. "She had a bit of human blood."

I started breathing again. "I would like to know more about her."

He nodded. "Yes. But not right now. After we finish Maxen's campaign, there will be time enough to delve into the past."

"One thing I know for certain," I said. "Prophecy will not play a prominent role in my reign. It may have its place at times, but I don't believe it should be followed so dogmatically as Marisol followed it. We owe it to the hidden ones to approach things with more logic. I don't want to ever again call upon our people to make that kind of sacrifice based on nothing more than a vision."

Oliver didn't disagree. He left a few minutes later, and I stood alone in my living room, staring at nothing as I pressed my hand to my abdomen, pushing back at the curious tightness in my middle.

So much had happened. So many important things were yet to come. And the most curious thing was that it had all become so terribly personal for me.

The ring of my house phone pulled me from my emotional musings.

"Hello?" I answered.

"Your Majesty," came the voice of Jaci, one of my personal assistants. "Your sister is outside the fortress, demanding entry."

"Nicole?" I asked in confusion.

"No, a Duergar woman. Says her name is Bryna."

"I'll come to the foyer right away," I said and hung up.

With my ever-present guards on my heels, I hurried from my quarters.

Chapter 24

MY GUARDS INSISTED on following me through the doorway to the exterior of the stone fortress.

In the slanting light of the Bay Area afternoon, I found my half-sister Bryna Marcourt waiting impatiently with her arms crossed and one hip pushed out to the side.

"I told them who I was," she burst out when she saw me. She threw her hands up in the air.

She couldn't have really expected to be let into the stone fortress just on her claim, but it seemed she needed to blow off a little steam. In fact, it appeared Bryna was rather on edge.

"I wanted to come myself to escort you in," I said patiently. "But for my guards' piece of mind, could you tell us why you're here?"

Bryna rolled her eyes and distractedly pushed the fingers of one hand into her long platinum-blond hair.

"Um, because I have nowhere else to go," she said. "I can't exactly go back to the Duergar palace. I'm a traitor."

No wonder she was agitated. She was homeless.

"Right. Okay. I'm sorry about that. You're absolutely welcome to stay here."

"She's a spy and a sworn Unseelie," growled one of my guards, a woman with huge quads and thick hair pulled back into two tight braids. She was around Oliver's age.

"Yes, she's a spy," I said. "She's also my half-sister. She came to my aid during the Battle of the Gods." I turned to Bryna. "I'm sorry, but I have to ask some pointed questions. Are you defecting from the Duergar kingdom?"

"Duh. Yes. They don't know that yet, though."

I smothered a noise of irritation at the back of my throat, trying to keep in mind that she was in a difficult spot.

"Okay. Do you mean the Carraig Sidhe people or kingdom any harm?" I asked.

"No, of course not."

"Are you looking for a temporary place to stay?"

She shrugged a shoulder, and her gaze angled off.

I planted my hands on my hips. "Could you just spell out for me why exactly you're here, Bryna? I'm happy to help you, but you gotta give me something."

She huffed, shifted her feet, and mumbled a few words.

"Could you repeat that?" I asked.

"I *said* . . . I wanted to see if I might join your realm," her voice trailed off to a near whisper.

I pulled in my lips and bit down for a second, until I could control the smile that threatened to spread over my face.

"You want to be one of my subjects?" I asked.

She sighed loudly. "If you insist on putting it that way." She finally faced me. "Look. I thought this would be the safest place. And I heard that Nicole is, you know, expecting a baby. I just thought . . ."

The breeze of a raven's wings could have knocked me over.

I couldn't help grinning. "You want to be an auntie to Nicole's baby!" I crowed.

Bryna's cheeks reddened, and she glared at me. "Nicole is my sister, too."

I went to her and threw my arms around her neck. She stiffened at first, resisting, but then briefly returned my embrace.

"You have a family here," I said. "Let's go inside."

I took Bryna and my two guards through the doorway into the stone fortress.

"We'll get you set up with an apartment," I said.

"And what of my oath to the Duergar realm?" Bryna asked, looking around a little nervously.

"That's something we'll have to figure out. It was already on my mind even before you arrived."

Her attention sharpened on me, and a sly smile replaced her trepidation. "For Jasper?"

"Shh!" I hissed. "He and I haven't talked about it yet. But maybe you could help persuade him? The two of you are close. If he knows you're going to be here too, it'd benefit my case."

She giggled. "You're not going to need my help, I suspect. But I'm at your service, Queen Petra." She stepped back and made a surprisingly beautiful curtsy.

I went to one of the house phones in the foyer and called Amalie's office to let her assistant know we needed a living quarters for the half-sister of the queen. Then I rejoined Bryna. My guards were still eyeing her suspiciously.

"Someone will be here in a few minutes to get some information from you. If they don't have a proper place to put you right away, they'll find you some temporary quarters." I peered at her, suddenly realizing she'd arrived with nothing. "Were you able to escape with any of your possessions?"

She shook her head and then shrugged. "No, but it's fine. A spy is always ready to abandon her life at a moment's notice."

"Were you actually a double-agent all along?" I asked.

"Yeah," she said, looking pleased.

"Was sending a wraith to kill me in the netherwhere part of your double-agenting?" I asked.

Her smile faded, and her gaze shifted downward. "At times I let things get too personal. I'm sorry I tried to have you killed."

"Seeing as how I survived, you're forgiven," I said wryly. I brightened. "The Carraig aren't exactly built for spying, so if you're interested in continuing in that line of work, we'd be glad to have you do it."

Her eyes lit up with a genuine smile, and she seemed to relax slightly. "Thank you, Petra. That means more than I can say. I knew it was the right decision to come here."

My lips parted in surprise at her willingness to show such vulnerability. "You're welcome, Bryna."

I left my half-sister in the hands of a couple of fortress pages and went to find Maxen. Oliver's mention of Melusine had reminded me that I needed to check in on her. After the battle was over and I'd told Eldon how Melusine's doorway had gotten blasted away and then we'd seen no more of the Fae witch after that, he'd vanished in a cloud of gloaming, off to look for her. He'd found her unconscious at the fortress, having defeated a band of assassins sent by Periclase, and whisked her away to his home. Problem was, I had no idea where he lived, and though we knew Melusine was alive, we didn't know what state she was in.

The Old Ones could take care of themselves, of course, but Oberon's sky iron sickness had showed us that they weren't completely invincible.

After I set Jaci on the task of tracking down Maxen for a Melusine update, a page arrived at my office with a scroll. He was slightly breathless, indicating he'd run all the way to me.

"I was told to hurry," he said, extending his hand.

"I appreciate your efficiency," I said and dismissed him.

When I broke the seal and saw the handwriting, my heart bumped. It was from Jasper. I'd been awaiting communication from him, as he'd had to disappear quickly at the end of the battle. My uncle, Darion, had survived, and Jasper, like Bryna, was still technically a Duergar subject. Jasper had gone into hiding with Drifte, fearing reprisal from his sworn kingdom. Jasper wasn't as skilled as Bryna at slipping through places unseen. And after he'd been outed as Finvarra's blood son, everyone in Faerie knew Jasper's face.

His note said he was requesting entry into the fortress but would be coming from a secret location and would arrive by Great Raven. He didn't say when.

Jaci appeared in the doorway of my office. "Your Majesty, Lord Maxen is here."

"Please send him in," I said.

Maxen came in and shut the door behind him and then sank onto a chair opposite mine across the desk.

"I originally wanted to talk to you about Melusine and how she's doing, but I just got this." I passed the message to Maxen.

"Alert Oliver and Shane, and tell them to give orders to not shoot down any of the big ravens," he said.

"That's it?" I asked. "We don't have to, I don't know, turn on the airspace so the Great Ravens can come here?"

He shook his head. "The raven doorways—whether for messengers or the Great Ravens—are always open to them."

"That seems a . . . vulnerability," I said, suddenly concerned.

"It is. That's why we need to tell our people not to attack if one pops into our realm."

I lifted the phone and gave Jaci the urgent message to pass to Oliver and Shane.

"So, we'll have two exiles here," Maxen said.

I nodded. "I know it's against tradition and protocol, but one's family with nowhere else to go, and the other is . . ."

The corners of his mouth widened slightly. "What? What exactly is

Jasper Glasgow?"

I shook my head and dropped my gaze to my desk. "I'll have to see what he wants." I looked up. "I hope you're not offended that I want to allow them to swear fealty to the Carraig."

"No, I'm not, personally," he said. "But there may be some contention within the realm."

I grumbled under my breath. "More strife. That's just what we need here."

"Well, at least with Bryna and Jasper, there is some stone blood. Bryna is a descendant of Periclase, who had stone blood, and Jasper has visible permanent stone armor. That may be enough to appease the dissenters."

I drew a slow breath in through my nose, my happiness over Jasper's imminent arrival dampened. "It will look like favoritism, though. Bending the rules for family and for . . . uh . . ."

"The queen's boyfriend?"

I gave him a withering look.

"How's Nicole doing?" I asked.

I'd only been able to briefly check in with my twin since the battle. She'd looked pale and tired, and I worried about how the stress of the events in Faerie—not to mention having Maxen in the thick of the fight in the Summerlands, and her potential future as High Queen—was affecting her health and pregnancy.

"She's healthy, generally speaking, but fighting a lot of morning sickness."

"The baby is one of the reasons Bryna wanted to come here," I said.

"Really?"

I nodded. "I think she really wants to be close to family, such as we are. And I told her we'd have something for her to do in the information trade."

"We can certainly use someone like her."

"We'll have to make her swear oaths from here to Sunday, though. She was a double agent. I don't know how she managed to pull that off, given how Fae can't lie to each other."

"That's probably something we'll need to have her disclose," Maxen said.

"Right, good thinking."

"There's something else," he said, his expression turning grave.

More? I tried not to wince.

"Remember the stone bloods who defected from the Stone Order and swore to King Sebastian?"

I suddenly recalled the conversation I'd had with King Sebastian in Druid Circle, the nightclub off the Vegas strip. It was the site of one of the first servitor attacks, and I'd saved Sebastian's life. Maxen had been there, too. Just before the attack, Sebastian had been trying to persuade me to swear fealty to him, and he'd talked about some of my brethren who already had changed their allegiance. I'd argued with him about his thin reasoning for wanting to claim all stone bloods as his subjects.

I'd been in that club chasing the vampire mark I'd been assigned by the Mercenary Guild. A chance crossing of paths, it had seemed, but looking back, it seemed clear that it had been the beginning. That encounter was the first step on the path that had led me back into Faerie. To Jasper. To my people and then to the Carraig Sidhe throne.

"Yes, I remember. It feels like eons ago when that was a topic of debate," I said.

I couldn't help thinking of Marisol. She'd been so riled up about Sebastian stealing some of her people. Back then, I'd thought it was better to let the unwise stone bloods leave. But from my position as queen, I understood her reaction. In her place, I'd have wanted to fight for every one of them, too.

"Do they have a safe place until we figure out how to help them break their oaths?" I asked.

Maxen shook his head. "They're seeking asylum with us."

I squeezed my eyes closed and rubbed my forehead. "Okay. We need to take them in. But they'll have to swear oaths that they will bring us no harm. We probably can't let them leave the fortress at all until they've sworn to the Carraig. I'll let Oliver know he needs to get the proper security precautions in place."

The rest of the day passed in a blur of administrative tasks and decisions. The Dobhar and Sylph who'd crammed into the fortress had begun moving back to their respective realms. I'd thought it was ridiculous that Moreau and Vida had insisted on coming into the stone fortress with their people, until I learned that Spriggan assassins had breached their kingdoms' respective strongholds right before the Battle of the Gods. The few officials left had been murdered, which I hadn't gotten word of until after the battle. Apparently, the Dobhar and Sylph oracles had been correct in advising their leaders to put themselves under Carraig protection.

The Dobhar left the fortress quickly and with chilly politeness, as their King Moreau was Maxen's biggest rival in the bid for the Summerlands. The Sylph, having publicly declared their support of Maxen, lingered a bit more. As much as I appreciated Vida's endorsement, I was past ready to reclaim the fortress for the Carraig.

As I worked, anticipation of seeing Jasper tickled at the back of my mind through the long hours. Little anxious thoughts chased my excitement at the prospect of reuniting with him.

Would he really be amenable to joining the Carraig Sidhe and swear-ing to me? Or would he want to be independent, perhaps like his wild shifter friend Drifte, and swear to no one?

Did he truly want a future with the two of us together? We'd talked about it, but only very briefly. And with all the changes in Faerie, maybe he would have different priorities.

By the time I got word that a Great Raven had landed in the practice yard, my stomach was a tight bundle of nerves. But I couldn't keep my feet from speeding up as I went out to meet Jasper.

Chapter 25

IF I'D BEEN at all worried about whether Jasper would be happy to see me, my anxiety was dispelled immediately. By the time I reached the practice yard, he'd dismounted the great black bird and stood talking to Maxen. Jasper spotted me, and a broad smile swept over his face, his tri-colored eyes sparkling as his gaze stayed glued on my approach.

I wanted to run to him but forced myself to keep to a stately walk.

Maxen turned and stepped back, and Jasper jogged the final ten feet or so that separated us. Scooping me up by the waist, he pulled me tight against him and spun me off the ground.

His lips met mine in a deep, but all-too-quick kiss.

"My apologies for ignoring protocol," he said as he put me back on the ground. He stepped away and bowed. "Your Majesty."

I knew people were watching, but I was too happy to see him to feel particularly self-conscious. My guards, however, weren't shy about keeping close, and I could sense their unease. I didn't entirely blame them. Jasper was an Unseelie, a sworn subject of our enemy, and blood son of Finvarra—though he'd killed his father to help the Seelie. On paper, according to some, perhaps, Jasper could have been an enemy. But he'd fought for the Seelie in every way you could ask, and his timely arrival with the Chalice of Dagda had helped turn the tide in the Battle of the Gods.

"You're welcome here," I said, my voice carrying. "And you have our eternal gratitude for the part you played in the Summerlands. You certainly are a friend of this realm."

"I thank you for your hospitality."

I stepped closer to him, lowering my voice. "We have much to discuss. I hope I can get a bit of your time soon."

"Yes," Jasper said, also hushed. "We have things to speak of. But I hope there will be time for things that involve no speaking at all."

I snorted a laugh at his phrasing, but the proposition quickened my pulse.

Maxen's attention was caught by something behind me. I turned to see a fortress page hurrying our way. She stopped in front of me, dropped a curtsy, and offered a scroll. I recognized King Moreau's black wax seal right away.

Magic shivered in the air as I opened the document and quickly read it.

I looked up at Maxen. "Moreau and a few of the others want to convene a council of the Seelie rulers to vote on who will take the throne in the Summerlands. He wants to do it tonight."

"That seems sudden," Jasper said.

I flicked a worried glance at him. "I agree."

Maxen leveled his chin. "I have no argument with voting tonight."

"No, we can't," I protested. "We don't know that we've secured a majority."

"We have the Sylph," Maxen said. "Also the Gnomes. I don't think we'll ever get Delun on our side, but I believe Corrain will vote with Vida. We get a vote. That's four for us. Two for Moreau."

"*Maybe* four," I said. "Corrain hasn't endorsed you publicly. Or even privately, for that matter. Damn it to Maeve that the council will be an even number of members. I'm afraid we'll end up with a tie."

"It was supposed to be seven," Jasper said quietly.

He was right. The Spriggan would have been represented, but Trey

238

had defected to the Unseelie. He probably would have voted for Moreau, anyway.

"Can we refuse to convene?" I asked.

"Not if a majority have already voted to meet," Maxen said.

I cursed under my breath. Uneasiness settled in the pit of my stomach, and I couldn't shake the idea that we needed more time.

We spent the last few hours before the council meeting trying to get audiences with Delun and Corrain. But our messages were met with silence, and when Maxen went into the Kelpie and Baen Sidhe realms in person, he was refused.

By the time we had to ready ourselves to go to the Summerlands, my insides felt like a tangle of live wires.

Arriving at the Summerlands with Maxen, Oliver, and a handful of other Carraig dignitaries, I couldn't help replaying some of the battle in my mind. No one had seen or heard from Morven since he'd dissolved away, and sadness tugged at me. I'd never been truly comfortable around the Ghille Dubh, but he'd given his life for our cause, and I wished I could thank him one more time.

We'd come through a doorway on the grounds outside the castle, and we all fell silent as we snaked our way through an obstacle course of craters left by the sky iron boulders. Seelie from all kingdoms had worked to remove the giant chunks of toxic metal, rigging up lifts to maneuver the sky iron outside the wall bordering the castle grounds. The dreadful throb of the stuff emanated from the right. I couldn't see the pile of meteorites the Tuatha had rained down on us, but from the sheer force of the pulses, it was obvious iron was piled not far beyond the wall. We needed to get the toxic metal to the caves soon. Otherwise, whoever ended up living in the Summerlands would go mad with such a volume of sky iron so close.

The sun had set, and workers from all Seelie kingdoms who had come to clean up the wreckage in the castle had lit candles, torches, and lamps to illuminate our way to Oberon's study, where the door was thrown open.

When our party arrived, I discovered we were the last kingdom to get there. That somehow felt like a disadvantage, and I felt a little stab of anxious dismay. Some of the conversations stopped abruptly as we approached the kings, queens, and diplomats gathered around the cold hearth.

When I caught sight of the recently crowned ruler of the Cait Sidhe, green-eyed, lithe Queen Yasmine, I frowned and stopped short. The cat shifter kingdom hadn't contributed full forces to the battle and were therefor not eligible to vote.

Yasmine came forward, the diaphanous, layered brown skirt of her dress floating behind her heels.

She stopped and curtseyed. "Your Majesty. I requested to attend as a spectator only. I'm here on behalf of all the unrepresented Seelie kingdoms."

Beyond Yasmine, back in the crowd, someone was waving frantically. I sucked in a breath. It was Lochlyn, my roommate and best friend in the years I'd lived on the Earthly side of the hedge. It seemed like a decade since we'd spoken, though it had only been a couple of months. I resisted the urge to sprint to her.

Instead, I returned Queen Yasmine's curtsy. "That seems fair," I said. "Your presence is welcome."

She drifted away, and my delegation and I joined the group.

Lochlyn sidled up to me, her catlike eyes sparkling. She was a Cait Sidhe subject and must have been chosen to accompany her queen. I couldn't imagine why, as she was about as far from being a politician as a Fae could get, and she hadn't lived in Faerie for a decade. Perhaps she'd begged for the appointment because she knew I'd be there. Or maybe Yasmine knew of my friendship with Lochlyn and wanted her there to ingratiate the Cait Sidhe kingdom to me. Either way, I was happy to see her.

Lochlyn curtseyed and then pulled me in for a side hug.

"You're the last person I expected to see here," I whispered, with warmth of happiness rippling through me as I briefly wrapped my arm around her waist. "Can we talk later?"

She nodded enthusiastically. "Absolutely, Your Majesty."

Lochlyn gracefully moved back to Yasmine and the other Cait Sidhe.

The glow from being reunited with my dear friend faded as I faced the room.

Vida stepped away from the other Sylph, going to stand directly in front of the fireplace.

"We must choose someone to lead the meeting," she said, her rich voice carrying. The chatter in the room quieted.

"I nominate you," I said quickly before anyone else could speak. It didn't really matter who was in charge, but I liked the thought of having an ally in charge.

Vida's brows raised, but she looked pleased.

"I second," Lawrence said.

"All in favor?" Vida asked.

Everyone but Moreau said, "Aye."

He was standing with his arms folded, his face uncharacteristically stony. Clearly, he was not pleased about Vida's change of heart. She'd probably damaged the Sylph-Dobhar relationship permanently with her endorsement of Maxen, but that was a concern for another day.

The anticipation in the room amped up, and there was some maneuvering as Vida asked the rulers to come forward. I touched Maxen's shoulder, and we traded a glance before I joined the other kings and queens.

"We have two nominations for the High Court, as far as I know," Vida said. "Moreau McLean and Maxen Lothlorien. Anyone else want to throw in?"

She looked at the Kelpie King Delun, who'd had himself in the running for a brief time. He didn't answer. No one else piped up.

My pulse accelerated. I wanted Maxen to win, but most of all, I wanted this to be settled. If we had a tie, it could drag things on for who knew how long. Worst case, it could cause such strife among the Seelie that there could be an inter-court war. We needed peace.

"I'll now go around and ask for your votes," Vida said.

She started with Lawrence.

"Maxen Lothlorien," said the Gnome king.

Next was Delun. "Moreau."

My turn. "Maxen."

Moreau's icy demeanor cracked a bit. He gave a small smile when he said his own name.

We had two votes for each.

"Corrain?" Vida asked.

The Baen Sidhe queen squared her shoulders. "On behalf of my people, I cast my vote for Moreau."

My chest clenched.

Vida voted for Maxen, as expected.

"A tie," she said with a sigh.

"How do we break it?" Lawrence asked.

"We will break it for you," came a voice from the doorway.

Everyone in the room turned. My mouth fell open. Walking into the office, side by side, were Oberon and Titania.

I was tempted to rub my eyes like a cartoon character to be sure I was seeing what I thought I was seeing.

As always, the Old Ones were ethereal and larger than life. But Oberon was pale, his trademark muscular frame thinned, and even his hair seemed to have lost its luster.

Titania's hallow eyes were the only thing to betray the stress of Oberon's sky iron sickness.

"King Oberon," Lawrence exclaimed. "Have you come back to reclaim the High Court?"

The former High King and Queen joined the ring of rulers, and we all gave them some space.

"No, I haven't," Oberon said. "It's time for me to retire and allow a new era to unfold in Faerie."

"Forgive my impertinence, King Oberon," Delun said. "But you don't have a say in this vote."

Oberon crossed his arms over his wide chest. "I do if you can't make up your minds. I caught wind that there would likely be a stalemate. That's unacceptable to me and to the Fomoire. You need to decide. Faerie deserves an answer."

I looked around at the other kings and queens.

"He's right," came a voice from behind me. It was Maxen. "For the good of the realm, I will take myself out of the running. We need to move forward, and we need someone here in the Summerlands in order to do that. Moreau can have the—"

"No, don't do that, Maxen," Corrain cut in, moving into the center of the circle. She looked around at all of us. "I change my vote. I'm for Maxen Lothlorien."

Moreau and Delun both started talking, their voices raised. From what I could catch, they were trying to remind Corrain of a deal they'd struck, which her change of vote would nullify.

"I'm fine with that," Corrain raised her voice over them. The two men quieted. "My gut told me to go with Maxen, and I should have listened. I'm sorry, but it's the right choice."

Vida looked at Oberon and Titania, as if expecting some pronouncement from them. When none came, she gave her head a little shake.

"All the other votes stand?" she asked.

"Yes," the rest of us chimed.

"Then Maxen Lothlorien will take the throne of the High Court," Vida pronounced.

"Wise choice," Oberon said. "With that decision, the Fomoire will allow the Carraig to keep the power of the gods. And I daresay you'll need it to keep the Unseelie at bay."

I gaped at him. "We'll continue to have the magic of the Fomoire?" I asked.

He nodded gravely. "All Carraig bestowed with the gift will continue to have it. But as you die off, so will the Fomoire power."

That was sobering. But I didn't want to think about death. Maxen had won. With ragged relief, I flew at him and engulfed him in an embrace.

"By your willingness to give up the throne, you just proved to everyone you're the right choice," I whispered to him. "I'd say you're brilliant, but I know it was pure sincerity."

Then I had to let him go, as others were coming up to offer their congratulations. Delun and Moreau stayed where they were, speaking in low tones to each other and avoiding looking at the rest of us. They'd go home and lick their wounds, but the majority had spoken, and the losers had to accept the result. Considering the bonus of the Fomoire power and how useful it would be in protecting Seelie interests, I thought things had landed extremely well for all of us. I hoped Moreau would come around to see it that way, too.

There was still much to discuss, but we agreed to wait until the next day to begin making those decisions.

There was nothing left to do officially that night, but everyone seemed slow to depart. Finally, Oberon hastened the process, asking all but me and Maxen to go back to their respective realms.

Once Oberon, Titania, Maxen, and I were alone, I turned to the former High King.

"How are you, truly, Your Majesty?" I asked.

"I'm sick and broken down," he said frankly. "I was able to come here only under the power of a dose of extremely strong healing magic.

But it wears off quickly, and each time after, I'm worse."

"Is there anything we can do?" I asked.

"There may be something in the universe that can save me, but it's not your job to find it." He leaned heavily against the edge of his desk. "I don't have much time until the sky iron takes over my mind again, so I will be brief. I'm assigning all of my former staff to you, Maxen. I have no need for so many people anymore."

Titania had moved to his side and taken his hand.

Oberon glanced at his longtime love, and she gave him a smile touched with sadness.

"Titania and a few friends are all I need now," he said. "Where we're going, we won't have use for scores of attendants."

"I can't tell you how much I appreciate such a gift, Your Majesty," Maxen said, clearly moved. His blue eyes were misting. "Our realm is too small to supply enough people for both the Summerlands and the stone fortress. It was one of the things that was weighing on my mind very heavily."

Maxen had briefly mentioned that we'd have to recruit many people from other Seelie realms to move to the Summerlands. It would have been a huge, daunting undertaking. But having a staff who already knew the castle workings would reduce the time needed to get up and running, not to mention ease the burden of assigning roles and training so many people.

"Now, I must go," Oberon said, pushing away from the desk.

He swayed, and Titania shifted her grasp to his arm, steadying him.

"Please take care, both of you," I said.

Oberon nodded, and Titania smiled at us before turning her attention fully to him.

Maxen and I watched them walk slowly toward the door. Then the two of us were alone, our guards having been sent out to the corridor to wait.

"This is all yours now," I said to Maxen.

He looked around, seeming to take in the grand study, furnished on a scale that was too large for us mere mortal Fae, with new eyes.

"It doesn't really feel like it. Not yet," he said. He turned to me. "Let's go home, Petra."

Chapter 26

MAXEN AND I arrived back at the stone fortress late at night. We said quick goodbyes, and he headed to his quarters, eager to see Nicole. News of Maxen's victory had already spread through the realm. I went to my own apartment, intending to find out where Jasper was.

But there was no need, because he was standing outside my door.

I smiled, feeling myself softening as some of the stress of the day rolled off me under his warm, golden gaze.

"You didn't need to wait here," I said, feeling bad he'd had to just stand in the hallway for who knew how long. "I was going to track you down as soon as I returned."

He shook his head. "I was fine. I didn't want to miss out on a single moment with you. Besides, I only got a few odd looks."

I opened the door, holding it while Jasper followed me inside. As soon as it closed, he wrapped both arms around me, lifting me and kissing me until I was breathless.

When he pulled back, his hands still at my waist, I sighed with deep contentment. But it only took a moment for outside concerns to begin creeping back in.

"The Dullahan skull and the Chalice of Dagda? Were you able to find safe places for them?" I asked.

"Drifte and his people are helping me with that," he said. "The artifacts are quite safe with them, and I will let you know where they'll be held when we figure that out."

"Thank you," I said, unconcerned about the vulnerability of the words. "Peace in Faerie depends on keeping them out of Unseelie hands. Unfortunately, the Duergar still have the Stone of Fal."

"It's definitely a concern," Jasper said. "But we have the Chalice to combat it, if Darion tries to use the Stone."

"We'll have to keep careful track of him," I said. "Carraig have never been great spies, but now we have Bryna, so that's a good start."

He grinned. "She and I caught up while you were gone. It's good to see the two of you growing closer."

"That's definitely overstating where Bryna and I stand," I said drily. "But her home is here now, so there's time for our relationship to thaw."

I wasn't sure Bryna and I would ever be very close, but Jasper obviously liked the idea, so I decided not to spoil it for him.

My stomach stirred nervously as I took his hand and towed him to the next room and one of the sofas there. We both sat.

"There's still the matter of, well, us," I said.

His brows lifted. "What's the problem with us?"

"No problem." I raised my hand to shove my fingers into my hair but forced it back to my lap. "I just . . . I guess I just want to talk about what kind of future you see for us."

His golden eyes seemed to deepen in color, sparkling warmly from within.

"The only future I see is with you, Petra Maguire," he said, his slight brogue deepening.

My heart thrilled at his words, my pulse racing.

"But there is one matter I must tell you about first," he said, growing somber. "It's something that could affect your feelings for me."

Cold tendrils reached through the warmth I'd felt mere seconds ago. My mind began to whirl, trying to think of what he could possibly be talking about.

"Do you remember when we were trying to save Oberon?" he asked. "When we were on the beach and needed a doorway directly to the Tuatha's stronghold?"

The chill gripped me in earnest. "The Lorelei," I said weakly. "You had to make a promise."

He nodded.

"What did you promise her?" I asked, every fiber of my being dreading the answer.

"My firstborn," he said.

I frowned, the words not making sense at first. Then the implication hit me. Jasper and I had never talked about having children. In fact, I'd never really thought much about it until I found out Nicole was pregnant. Even then, I wasn't sure I was mother material, or that I'd ever have the desire to have children of my own. But looking at Jasper in that moment, I realized with a rush of fierce desperation that I didn't want the option taken away. No. It was even more than that. My breath caught in my throat as it hit me with the force of a hurricane: I wanted to experience everything possible with Jasper Glasgow.

He was watching me, and something must have changed in my expression because he reached for my hand.

"My promise would not affect any children of ours, if we had them," he said.

"What?" I asked, too confused to feel any relief.

"It was a long time ago. I was young, not even finished with school yet. I met a girl, and we fell in love. She got pregnant and made it nearly to full term, but when the baby was born . . ."

Sorrow filled his eyes.

"Oh," I whispered, that one syllable weighted with sadness. "Oh, I'm so sorry."

"The baby's mother was part human, and in the human way had the baby cremated. I had some of the ashes. I took them to the Lorelei. She was furious, but it fulfilled the promise."

I just sat there a moment, trying to take it all in.

"So you were worried that I'd be upset you fathered a child a decade ago?" I finally asked. "And that you were clever enough to use something very painful to outwit the Lorelei?"

One of his shoulders moved in a tiny shrug. "I wasn't sure what you'd think."

I leaned forward, wrapping my arms around him and pulling him close. "What I think is that I'm terribly sad you lost a child. I'm so sorry I didn't know you'd endured such a tragedy. But you've made me realize just how deeply and completely I want to be with you."

He kissed me, then, with all the pent-up passion of the past many weeks. Then he scooped me up and carried me into the bedroom. After that, there were no more words for some time. We fell asleep entwined in each other's arms.

The next day, we gathered Oliver, Bryna, Maxen, and Nicole to announce to them that Jasper and I planned to get married. No one seemed surprised, and even Bryna appeared quite happy for us, actually cracking a smile and giving me a brief hug.

Before a ceremony could happen, we had to address the issue of Jasper's kingdom affiliation. For that, we sent a raven to Melusine. She sent word back later in the day that she was recovering at her cottage, and that Eldon had been caring for her. She promised to come to the fortress within the week.

The next several days were a flurry of preparing Maxen and Nicole to move to the Summerlands. All of the Seelie rulers had agreed it was best to occupy the castle as soon as possible to establish the Seelie power.

Maxen asked Jasper to work for him, and he agreed under the condition that he could still live with me in the stone fortress.

When I summoned Amalie to my office to offer her Maxen's former job as the kingdom equivalent of head of state, she jumped at the opportunity with even more enthusiasm than I'd hoped.

By the morning that Melusine made it to the stone fortress, Maxen and Nicole had already taken up residence at the Summerlands castle. I missed having Maxen's knowledge and skill close at hand but found I wasn't as afraid as I'd expected to rule the Carraig Sidhe without him nearby.

I hosted Melusine in my quarters, the two of us sitting out in my courtyard in the sun, her with tea and me with a mug of strong coffee.

"Are you still feeling the aftereffects of the battle?" I asked.

When the doorway she'd opened had been suddenly blasted closed, she'd absorbed the magical blowback.

She brushed a hand through the air. "I'm nearly back to my old self."

I gave her a sly look. "It sounds as if Eldon has nursed you well."

She gave me a prim glance, straightening the black lacy edges of her bell sleeves.

"So, the two of you are . . .?" I pressed.

"Well, we are the only two of our kind, so it does make a certain sort of sense for us to be together, doesn't it?" she said it in an offhand way, but her pale cheeks pinked.

"The Fae witch and the Fae sorcerer," I mused. "It certainly is a nice fit."

I could have teased her further but decided to let her off the hook.

"You really believe you can break Jasper's and Bryna's oaths of fealty?" I asked, changing topics.

She squinted into the distance. "I believe so, yes. The task may be easier because the man they swore to is dead."

"But fealty passes to the next ruler," I said.

"That's true. But there's something in the oath that changes when that happens." Her strange orange eyes were flitting around, as if she watched something dart through the air that I couldn't see. She sank into her thoughts for a moment. "Yes, I believe it will be possible to sever it. It also helps if they both strongly desire to break the bond."

"How soon can we do it?"

"I will need to go back to my cottage to consult some of my magical manuals, but I think I could be ready tomorrow morning."

A smile spread across my face. "That sounds perfect."

At dawn the next morning, Melusine arrived in one of her signature black velvet gowns. Eldon came, too, dressed in a matching suit. They were quite the striking couple.

In the privacy of my quarters, Melusine, Eldon, Bryna, Jasper, and the Spriggan subjects who'd defected gathered in my formal sitting room.

The Fae witch wove strands of human and Fae magic for several minutes, winding her power around each of the oath breakers. Some of their faces began to contort in pain, their breath coming faster, but to their credit, no one cried out or stumbled. After about fifteen minutes, there was a burst of sparkling Fae magic like a tiny fireworks show. The residual mist cleared, and the newly free Fae looked around with glassy eyes, blinking hard.

Melusine brushed her hands together. "Done and done," she said with satisfaction.

"Will it harm them to take a new oath right away?" I asked.

"Not at all," she said.

Good thing. We had the oath of fealty ceremony scheduled for later that morning. After consulting with Oliver on the topic, we'd decided it would be best to minimize the delay between oaths. Because our new subjects were coming from other realms, we planned to have them take extra loyalty oaths as a precaution.

Before the ceremony, I got a call from my assistant informing me that Lochlyn was in the foyer. She was on the short list of foreigners who were allowed inside our walls automatically. I asked Jaci to have Lochlyn escorted to my quarters.

After I invited her in and closed the door, she let out a little shriek.

"You're engaged!" she exclaimed.

"Well, it's not like I have a ring or anything," I said.

I'd sent a raven with a message to let her know about me and Jasper. I definitely *hadn't* used the word "engaged."

"But you're getting married," she beamed.

I cracked a smile. "Yes, we are. I don't know when, but those details will work themselves out."

She gasped with exaggerated shock. "How can you be so flippant? This is the wedding of a queen, Petra! It doesn't happen very often." She flopped on one of the sofas, curling her long legs under her. "It's going to be the Fae wedding of the century."

I held up my hands. "Whoa, slow down. It's not going to be some crazy circus event. We just want to do something quiet and intimate."

She hummed, looking at me though slitted eyes. "We'll see about that."

"Moving on," I said, giving her a mock annoyed look. "You didn't have to come in person."

"Of course I did! I wanted to congratulate you. But I have other business here, too."

"Oh? What's that?"

"Lord Lothlorien—I mean King Maxen—asked me to meet him here to discuss a job at the Summerlands."

Maxen was back at the fortress for the morning so he could witness the swearing-in of our new subjects.

"He wants to hire me as an entertainer," she said.

"Are you okay with living full-time in Faerie?" I asked.

She nodded. "I've been spending more time on this side of the hedge, and it really feels like coming home. I think I got all my rebellion out of my system." She gave a little giggle.

"You and me both," I said.

"Actually, you're one of the reasons I wanted to come back. One, so hopefully we could see each other more. But also, I figured if you could be happy back in Faerie, I could find peace here."

"I never thought I'd live in Faerie again." I looked around. "Even now, I have moments where I can hardly believe this is my life."

"But it's good?"

"It's challenging, frustrating, sad, terrible, surprising, and wonderful all at the same time."

She smiled and then glanced at the clock on the mantle. "I need to get to Maxen. But we must talk about your wedding." She clapped her hands under her chin and stood. "So much planning to do."

"No planning," I said.

"Yes, planning!" she trilled.

She slipped out the front door before I could argue further.

An hour later, I was in one of the fortress's small ceremony rooms. Maxen served as the officiant for the fealty ceremony, since he knew the ins and outs of the protocol.

One by one, each person swore their oath to me. Bryna gave me a little wink when she finished. Jasper went last.

The sound of his voice and the sincerity in his eyes made my heart swell.

We had an early dinner that evening, where Jasper and I dined with Oliver, Bryna, Nicole, Maxen, and Lochlyn. Afterward, Jasper took me to the courtyard outside my quarters.

"I have a surprise for you," he said.

He pulled out his whistle and gave it several short blasts. A moment later, two forms darker than the twilight sky appeared above us. With gentle rustles of air and feathers, the Great Ravens landed lightly on the grass several feet away from us. I recognized Mohawk, the Raven I'd ridden many times before.

"Where are we going?" I asked.

"If I told you, it'd ruin the surprise."

He helped me onto Mohawk and then settled himself on the other bird. I grabbed fistfuls of Mohawk's glossy feathers and leaned low across her back as she hopped a few times and then took flight.

The two birds almost seemed to dance with each other as they spiraled upward. Once the fortress was far below, Mohawk eased into a straight flight path, following the other bird. Jasper's Raven winked out of sight, disappearing through an invisible doorway known only to the great birds. A few seconds later, Mohawk took me into the cold of the netherwhere.

We drifted in the chilly void between doorways briefly and then emerged into a night sky that was cooler and drier than the one we'd left. There, night had not yet fallen, and I squinted at the low-hanging sun, the lower two thirds already hidden behind the distant mountain range.

Mohawk set down on the highest of the foothills below us, coming to a hopping landing next to Jasper's bird. He came and offered me a hand, steadying me as I slid to the ground.

"Where are we?" I asked, slightly breathless from the flight.

"One of the wild realms," he said. "Drifte and his people have claimed it."

He pointed off to the right, and I spotted several thin trails of campfire or chimney smoke rising above the forest.

When I looked back at the distant mountains, my breath caught.

"There's no snow," I said.

"No, it's already melted away here. The places where winter had started to take hold are changing, warming. Summer will once again reign in Faerie."

Jasper slipped his arm around my waist, and I leaned into his side.

Joy spread warmly through me. "That somehow makes our victory seem even more real."

"I agree," Jasper said. "I thought coming here to watch the sunset would be a nice way to celebrate."

"It's perfect."

I couldn't help smiling as I watched the sun shrink and then disappear over the horizon. The blue of the sky deepened, and purples and pinks began to paint the undersides of the distant clouds. There were many duties and challenges awaiting me back home, but in that moment, I wasn't sure I'd ever felt so content.

"Do you like the view?" Jasper asked.

I looked up at him, and his golden eyes seemed to glow in the fading light.

"It's incredible," I said.

"I'm glad you approve." A smile tugged the corners of his mouth wide. "Because it's ours."

I turned to him fully. "What do you mean?"

"I made a deal with Drifte," he said. "I'd like to build a cabin here. Something small and comfortable, a place for us to get away. How does that sound?"

I leaned into him, slipping both arms around his waist and savoring how solid and warm his body felt against mine.

"That sounds absolutely perfect," I said.

We stayed there on our little mountain, watching as the colors of sunset gave way to a sky strewn with stars.

I'd spent so much of my life running away from Faerie and resenting its obligations. But as I stood there with Jasper, feeling the faint shiver in my veins that was my magic resonating with the magic of my homeland, I couldn't imagine being anywhere else.

**Look for *The Oldest Changeling in Faerie* by Jayne Faith,
the next book in the Stone Blood Series!**

About the Author

JAYNE FAITH WRITES fantasy set in the real world. She's a meditator, dog lover, TV addict, clean eater, homebody, sun baby, and Sagittarius. Her superpower is her laugh. She owns way too many colored pens and pairs of jeans. Visit her website at www.jaynefaith.com, where you can sign up for her VIP list and get free books.

Also by Jayne Faith

Ella Grey Series
Demon patrol officer Ella Grey beat death after an accident on the job, but something followed her back from the grave. Will it eat her soul or become her greatest ally?

Stone Cold Magic (#1)
Dark Harvest Magic (#2)
Demon Born Magic (#3)
Blood Storm Magic (#4)

Tara Knightley Series
Between paying off a debt to a Fae mob boss, working as a professional thief, and keeping up with her busy three-generation household, Tara Knightley barely has time to eat and sleep. But now she's going to have to choose: her family, love, or her freedom.

Oath of Blood (prequel)
Edge of Magic (#1)
Echo of Bone (#2)
Trace of Fate (#3)
more to come

Stone Blood Series

When vampire hunter Petra Maguire discovers she has a secret twin who's been kidnapped, she's determined to rescue her. But it could spark a magical war.

Blood of Stone (#1)
Stone Blood Legacy (#2)
Rise of the Stone Court (#3)
Reign of the Stone Queen (#4)
War of the Fae Gods (#5)
The Oldest Changeling in Faerie (#6)

Sapient Salvation Series

An innocent young woman fighting to survive in a foreign land. A powerful overlord longing to leave his dark past behind. The moment they meet, worlds clash as forbidden love ignites.

The Selection (#1)
The Awakening (#2)
The Divining (#3)
The Claiming (#4)